# THE TAKING OF THE HIKE

TIMOTHY J. MORIARTY

www.ten16press.com - Waukesha, WI

The Taking of the Hike
Copyrighted © 2018, 2020 Timothy J. Moriarty
ISBN 978-1-948365-93-2
Second Edition

The Taking of the Hike
by Timothy J. Moriarty

For information, please contact:

www.ten16press.com
Waukesha, WI

Edited by Carolyn Washburne

For the Amazing Connie,
whose arrival ushered in the best of times

# Chapter 1

Lyle's timid waiter's eyes stared blankly ahead. It was a lazy attempt to fight through the ozone-like haze of moments that hung between sleep and consciousness like a fuzzy eye chart. Not exactly optimal, but for Lyle, the historical path of least resistance had been not to mind. And while his pillowed head lay comfortably still, his short, slender body—somewhat obedient in tow—twitched periodically, a new and minor spastic nuisance for which he had no current concern or explanation.

For now, he lay nicely cocooned beneath soft satin sheets and a large, furry bedspread. Its loosely stitched patterns coalesced into a super-size likeness Lyle could only imagine resembled a giant teddy bear, with all its soft and snuggly goodness, covering him from head to toe.

Lyle drew in the fresh morning air in a slow and even way, his lungs perfect and efficient bellows. Each shallow, waking breath offered a hypnotic suggestion—it reinforced the comfort, the goodness. And Lyle and comfort were old friends.

As the newness of the day began to refresh Lyle's tired mind and focus his sleepy eyes, he quietly began his morning ritual, re-familiarizing himself with the things in his room, his favorite things, the things that had brought him consummate pleasure and joy throughout all of his twenty-two years of uneventful life. He saw a large Raggedy Ann doll resting peacefully in a rocking chair at the foot of the bed, a volleyball, a pair of bright yellow tap shoes, and, on the wall directly above his head, a poster of a picturesque mountain stream on a sun-drenched summer day. In the poster, a young woman, streamside, craned mightily to see her reflection in the eddy before her. The poster read:

A penny cast into a stream,
From patient, faithful hands,
A shiny copper hope, a dream,
For all true loves demands.

How beautiful, Lyle thought, until he realized he had never seen any of these things before.

"Aaaaagh!"

Gone for Lyle was the safety he always felt in the sameness of his own room and his own things: his Luke Skywalker pajamas; the small wooden plaque he received for spelling "'turpitude" correctly when he was in the sixth grade; his two favorite and only books: *Rootabaga Stories* by Carl Sandburg and Rudyard Kipling's *Kim*; even the photo of himself and Alderman Peabody shaking hands at last year's Fourth of July parade, the grand prize for his winning essay, "Why This Country is Great." Lyle had cautiously clipped the photo from the pages of the Town Examiner on July fifth and beamed with pride whenever he looked upon it. All that was mysteriously gone for him now, lost somewhere during the night, a night that left him in a strange double bed.

Lyle rubbed his eyes.

Fear can be an odd sort of a thing, he felt, arriving as unannounced as a bolt of lightning, the shock and the shiver of the initial jolt just as quickly giving way to tingly and lingering suspicions as to one's bravery. He feared that someone might have heard him scream, or, worse, might come into this bedroom and find him quivering beneath the covers. Worse still, a feeling of dread, as if he were about to be waylaid, fell upon him, as his impish imagination instinctively chartered a course that had that same someone rushing toward him, aghast and in a frothy hither, frantically screaming, "Egad! Who are you . . . ! And what are you doing under Mr. Buggles?!"

Such thoughts were random and scattered and troubling but beginning to ebb when Lyle saw that he was naked, save the boxer shorts his mother had given him on his last birthday. They bore the inscription, "World's Greatest Son." Somehow, he figured, Mother wouldn't understand this situation, God bless her recently departed soul.

He bristled with a cosmic blend of confusion and goose bumps.

Clearly Mother Speckman would not have understood. Of this, there could be no doubt. No doubt at all. A straightforward explanation of events to himself was clearly needed—Mother would have accepted no less—and his understanding of same, clearly the first impasse, and the first bridge to cross. It seemed an odd dilemma, as if the quiet warmth in his cocoon were pressing upon a blackened, undeniable cold. It was as if a need for discovery of the dark unknown had been magically and genetically awakened—until the blissful appearance of a familiar and remarkable ease came wafting upon him, a simple rationalization like a thousand before: It was okay if Mother would not have understood, because he himself did not understand. Such common ground, he felt, always brought a certain safety to relationships, especially any relationship where sex and his virginity might have been concerned. Best not to poke the beehive, he concluded. Better to allow events to reveal themselves to him in a natural and unforced way, he reasoned. And if that way happened to be in his distant future, so be it.

He sighed in his warm place. There was joy in relief.

Lyle, however, had not counted on the short life expectancy of his most recent rationalization. Nanoseconds, really. A fruit fly enjoyed eternity by comparison. And in no time at all, he felt the urge—the urge to poke the beehive. He succumbed to the idea like no other, gladly and willfully, and set about for a vivid recollection, a vibrant stroll through the previous evening's events that might illuminate any detail—noble, lurid, or otherwise—of his curious and possibly promiscuous behavior. Not unnoticed, his recollection also meant that he didn't have to get out from underneath the covers, as did his only other option—exploration.

Lyle graciously allowed his mind to drift backward to the previous evening, back to the moment where evenings always began for him at Grossman's Neptune Club: arriving at exactly 8:00 p.m. to prepare for the restaurant's late dinner crowd.

Places must be set, silver and belaying pins must be polished, knots tied correctly, and relatively fresh sea anemones must be set in slim, crystalline vases and centered at each table. Time, then, to punch in.

Lyle regarded the time clock with about as much kindness as a postman who gets bitten by the same German shepherd daily, recalling one instance where it refused to print the times on his card and instead printed only the days, suggesting only that, yes, Lyle was there "sometime." Or another time when it printed only the minutes and not the hours, thus cheating Lyle out of all but one of the hours of his shift. Yet despite the confrontational nature of Lyle's relationship with this device, management refused to hear Lyle's complaints, discharging them as whining. "Be a man," they said.

No wonder then that Lyle felt helplessly bound to the clock, as if the firm stamping sound it made just sentenced him to its service for yet another dutiful evening. Lyle knew this feeling was not uncommon, but, rather, one that had special significance on this particular evening, as Lyle also noticed a freshly typed memo bound by a golden frame and covered with a thick piece of plate glass. It was placed directly beside the time clock.

A sentinel of rules had been given to the time clock king. Lyle began to read the rules, praying as only a dutiful servant would, that he was in compliance.

RULES:

1. Waiters must be well groomed. Hair must be neatly trimmed. Hands and fingernails must be manicured so as to suggest a professional delicacy that is a waiter's job.
2. Pants must be pressed and shoes must be polished.

And so on and so forth, down the list, until Lyle came to number ten. The curious number ten, as Lyle remembered. It said:

10. Remember: SMILE! You LOVE your job.

Without wanting to make too much fuss, Lyle recalled, he approached his boss, Mr. Grossman, ready to suggest that, in his own case at any rate, the word "love" had been incorrectly used —or, at the very least, used in far too general a context. To be honest, Lyle felt, there were any number of other words that would better describe how he felt about his employment, words he would keep to himself. At this point, Lyle wondered if he hadn't in fact started to think of the words "time clock" as being synonymous with the word "job." It was, in his mind, a beastly, pernicious contraption.

"Speckman! What's your problem now?" said Mr. Grossman, clipboard in hand, kicking another waiter in the tail, sending him on a fly out of the kitchen and into the dining room. "Aren't you at work yet? Why do I always catch you hanging around the time clock? Are you a clockwatcher, Speckman? Are you one of them?"

Grossman's voice assumed an air of abject disgust, as if he was, for the first time in his life, in the presence of a complete untouchable, a social outcast of the lowest depths. His deep-tanned face scowled; it was aged and weather-worn, as if years in the sun and wind had chiseled leathery wrinkles into his face, around his eyes, and into his brow that bunched into basset-hound-like flabby rolls of flesh when he squinted.

"No," was Lyle's weak reply.

"Good. Damn good. Wouldn't want any clock watchers on my team, Speckman," said Grossman, his voice returning to its normal state, a gravelly self-assuredness often found in people attempting to sound authoritative. Grossman was obviously relieved. "You're lucky I've got a soft spot in my heart for waiters, or there'd be hell to pay," he added.

Lyle watched as Grossman turned his attention to his clipboard, and he surmised the first of the night's pop inspections was imminent. Lyle could only hope his assigned task was a reasonable one, something a landlubber could fathom. In the past, he had been lectured about the ways in which dusty conch shells and the tarnished tines of the twin tridents above the entrance to the dining room failed to convey the mystery, majesty, and enchantment of the Seven Seas, something Grossman's Neptune Club clearly aspired to. No matter that the giant wooden figurehead of Flying Pegasus at the Club's entrance, the closest thing Grossman had to a prow, frightened small children and the elderly. No matter that Lyle often struggled with the clarity of Grossman's commands, like the time he ordered a complete repositioning of the Club's loose décor—fish netting, life preservers, driftwood, parts of an old footlocker, a damaged signal buoy, etc.—with the command 'Flotsam to the leeward and jetsam to the windward! Double time!' Lyle did the best he could. As always, he hoped for compliance, compliance, compliance . . .

"It's the rules," Lyle blurted.

"Damn heads-up of you to notice, Speckman. What this restaurant needs are more go-getters like you. Why, if I had a few more like you, I could whip this wait staff into a crack serving unit. But it takes discipline, Speckman. Discipline. You do what you're told. Learned that in the Merchant Marines. Now what do you want?"

Grossman stood next to Lyle, his apish frame slouching under his crew cut, but still towering over Lyle's wisp of a trembling body.

"Well, speak up, boy. What is it?"

Lyle felt the word "love" on the tip of his tongue and was only seconds away from confronting Grossman on the wording of the rules—politely, and, if necessary, apologetically—when Nick Sparelli, another waiter at the restaurant, strutted into the kitchen from the dining room. Nick loved to strut, allowing for the firmest, loudest, most even-toned emanations to be made by the cleats on the bottoms of his boots against the sandstone-colored linoleum. "The day you carpet the dining room is the day I'm out of here, *capisce?*" he often said in that invented dialect, the one he used to tell everyone he was from New York where, as he said, "all the real Italians come from." No one cared that he was from Kansas or pretended to notice when he dyed his blond hair jet black and darkened in his eyebrows with the maître'd's reservation pencil. Everyone pretended the old Nick Sparelli just quit.

"Monsters," Sparelli said. "Not human. No other words. Adolescent wolverines, maybe. And they're eating at my table right now. Look at me," he said, pointing to his tuxedoed shirt, which was now decoratively spotted with a vicious-looking pasta sauce. "They've got this little munchkin of a kid, must be three or four years old, and they order him meatballs.

Meatballs! They put a big plate full of juicy, sauced-covered, throwable balls of meat right in front of his grabby paws! What did they think was going to happen? Can you believe it? Can you believe the intelligence of some people? Who teaches these children? Monkeys? Some people should teach their children some manners. We should have a height requirement, at least . . . And if they do bring these dwarfish mutants into my restaurant, they should at the least have the decency not to feed them anything fist-sized. Maybe a nice Virginia ham."

"Sparelli!" Grossman yelled. "I don't see a smile! Can't you read the rules? Look at Speckman. Speckman's smiling."

Nick half-glanced in the direction of Lyle, feigning a smile. He said under his breath, "Figures."

Nick had never been a close friend to Lyle, despite their closeness in age. Nick was a year older and in no way considered Lyle a peer. It was a distance that had seemed to become even more expansive since last weekend, that wild weekend Nick told everyone about firsthand—everyone but Lyle. Lyle's only information of the events came accidentally as he was trying to unbend his time card from the time clock and overheard Nick retell the story to Butch, the liquor salesman (something about bars and drinking and laughing women). Lyle recalled seeing, however, that Nick showed Butch his newly tattooed forearm: a naked lady wrapped in snakes over the words, "Don't Tread on Me." Nick was tough, Lyle felt—too tough to pal around with guys like himself.

"I still don't see a smile, Sparelli!"

"Smile? I'm not going back out there without combat pay. And what's more, get this, they've got the nerve to ask for more meatballs! Can you believe it? Where's my hot sauce? Which one of you bleeding hearts stole my hot sauce?"

"Sparelli! Now get this and get this good: You're going back out there and you're going out there with a smile on your face. Do you get that, mister?"

Lyle saw Nick's eyes widen, as if he were feeling the force of Grossman's words against his face, powered by explosive salvos of saliva.

"Yes, sir, Mr. Grossman, sir," Nick said facetiously, as he wiped his face dry with his shirtsleeve.

"Don't get smart with me, Sparelli. Are you trying to get smart with me? You get smart with me and I'll . . ."

"You'll what?" Nick said defiantly.

It was at that precise moment that Lyle noticed a glazed and far-away look appear on Grossman's face. It was as if he were suddenly overtaken by an unseen and immutable force, a malevolent spirit or a jaunty memory, some inexplicable presence that froze his facial features in an unnatural and contorted way and sent his thoughts to some unknown hinterland. Lyle had seen this before. From time to time, amid the harried activity of the late dinner rush or the jabbering confusion and wheeler-dealing offered by traveling vegetable salesmen, Grossman had shared the bygone and disjointed tales of his time as a young lad in the Merchant Marines to anyone within earshot, the briny sea air and rolling swells the backdrop to every edgy, life-altering adventure. Usually a shriek would follow, but not always. Lyle knew almost anything could come next.

"And I'll . . . I'll fire Speckman, that's what," Grossman said.

"What?" Lyle squeaked incredulously.

"Sorry, Speckman," Grossman began, "you're out."

"But I didn't do anything!"

"Don't whine, Speckman. Be a team player. For once in your life, be a man. Now get out of here before I call a cop. Grossman's Neptune Club is no longer in need of your services. Shove off."

The clarity of Lyle's recollection suddenly arrested his normal breathing functions as he, lowering the bedspread to his chin and gasping for air, wheezed, "Heavens . . . I've been . . . let go."

The tiniest tear appeared in the corner of Lyle's eye, failing to glisten in the dim morning light and begging permission to fall from Speckman eye to Speckman cheek. Grabbing a corner of the soft satin sheet, Lyle blotted.

"Dismissed," he whispered, the softness of the word in direct conflict with the Speckman constitution, which at this very moment spun and whirled and heaved with all the undulation of an undigested egg salad sandwich. It made Lyle nauseous. Still, dismissal alone, he reasoned, would not account for his change of sleeping venue, and Lyle returned to recollection, searching for those missing pieces that resulted in the disheveled embarrassment that was now his life. He closed his eyes.

Lyle remembered walking out the back door of the Neptune Club, the warm summer night a small consolation to his current problem: both tires of his bicycle had somehow became lifelessly flat, deflated in the same moments that it took to suck the air right out of his employment. Standing over

11

his bicycle, Lyle moaned, "Not you, too." He remembered he walked away without looking back.

Lyle walked down US highway TBNL (To Be Named Later), the latest in redevelopment projects promised when Alderman Peabody took over. "I give you seven miles of growth and prosperity," Peabody said at the dedication. Nobody came to the dedication but Lyle and the photographer from the paper (rumor has it he was Peabody's nephew, Ed, from Iowa) and only slightly more decided to take him at his word as to the "growth and prosperity" part. After six months, there were no new businesses. The only residents on either side of the highway remained Grossman's Neptune Club, Ray's Cut-Rate Liquor, and an unassuming little café called Eat, entrepreneurs who had staked their claim and attempted to seek their fortune as many as ten uneventful years ago.

The proprietors of these establishments put the blame solely on Peabody's failure to name the highway as reason for the conspicuous absence of other businesses and clientele, citing that it was hard for people to find them if they didn't have an address. Peabody, however, steadfast in his resolve, promised that the contest for the naming of the highway was nearly over, saying, "I am close to a decision." Lyle could only hope Peabody liked the suggestion he sent him several weeks ago, "US Highway America," and felt that, since he had just won the Fourth of July contest, another Speckman win wouldn't suggest favoritism. He could only hope Peabody's decision was imminent.

As Lyle walked down the highway and toward home, oblivious to the miles that would have to be covered before he could shelter his embarrassment in the comfort of his own home, he began to look soulfully to the sky and to the heavens. It seemed the only companion to provide comfort and solace to his wounded feelings would be found in the sparkling diadems of the dark and ancient sky, silently, like some unknown, welcome presence, a mysterious and compassionate nameless friend. Lyle couldn't explain the feeling, but now, of all times, felt that a wish or a prayer upon a star couldn't hurt. He saw it work once in his favorite movie (something about a cricket). He then felt the sky, a great expanse above him, and a constant before his changing life. This was the sky of Caesar. Of Napoleon. Of Alexander the Great. They, too, had stared and wondered. Perhaps they also wished. All great men and himself present beneath the sameness of the ancient sky. Mystically, Lyle started to call out the constellations.

"Orion the Hunter! . . .

. . . Cassiopeia the Something! . . .

. . . And another thing that looks like it's got swords and shields and chariots and other manly things! . . .

Yes!" Lyle yelled into the night, for the first time in his life realizing that unemployed waiters don't get constellations named after them—men of action do.

Tonight would be the turning point in his life, he remembered, a blessing amidst the recent unpleasantness. Lyle began to run down US TBNL, his eagerness void of any direction other than forward, his mind a constant quartet of Caesar, Napoleon, Alexander, and Speckman. Somehow he was sure to take his place among the great ones, if he only remembered that they were all one under the ancient sky—if only he remembered to show a little aggressiveness. Maybe Grossman was right, he thought, maybe it was time to stand up for himself and be a man. Ray's Cut-Rate Liquor was just ahead.

Lyle entered Ray's on a full run, the color gone from his face and the lack of stamina in his legs making him walk like a marionette with the strings tangled. "I'd like a beer," Lyle said breathlessly to the man seated behind the counter.

"Looks like you've had enough," said Ray, his eyes surveying every inch of Lyle.

"No, you don't understand. I'm not the least bit impaired."

"Of course you're not," said Ray, his economy of words a stark contrast to the massiveness of his form.

Lyle paused to catch his breath and noticed a framed snapshot of what appeared to be the man behind the counter in a wrestling ring. Lyle quickly and cautiously compared the features of the man in the photo with those of the man seated firmly before him: sloping forehead—sloping forehead, shaved head—shaved head, intently maniacal stare—intently maniacal stare, height and weight relatively equivalent to a small building—height and weight relatively equivalent to a small building. Lyle was still unsure, though, until he saw the nameplate under the photo. It read: Death Ray Drake Inter-Time Zone Champ. It matched the nametag on the man behind the counter.

"Have they named anything after you?" Lyle asked quizzically. Ray didn't answer. "Never mind. Back to the item at hand. Now that I've caught my breath and you can see that I'm not impaired in the slightest degree, I would like to purchase one can of alcoholic beer beverage."

Ray shook his head slowly.

Remembering Caesar and Napoleon and Alexander, Lyle said, "And if I insist?" Ray got up off his stool. Lyle noted that, had they been outside, Ray's broad shoulders could have blocked out the entirety of the sun. He gulped. "Champ?" Lyle offered sincerely.

Ray eased himself back onto his stool, and Lyle felt victorious, as if Ray was calmed by the gentleness of his words and the kindness of his smile, the result of manly Speckman overtures in action, obviously. Alternate scenarios quickly supplanted those thoughts, however, and Lyle soon feared an ominous uncertainty common to him: He had no way of discerning the absolute truth.

A raised eyebrow and scant glance from Ray suggested to Lyle he was to leave, and he prayed it wasn't by some overt act of physical violence. He had heard that Ray didn't like whiners—he liked headlocks. Lyle's imagination commandeered the moment, and what it might take for Ray to remain on his stool, stay stuck in his corner. Lyle imagined that Ray had already thrown out the only three people who came into his store that day, two unintelligible liquor salesmen and one Boy Scout trying to sell him a Christmas wreath. Any further display of anti-community sentiment, he figured, could only jeopardize his future business success, a success that was virtually guaranteed as soon as the highway was named and he received an address. Positive word of mouth was then necessary to balance the day's ledger, of course. Pleasantly, Ray sold Lyle one can of beer, remarking, "Have a nice day," as Lyle walked out the door and headed for the highway.

Lyle put the can of beer in the deep front pocket of his baggy black pants, spoils to be savored. It was the first reward of his new aggressiveness, the new Lyle Speckman, and deserved to be imbibed with pomp and circumstance. Surely, Lyle felt, some type of ritual was in order. For now, though, Lyle continued walking, a course guided by his allegiance with the majesty of the stars, as well as the painted yellow centerlines of US Highway TBNL.

Lyle stepped smartly and with purpose, each step awakening a new and natural sense of things. He felt the rhythm of his quick step feed new warmth in his heart, an inner warmth to collide with the cooling night air in a gradual and elegant sort of way. Each tiny speck of bright starlight, sparkler crisp, a pulsing hypnotic jewel, the remnant of an explosive birth and unknown light years journey, met his eye in a brilliant and wordless way. An extraordinary brilliance. Each seemed to offer a faint iciness into the darkness, faint enough to suggest that the warmness of the day had somehow been smoothed over by its viceroy, calming it without incident, as if it were the most normal thing in the world. Feeling the confidence of a great man alone on a road untravelled, Lyle walked in the direction of Eat.

Eat was the second of the three legacy businesses to occupy a space along the side of US Highway TBNL, arriving pre-fab via truck from parts unknown many years ago, only one day after the opening of Grossman's Neptune Club. "Competition is good," it was rumored to have been said at the opening ceremony, during which a prominent local official symbolically ordered and drank, "the first cup of joe." It made a nice photo.

As the story went, onlookers at the time, one elderly waitress who couldn't speak English and the man who came to hook up the neon sign, seemed politely unimpressed and continued about their business during the entire ceremony. She stood behind the counter, staring out the window, daydreaming, the fingers of her hand mindlessly twirling a ball-point pen like a majorette's baton in slow motion; he sat on the floor, legs stretched out in front of him, a genuine look of confusion on his tired face as he traded glances between the wall socket and the sign's electrical cord, a cord that dangled two inches short of its destination. Over the years, legend grew of this tradesman's dedication and skill in the harnessing of the volt and the amp and the inert gas. He was rumored to have worked long into the night to solve the problem, his ingenuity incubated from sheer perseverance, his talent as magical as electricity itself.

It was only a short distance from Eat when Lyle saw that neon sign, its letters flickering an unnatural redness into the night, when he felt an uneven smile come on. He could see that the café was open, and that pleased him. He could see that the café was empty, and he felt deflated that no one would see him in his new found stature, his new pride. There were no idle men chin-wagging. There were no mysterious out-of-place dowagers (the kind that seem genuinely impressed by self-assured young men), their dentured smiles and vivid memories and hand-crocheted shawls conspicuously absent. There were no young people whatsoever—maybe it wasn't a good place to hang out and waste time. There were no bachelors dining out. There was no one who didn't have someplace else to be. Only a young waitress was there, brewing coffee.

Lyle entered and took a seat on a stool at the counter. It was the first time in a year that he had been in a restaurant other than Grossman's, a detail that didn't seem in the least bit odd or peculiar to him. But then, Lyle figured, no longer being in the employ of the Neptune Club should have automatically freed him from any obligations of loyalty or allegiance. Thus, he knew he was feeling the proper emotion when he felt absolutely no guilt, absolutely no terror, no oddness. Lyle's realization made him want to giggle. With a flick of his wrist, he spun the seat of the stool next to him and watched it race around in circles, a blur of yellow vinyl wobbling noisily atop a single stainless steel leg. As the seat slowed, Lyle smartly slapped at its side, encouraging more revolutions, more speed, faster, faster, faster . . .

"May I help you?" she said.

"Uh . . ." replied a shocked and embarrassed Lyle, the metally slick tones of ball bearings slowing to a halt next to him.

"We only have coffee today," she said. "I hope you don't mind, but the cook had to go someplace. I'm not exactly sure where he went, but he told me to be in charge. He also told me not to use the grill until we got the fire extinguishers recharged. You don't mind, do you? The coffee's fresh. I just made it."

Lyle suddenly remembered the last cup of coffee he had. Nick Sparelli gave it to him while on a work break one day, saying, "This is just how Momma Sparelli makes it in the old country. She uses the husks." Lyle felt a lump in his throat. "No, I . . . I'm just looking," he said.

"Okay," she answered, as she walked back in the direction of the brewing coffee pot.

Lyle got up off his stool and began to pace. Just looking, he thought, what a dumb thing to say. He paced back and forth near the neon sign, its incessant buzzing and powerful red glow distracting him from once again staring out into the night.

In a manner of few instinctive and annoying seconds, Lyle turned away from the window. He realized he had been watching her reflection in the glass in front of him, a brightness in the window beyond the red glow that wouldn't let him see the darkness outside, only the light behind. His elation at breaking free of Grossman—which only recently became the aggressive-Speckman-rationalization-version of what had happened during the evening—had given him a feeling of control that, to be honest with himself, he didn't feel in his conversation with the waitress. He could see that now, in reflection.

Elation, confidence, and vibrance were good, he felt, but as just evidenced, useless without self-control. Caesar had self-control. Napoleon had self-control. Alexander had self-control. So will Speckman, he proclaimed to himself.

Lyle stood next to the sign stoically: shoulders back, head held high, the whiteness of his ruffled shirt suffocating an otherwise thrown-out chest. This was the exact position that Grossman, on Lyle's very first day of employment, showed him for "observing." The man did have some good ideas, Lyle conceded.

Lyle watched her and began to replay in his mind what had happened only moments before, intent upon the precision of observing detail. Having all the facts, all the details, was the only way to efficiently orchestrate a situation of total control, he reasoned. Still, he didn't want a conversation with a waitress to turn into a military exercise—only a moment in which a complete stranger, a waitress, would give him the benefit of the doubt as to all matters relating to his pride, self-confidence, and competence. That's all.

He recalled the yellow stools in front of the counter, eight vacancies and the last of the barriers, the last detail to concern himself with; he had been there before and forced retreat. He noticed the emptiness of the café's walls, beige and a plainness that seemed to reflect a dull light off the stainless steel of the grill and the coffeemaker. After years of operation, Eat had taken on a look that suggested age without use, a newness of a past time that had been consciously passed by in favor of, it seemed, anything else. The only recent addition seemed to be a small cardboard stand, filled with colorful informational brochures about Alderman Peabody's redevelopment projects, apparently a free gift from the Chamber of Commerce and worthy of its prominent position beside the front door. Lyle also noticed the neon sign, a humming about his head and a crackling about his ankles. He looked down and saw that two small pieces of what appeared to be a rusted coat hanger had been soldered to the prongs of the sign's electrical cord, pieces of wire that were then stuck into the wall socket, causing the occasional arc of electricity from socket to hanger to prong. How resourceful, he thought.

And Lyle saw her.

He watched her, her young delicate frame veiled by a clumsy red-and-white checked dress, a uniform that attempted by association to make her look like a waitress. Her short, dark hair fell loosely about her collar, and Lyle could see the reflection of her face in the coffee pot, remembering the averageness of her features when she first said, 'May I help you?' The much-too-wide-open eyes and the uneven smile made a picture that Lyle didn't think quite matched, yet seemed honest in the way he always trusted without explanation the things that gave him pleasure, the things in his room.

Bravely, Lyle walked back to the counter and sat down. "Nice weather, isn't it?" he said.

"Yes, it's very nice," she said, moving toward Lyle. "Dark, too."

"Yes, I think it's very dark."

"Do you think it's darker than usual? Tonight, I mean."

"I don't know," she said. "I work most nights."

Her tone indicated to Lyle her genuine displeasure with having to work nights, and he feared it may become a stumbling block to a conversation he was beginning to enjoy. He could only hope her conversations with other patrons were far too infrequent, perhaps less noble, and he hoped he impressed upon her his finest gentlemanly qualities in an instant, though he couldn't name a specific one off the top of his head. He wanted her to magically see qualities that had nothing to do with the sparse words coming out of his mouth, an awkwardness in his demeanor that would somehow, miraculously, make her smile. He hoped she would like that.

"Nice and bright in here, though," Lyle said, noting the name "Jane" on her nametag.

"Yes. The boss likes it bright in here. He says it's good for business. Sometimes the cook likes to turn down the lights and watch the flames shoot from the grill, but since he's not here tonight, I decided to leave all the lights on. Every one. I don't think he'll mind."

"No, he won't mind . . . This lets everyone see the yellow vinyl stools and the beige walls and the way the workman cleverly mounted the neon sign." Lyle felt himself on a roll. "No, Jane, is it? I don't think anyone will mind."

"Janet," she said.

Lyle didn't know what to say.

"My name is Janet," she said with a casual smile.

"But your nametag says Jane."

"I know, but my name is really Janet," she said.

Lyle noted she sensed his confusion.

"You know those little nametag things that print your name on a little piece of plastic? Well, the tiny thing inside it broke after I printed the 'e' and I couldn't get it to work anymore. I tried to write the 't' on with an ink pen, but it kept smudging off."

"Oh." Lyle took a quick breath and looked directly at her, his eyes pleading that if, for some incomprehensible reason, his next supposition was incorrect, she would nonetheless nod and grin approvingly. "Janet, then?"

"Yes." Janet paused. "No one who has ever come in here before has called me by my real name. This is the first time," she said, as her smile broadened and she turned coquettishly away from Lyle. "Even the cook calls me Jane."

"Really?" Lyle said in a high-pitched tone of excitement.

Sensing a momentary lapse of control, Lyle lowered his voice a few octaves into what he considered his most manly range. "Is that so?" he continued.

"Even my friend, Deb, calls me Jane. She says it suits me. What's your name?"

The question hit Lyle like an emotional sledgehammer between the eyes, a blow so severe as to make the "Grossman Incident" seem all but forgetable. For the first time in his life, a woman other than his mother had shown an interest in him. The potential ramifications startled Lyle. She asked him his name for the purpose of . . . ? Wheels turned inside Lyle's head, and he felt himself getting dizzy. He got up off his stool.

"Did you forget?" Janet said, as a playful giggle escaped.

"Uh, no. I didn't forget." Indeed, Lyle remembered only too well. Now, of all times, he wished he had an impressive-sounding name, as if purely resonant tones in tandem with a convincing inflection could themselves carry the confidence and masculinity of the speaker. Somehow, he felt, "Lyle Speckman" didn't quite measure up to the standards of his new self-controlled aggressiveness. He could only think of names he considered tough, hard-sounding. He thought of Nick, Nick, Nick . . . "My name is Ray Drake." The words seemed to dribble from his mouth, contrary to their desired effect.

"Oh, are you the wrestler? From down the road?"

"That's me," Lyle said proudly, only a split second before he could get his hand in front of his mouth. It was a feeble attempt to stop this self-induced carnage of character.

"I've heard of you," Janet said. "Aren't you the champ, or something?"

Lyle winced. "Oh, you know how it is." He felt an unbearable pain begin to swell within him, choking his thoughts and distracting him from Janet.

Janet stood behind the counter, her only official duty her simple presence, as she watched Lyle. He had developed a nervous tick in his right leg, causing him to tap his foot furiously as if keeping time to some imaginary brass band he searched for with his stares somewhere among the ceiling tiles.

"I saw you wrestle on TV several months ago," she started. "My girlfriend was watching; she's the real fan. She knows all the players and all the outfits everybody wears. She says she knows just everything about wrestling. You should meet her. You look a little different in person, though."

"Well, you know what they say about TV adding a few pounds." Lyle began to feel a heavy dampness about his body, as if the nervous sweat that now seemed to be gushing from his pores was about to envelope him, soaking his clothes and making them feel like the deadest of weights. His right leg felt like an anchor.

"You looked a little taller on TV, too."

"Uh . . . I was taller. I mean, I used to be tall. I lost my height in a car accident."

"Oh," she said, in a manner that suggested she didn't know whether or not to be curious or sympathetic.

Lyle took another deep breath, wiping the sweat from his brow with the back of his hand. And only when he was sure he felt that the worst was over, a moment where he could begin to look for the silver lining in this, his most recent encounter with what seemed his own personal black cloud, did he notice the coolest trickle of water inching a path down his leg.

He put his hand in his pants pocket and felt the once ice cold beer, now a tepid reminder to a happier time, itself sweating and soaking Lyle's pants in a most unflattering and embarrassing location. He could only think about what would happen if she noticed. The mental picture frightened him. Without excusing himself, Lyle sped off to the men's room, an inaudible "Oh, gosh" leading the way.

Lyle closed the door of the men's room behind him but was careful to not lock it. He felt himself becoming faint and quick-breathed and thought that, in the event of hyperventilation, a fast and immediate exit would best serve to save face and, perhaps, life.

He took off his pants, setting the warm can of beer on the edge of the sink and pulled several paper towels from the dispenser on the wall. The mirror above the sink captured the image of the beer can, providing Lyle with twice the opportunity to view what he felt was now a failed symbol of his new aggressiveness. Once in reality and once in reflection, the can now seemed to Lyle a most despicable victor, claiming victory over him by attrition and now tormenting him with silence. He hated it.

In a blur of motion, Lyle lunged at the can, grabbing it firmly with one hand and ripping the pop-top open with the other, sending a warm explosion of beer and foam into the air that looked like the grand finale to the Town's Fourth of July fireworks. Lyle wanted to "ooooh" but instead vengefully guzzled the remaining contents before he crushed the thin aluminum can by thrusting it soundly into his forehead. He fell to the floor with a thud, moaning. So much for ritual.

Lyle opened his eyes, snug in his cocoon.

Once again lowering the furry bedspread to his chin, Lyle stared at the ceiling. He rubbed his bruised forehead with the tips of his fingers and felt the slyest of smiles come to his face. He could remember nothing else but relied upon his powers of deduction and observation to fill in the obvious. "Yes," he said aloud, "I met a girl."

# Chapter 2

"So, what are you saying? Is old man MacNamara here, or not?" Nick heaped his stained shirt on the counter, highlighting a blotchy redness with a point of his finger and a "what gives?" look on his face. "Look at this shirt. Just look at it. Pasta and meatball, tomato sauce everywhere. It looks like I was one of those shooting gallery ducks like they have at Coney Island. Only instead of shooting corks out of little tiny air guns, some miniature Fascist unloads with a fistful of meatballs, and then he laughs at me like he's a child of Satan or some three-toothed moppet from outer space . . . Weasily eyes, too . . . So is he here?"

Mrs. MacNamara stepped back from behind the counter, her customer's enthusiasm affecting her sweet grandmotherly face with wide smiles, a nod, and a wink. She picked up the shirt and headed into the back room, parting a thin curtain with her hand. Her leisurely pace displayed an opaque lack of urgency.

Mrs. MacNamara and her husband, Clancy, ran MacNamara Cleaners from a small building conveniently located right next door to the Chamber of Commerce. Mrs. M. rejoiced when Clancy had retired from his position of clerk at the Bank of Ireland in Limerick just the previous summer and felt that now, after a long period of tedious employment,

27

meeting a collection of unstuffy, completely different sort of people on a daily basis was not only in order, but something that should ascend rapidly to the top of his agenda.

This was a fine opportunity for Clancy to let loose the playful and mischievous personality she fell in love with so long ago, she hoped. America had afforded him this glorious opportunity, she thought, as well. And, as a means of showing her appreciation to their new country, Mrs. M. decided to mainstream Clancy into American retirement life. She already paid for the business from their modest savings, ensuring a pleasantly casual livelihood, while fighting off, as she had told him long ago, "that demon boredom." Magazine subscriptions, too, already started rolling in, and she made sure he made plans to have his picture taken for his senior citizen ID card. She couldn't wait for him to get his first discount.

The uprooting of her life in Limerick, she conceded, was a bit of a bother, so much so that Clancy promised, in a most solemn tone, not to do that sort of thing more than once every sixty-six years. On this point, there was ready agreement, and there would be no lively debate.

Mrs. M. also figured that, since she and her husband were recent émigrés, being so close to the governmental hub of the town could only serve to Americanize them more quickly, by osmosis if nothing else. She had heard things sometimes happen like that in America.

"Clancy, dear, there's a lad out front who's wishing t'speak with you."

Clancy sat on a stool in front of a large new telescope pointed skyward, the tassels of his still boyishly red hair gently falling over the eyepiece. He looked up. "And what might the lad be wanting?"

"He's got a stain."

"So?"

"Well, you see, it's like this: he's a bit of an odd fellow, with runny black eyebrows, who claims he was attacked by a group of miniature Fascists wielding meatballs. Insistent upon that, he was. I quite think his mind 'as skipped completely off the track and into the pebbles."

"You don't say. Right here in the store."

"Yes. Right out front."

"Imagine that."

Clancy picked up the open copy of his new *Astronomy and Alchemy,* studied the diagram on the page, and returned his eye to the eyepiece.

"And Clancy, dear . . ."

"Yes?" he said, without looking up.

"You know I am not one to pick nits, and I am certainly not one to debate you on matters celestial. However, I was under the impression, and I may be entirely mistaken, that peak stargazing opportunities presented themselves in the dead of evening. Has something realigned in the cosmos that is best seen at half past eleven on a Saturday morning? Shouldn't you wait for the darkness, dear?"

Clancy's eye was pressed hard to the eyepiece. He fiddled with the focusing knob. "Just a wee bit o' practice, that's all. Last night, I saw something in the sky I couldn't explain. The stars all seemed funny and jumping about like they were jockeying for position in the Derby. And it felt as warm to me as . . ."

"Clancy MacNamara! You went to the pub again! Didn't you!?"

Clancy got up off his stool, an innocent grin already two steps ahead of him. He blinked his eyes rapidly in response to the unfiltered sunlight and slinked over to the curtain that hung between the doorway. He peeked through a hole in the cloth. "Let's have a look at your maniac, shall we, love?"

Nick leaned against the counter, waiting. He was staring off into dead space when Janet walked in. She carried a shirt and pair of pants under her arm; they were bundled with a piece of string.

"Is there anyone here?" Janet asked, as she set her bundle on the counter.

"In back. All I asked was a simple yes or no question, and it sent her running with a stupid grin on her face. I figure she's got gas."

Janet at once seemed stunned. Her delayed response a thoughtful and polite, "Oh, I see." She coyly turned away, added a delicate smile, her eye contact with Nick broken by a subtle wave of her hand, brushing back her hair.

Nick, however, was apparently not one to waste an opportunity to display the more smooth and suave elements of his interpersonal skills. He sported a confident grin and threw out his chest. "You can never find a good Chinaman when you need one, can you?"

A polite but disinterested Janet turned her head, ever so slightly. "I beg your pardon," she offered.

"It's a laundry joke. Laundry—Chinaman, get it?"

Mrs. M. watched over Clancy's shoulder, through that

same hole in the curtain, and knew there was nowhere for Janet to go. She felt for her, trapped by her circumstance, as if one of her limbs had mistakenly entered the loopy end of a snare trap. She hoped for a spirited turn of events.

"You like jokes, don't you? I'm a funny guy," Nick said, as he nodded. "You like funny guys, don't you? Let me tell you how funny I am: 'Once I fed a cigar to a goat.'"

Janet put her hand to her mouth and let out a tiny squeak. As Mrs. M. and Clancy watched, they simultaneously cringed for Janet. If they could, they would have rendered her temporarily invisible. But for now, the drama was too intoxicating for them to interrupt or turn away.

"Okay, so you don't like funny guys," Nick continued. "I bet I know what you like. I bet you go for tough guys. Well, take a look at this." Nick stood beside her and stuck his newly tattooed forearm in her face. He began to flex the muscles of his arm. "See, I can make it dance."

Clancy whispered to his wife, "Mrs. MacNamara, you're quite right. The man is a loon. Stall the lad while I search for the Instamatic. I wouldn't want this one to get away. A fish out of water, if ever I saw one. Quite rare. *Imbecilious Moronicus,* I think."

"So, what do you say?" Nick started. "Am I one of a kind or am I one of a kind?"

Before Janet could answer, Mrs. MacNamara came out from behind the curtain. She set Nick's shirt on the counter. "Why, hello, Janet! How very grand to see you again."

"Hello, Mrs. MacNamara."

"And what have you got for us today?" Mrs. MacNamara

said, as she picked up the bundled clothes on the counter. "This doesn't look like your regular uniform."

Mrs. M. knew it would take about a second and a half for Nick to believe he had been slighted. She sensed emotions bubbling through him like a volcano. "Hey! What about my shirt?" he finally erupted.

Mrs. MacNamara answered Nick with a wordless eye-to-eye stare and a tilt of her head that seemed to say, without inflection or sentiment, plain and simply, unequivocally, "What?"

"What about my shirt?" Nick repeated. His tone suggested a substantial amount of experience in repeating himself.

"It's stained."

"I know it's stained, that's why I brought it in here."

"And you thought enough of Mrs. MacNamara to come to for a second opinion! What a fine, fine lad you must be," she said with a smile. "I'm so glad you came, as well. I do so love it when I can be of help to others. It makes me feel so useful. Can I get you some tea or crackers?"

"No," he said. "And useful, I know. I've got a grandmother who makes decorative planters out of bedpans. What I want to know is, can you get the stain out?"

"And are you so sure you'd be wanting the stain out, lad? Me own sainted grandmother had a stain just like that on her baking apron and said it kept the little people from stealing her desserts for years. The little people are so clever, you know. But they hate when anything's a mess. The wearin' o' that shirt is sure to keep mischief away and bring you the luck of the blessed. You shall age a fortunate man."

"Lady, I don't want to hear any song and . . . Luck? What kind of luck?" he said, interrupting himself again.

Mrs. M. surmised an idea was percolating inside of Nick, as if the elegant tickle of a cattle prod had nudged the active part of his cerebral cortex, jolting it awake. She felt certain he intended to follow this new electric thought to some fantastic conclusion—albeit one of his own imagination.

"Oooh, the strongest kind, me boy. Whenever there's a time you'd be wanting fortune to swing in your favor—and you're wearing the shirt, mind you —all you have to do is put one hand o'er the stain and shout 'MacNamara Cleaners!' three times loud."

"MacNamara Cleaners?" Nick asked. He was obviously lost.

"But of course. The luck won't work unless you shout out the name of the place where you heard the legend first. Common sense, really . . . like coming in out of the blistering sun. That sort of common sense. The most natural thing in the world, really. Shouldn't even have to think twice. ' Tis taught every small boy in Limerick. You wouldn't want to be wastin' the luck of an almost sainted legend now, would you? Casting it out, so to speak?"

"Gee, I guess not," he said almost immediately. His mind stumbled to reconnect with the bright idea he had only seconds ago. "But what kind of luck could I wish for?"

"All that your heart desires, lad."

"What if, just for the sake of argument, I would walk up to a certain, well . . ."

"Lass? With a twinkle in your eye?"

"What then?"

"Well," Mrs. MacNamara said, her voice a whisper. She put her hand on Nick's shoulder, gently leaning over the counter as if about to impart the secret directly into his ear. "As loud as you can, m'boy, 'MacNamara Cleaners!' three times loud."

Nick pulled back, unconvinced. "Wouldn't she make a face at me?" he said.

"Aye, lad, that she will. 'Twill be the good luck rushing into her and taking her heart by surprise. The shock of her own good fortune shone upon her face."

"Oh." Nick looked at the stained shirt atop the counter. He alternated reaching for the stain with each hand. It was the most curious choreography. "Is this a new legend? How come I haven't heard of this before?"

Mrs. MacNamara winked. "You will have the MacNamara guarantee by your side at all times."

"I better have. I won't be made a fool of, you know."

Nick took the stained shirt and walked toward the front window. Staring out into the street, he draped the shirt across his back as Mrs. M. watched. She was certain she tipped the first domino in some master plan of his, setting off a blitzkrieg of highly choreographed interpersonal maneuvers only he could conceive of. No amount of time, however, that had been allocated to any master plan by Nick was a match for his impatience. He grabbed the shirt and desperately tried to fit both arms into the correct holes. It was a breathtaking struggle between man and object, an object that ultimately succumbed to its aggressor's animation with little more than the occasional lint flake being lost forever into the atmosphere. Victorious, Nick buttoned.

Mrs. MacNamara began to unbundle the clothes in front of Janet. "Now, what have we here," she said. "Why, Janet! These are men's clothes! And they're smelling like they've been used to swab the pub floor with. You haven't fallen in with drunkards, have you? Sots? Oh saints, Janet! Tell a poor old wash woman that it isn't true!"

"No, Mrs. MacNamara, nothing like that," she said, blushing. Her eyes casually watched her own hands even more casually playing with the string that lay on the counter top. She tilted her head a bit to one side and began to wind the string taut between her fingers. "I've met a young man, though."

Mrs. M. smiled. "How grand, Janet, grand! And what might his name be? Do I know the fellow?"

"Hey! Is this thing on right?" Nick said, as he pushed his way in front of Janet. "How come I don't feel any different? Shouldn't I tingle, or something?"

"That part comes later, lad."

"Oh," Nick said. He stepped back from the counter slowly and began to leer at Janet. With his left hand, he brushed the hair back from in front of her face. He fiercely clutched his shirt with his right. "MacNamara Cleaners! MacNamara Cleaners! MacNamara Cleaners!" he yelled.

"Are you insane!" Janet snapped.

A blank look then overtook Nick's face and Mrs. M. was awed by ease of it, as if the muscles in his cheeks and brow were returning to a familiar and comfortable state, the evolutionary memory of a natural cluelessness brought on by the mildest of confrontations. "Hey! Nothing happened.

It's broke or something. Why didn't something happen? Are there other magic words?"

There was only a brief silence.

"But of course it won't work on her," Mrs. MacNamara began calmly. "Couldn't you see that she was here the whole time that I gave you the secret? She knows, lad, she knows. You've got to find a lass who's ne'er put ear to whisper of the tale if you hope for the magic to work. Virgin ears have no defense. Wide open as the first tulip on a spring morn, they are. 'Tis always been the way. Surely, an intelligent, worldly sort of man like yourself knows that, yes? The virgin ears? Do you know of tulips, lad?" Mrs. M. paused, then added a wink for good measure. "Why, of course you do. I can already see your worldly wisdom beatin' back the last few sprouts of doubt like a fine thoroughbred shooin' flies with 'is tail as I speak . . . Ah, but you're giving a poor old wash woman a bit o' the blarney, aren't you? Sure, you are."

A catatonic moment pulsed uncomfortably between the three as Nick, his right hand still frozen over the stain, said, "Don't look at me like that. I wasn't sure, so I had to try it out. I wouldn't want to make a fool of myself in public, you know. I've got a reputation at stake."

"Aye, I bet you do, lad. I bet you do."

"You bet I do," Nick said, as he strutted back to a spot in front of the store's picture window. The eagerness in his voice matched the intensity of his gaze, a gaze that methodically surveyed the streets and the sidewalks and the Town Square in front of him, searching expectantly for his first long-legged, legend-ignorant lady. "I'm Italian, you know," he added.

Mrs. MacNamara smiled warmly and turned to Janet. "So tell me about your young man, and don't you dare leave out the tiniest detail."

"Well, his name is Ray Drake and . . ."

From in front of the store, Nick's breathing became erratic and his ears pricked up like a frightened rabbit. "Ray Drake! Death Ray! Has he seen me!?" His voice quivered and his chest heaved in an undulating fashion, gasping for any and all air in the immediate vicinity. The panting became more violent with every strained breath. "Does it look like he's looking for anyone, in particular? Like, maybe, someone who very accidentally spilled Mexican hot sauce on his schnitzel and then tried to cover it up with jalapeños? Oh, gosh, tell me he's not coming this way! Somebody hide me! MacNamara Cleaners! MacNamara Cleaners! MacNamara Cleaners!"

Both women focused their attention on Nick. He was now sitting on the floor, huddled in the corner, his eyes closed tight enough to make his entire face shiver; it was a nice compliment to the spastic shaking of his right hand, which gripped the shirt directly over the stain.

"So anyway," Janet started again, "his name is Ray Drake and . . ." Janet continued, her voice trailing off into a whisper.

As Mrs. M. listened to Janet, she also noticed that Nick cautiously opened one eye and peeked about the shop. He looked right at them in a frightened way. He opened his other eye and inched his head closer to the window, appearing to ready himself for the briefest of glances out the window and into the street. A quick darting motion later and it was over—he had looked. There was no one in sight. The street was clear. Still clutching his shirt fervently, Nick got up off the floor. He seemed to smile at the stain faithfully, as only a devoted worshipper could, as if the secrets of the world had been revealed to him in the form of dried, reddish-brown, pasta sauce blotches. He let out a Herculean sigh.

"I am here to tell you that Ray Drake is a fake," Nick proclaimed, causing both women to sharply refocus their attention in his direction. "What do you think of that? And you can tell him that I said so. Nick Sparelli knows what's what." He headed for the door. "And another thing: He's bald." The steely clicks of Nick's cleats against the linoleum floor sounded him out the door.

"He's got hair," Janet said plainly. "Unless . . ."

"I've found it!" Clancy exclaimed, as he came stumbling quickly through the curtain. A shiny, new camera hung from a thin black string around his neck and bounced off his chest like the clumsiest of pendants as he walked. The eager smile on Clancy's face suddenly turned to sour disappointment, though, as he brought the camera up to his eye and focused on Janet. "You're not the maniac," Clancy said, as he lowered the camera.

"Thank you, no."

"But I thought . . ."

"Clancy, dear," Mrs. MacNamara began, "take this shirt and pair of pants in back. They've been soaked with the devil's brew and are in dire need of the MacNamara treatment."

Clancy paused as his wife handed him the clothes. He held them loosely and at a distance away from his body as if they possessed something that Clancy wanted no part of whatsoever. And then, with a look of sternest conviction, and in his most statesman-like voice, he said, "With a maniac on the loose? I, wife, in good conscience cannot tend to affairs knowing that the safety of every man, woman, and child is in jeopardy of contagion from this, this ne'er-do-well. I shall hunt him down, ferret him out, in the name of all that is righteously good and blessedly pure. I shall hunt him down to ensure that women and small children can lie safe in their beds at night. I shall hunt him down and snap his photo for all to see, plainly, his corrupt features and tortured face. I shall hunt him down for honor. I shall hunt him down for, for . . . Ireland."

"And?"

"I believe I shall make an informational sojourn to O'Connell's where, God willing, some of the lads may know of this maniac. A despicable place it is, true, but now, in our darkest hour, we should not be afraid of where the quest might take us. Alas, I'm off. Wish me Godspeed."

Clancy ran through the curtain and out the back door of the shop, dropping the clothes and accidentally setting off the camera's flash along the way.

"The man is a saint," Mrs. MacNamara said. "Stirs the pot a bit, he does. But a saint, nonetheless." The plainness in her voice cloaked the peaceful emotions on her face like a satiny veil she wore with grace, wit, and elegance. She shook her head slightly and gave a half-silent chuckle in the direction of Clancy's escape, picking up the clothes he had dropped and returning them to a place atop the counter. She pulled a small notepad from her apron and began to write.

Janet exchanged a knowing smile with Mrs. MacNamara as she was handed the claim ticket. As she put the ticket in her pocket, she noted the time. "Thanks, Mrs. M., I'll be back tomorrow. I promised Deb I'd meet her for lunch today. I hope Alderman Peabody lets her off early. I want to tell her all about Ray."

"I understand, Janet. I understand. My Clancy was a Ray not so very long ago."

As Janet walked out the door, Mrs. MacNamara recalled that very first day she met Clancy, that day thirty-five years ago when she walked into the bank and saw Clancy fumbling with stacks of pound notes behind a barred teller's window. The sullen look on his face suggested the tedium that was his daily work routine, while his boyishness reflected brightly off rolls of gold and silver coins, offering an impish, playful quality into that land of high seriousness.

Yes, she thought, it all began in such a hopeless, helpless way so long ago. And now this. Her recollection turned the days and the years into notes as well, only musical, and she felt them pass by and through her like warm sunlight. And this she could now see in Janet, in her expectations, and in her beginnings.

# Chapter 3

Six quick breaths filled Speckman lungs with air, invigorating and vilifying Speckman spirit, while a simultaneous barrage of pumping legs and thrashing arms worked their way through soft satin until, sheet shed, they heaved the furry teddy bear spread off Lyle's body. It fell to the floor in a heap beside him, and Lyle mindfully stepped over it as he got out of bed and began to stretch.

Arms reaching high and fists clenched, twisting, Lyle felt the taut muscles of his body awakened by his movements and relaxed by his exercise. He walked over to the bedroom window and gently parted the drapes with his hand, looking out into the morning sun, his squinting eyes not used to the radiance.

Before him in the distance, like a land perceived from a place farther than the eye should be able to see, Lyle saw the tip of the spire, a whited minaret, which broke open the cloudless sky above the Chamber of Commerce building. Below it, but out of sight, he imagined he saw the silvery ball atop the town flagpole, a flagpole that was long ago dedicated and set firmly in concrete beside the steps of the building. He had often felt the pole was too tall for the height and stature of the town's meager skyline, its ball inching toward the third and top floor of the Chamber of Commerce, extending almost coldly to a height just above that of the tallest and only tree in the square, the old oak. Yet colorful flags still flew from it and tossed about freely and whimsically in the breezes that often stirred within Town Square and within the dreams and loose summer minds of those who spent time looking out their windows, entranced by the vibrance and naturalness of simple motion, empowered by that which they could not see.

He noticed then that he couldn't see the tree, that oak, or see it move before him or hear the sounds that came from the soft summer leaves as they met, windblown and familiar. What he called the mighty oak in his boyhood was now uncomfortably out of sight, left only to be imagined like the pictures of the flagpole and the flags that even now, after only an instant, he seemed to forget, their images fading like the past forgotten winds that gave them life.

Long ago, he heard stories about how the founding elected fathers wanted to chop the tree down in the name of progress and civic-mindedness, hoping to avoid the future political embarrassment that was sure to result as the town grew and needed the space to expand into an industrial Mecca for the world. Surely there would be no room for old oak trees, and the sooner it was removed, the better, became the thinking of the day. Only when confronted with a rumor that aged oak wood is among the hardest to cut and would take innumerable man-hours to saw through, along with the many added expenses in the equipment department: broken saw teeth, axe sharpening fees, wagons to haul the wood, etc.—and God forbid slivers in the men themselves—was an alternative community good decided upon: The Town would build a huge square around the tree, dispelling previous rumors that the tree was to be cut down as "blasphemous" and "not conducive to the policies of this administration and nature." During the dedication of the tree to the community, attended by all in the spirit of strength and brotherhood, it was rumored to have been said, "No man shall put a mark upon this tree, this paragon of history, this, this, really big old tree."

And as Lyle tried to draw the picture of the mighty tree in his mind, the tree flanked in contrast by its silvery-hued neighbor rooted in cement only feet away, did he come to be there on a fine spring morning as a boy, penknife in hand.

"I'm moving tomorrow, Lyle," she said.

"Yes, I know."

"So, are you going to do it? I think it would be the sweetest most darling thing anybody ever did for me in my whole life, and I'll just die if you don't, and if you don't hurry, we'll be late for school."

"I have to think."

"Lyle," she implored, "this is really important. Come on."

"But . . ."

"Oh, I knew you wouldn't. I hate you, Lyle Speckman. I'm moving tomorrow and I'll hate you forever," she said, her tender voice clipped as if in the only proper response to her state, her ten-year-old eyes awed by exactly what she wasn't seeing.

Lyle remembered watching her walk away and the feeling of the sharp bark pricking through the back of his shirt as he leaned against the tree for support. He remembered so clearly all that he didn't know how to say and just how he wanted to say it, and how in that moment, he lost his chance to become a part of her life forever by the peaceful act of closing his knife and returning it to his pocket, safe. Had it been so long ago? Had it been the right thing? He thought it funny he wondered whatever happened to the knife.

The sun became hot against Lyle's face, and he pulled his hand away from the window, letting the drapes fall back to block the rays. He turned passively to look for his clothes and, not seeing them immediately, his mind lurched forward into contemplation, then panic-stricken, past the moment where look became search and vaulting Speckman mind directly into fear.

Lyle dropped to his hands and knees and, as he crawled on all fours, felt the nap of the carpet beneath him, its baby blue softness lost to friction and the heat generated by his locomotion. As he looked under the bed, in his mind the traditional hiding place of the ages, he sneezed a gargantuan sneeze as a rush of dust and dust balls raced into the void created by the frenetic inhalation of his nostrils.

Nothing there.

The bedroom, he then noticed, was all too clean, too tidy, save the heaped spread beside the bed, to suggest that something, namely his clothes, had been hidden. A rational man could now plainly see that they had been put in their proper place, wherever that might be, and he need only find that place, that home, calmly, reassuringly. Brushing the dust and lint from his body, he stood up and walked over to her bedroom closet.

Once again, Speckman lungs filled with air, a cool whishing sound being made as he sucked the new breath past his gritted teeth. He opened the pair of louvered closet doors quickly, and with both hands, his head and eyes turned slightly aside as if not completely willing participants to the action but accomplices to the fact nonetheless. The doors opened easily and with a clicking sound, like the turning of a key in a lock, and Lyle knew he had gone past that point of no return and now had no choice but to look inside and survey the contents.

He saw what he assumed to be several of Janet's work uniforms on hangers to the left, the red-and-white check of the pattern jumping out at him, arresting his eyes and diverting their attention from the assorted odd collection of house dresses, slacks, and blouses that remained to the right. It was the second time in two days he saw that uniform, and he once again felt the shock and flutter of excitement as if seeing it for the first time. He touched the fabric with the tips of fingers, tracing a delicate line from shoulder to waist.

The ensuing hanger-by-hanger search proved fruitless, and Lyle resigned himself to the fact that his shirt and pants were not there. As he stood in front of the closet, though, head down, chin to his chest and his hand to his forehead in deep thought, out of the corner of his eye he thought he recognized, tucked away behind a pair of white pumps, the familiar glint of a shiny black oxford. His oxford. Upon closer look, he indeed found both his shoes, left placed neatly next to the right, a balled Speckman sock serving as impromptu shoe tree for each. A quizzical smile then came to his face and he didn't quite know why. He dispatched this curiosity, this spastic grin, as quickly as it came and proceeded to sit on the carpet fitting foot into sock into shoe, thinking that, yes, she had passed this way only recently.

The discovery of his socks and shoes, though not the primary objective of his quest, filled Lyle with the bravery and incentive to press on, go forth. Well-postured, he stepped boldly out of the bedroom and into the living room, a cold rush of adrenalin colliding with him as he passed between the doorjamb. His eyes became alert, and all his other senses bristled with the anticipation of the hunt, and he felt a tension in his neck that seemed ready to make a squeaky, stretching sound at any second. Then he saw Janet's things, her possessions, as if he were privately staring at each separate item, and the same uneasy feeling came over him as when he had opened her closet door alone, without her. A silence gone mad with conscience seemed to try and work its way into his head, and he didn't know if he had the will or the right to fight it. Confused, Lyle sat down on the sofa to think.

Around him, he felt Janet's things, as if in them, they possessed a quality that would somehow know he felt uncomfortable, that would somehow know and tell Janet of his false bravado. He sensed her sofa as if about to envelope him, its crushed velour creeping along the peach-fuzzy hair of the back of his legs; her loveseat too personal, too daring to approach. Emerald green plants, in colorful polka-dotted pots hung from hooks in the ceiling, their eerie flowered vines like strips of Venus flytraps reaching for the floor. They seemed to suck the oxygen, and anything else that might venture too close, right out of the air. On wall shelves, ceramic toothless tigers and elephants and giraffes paced silent footsteps, each casting a furtive territorial eye in his direction. The kitchen, modest and also neat, but white, all too white and too pristine to approach without approval from Janet, was, in his mind, definitely off limits. In front of him, resting atop a keen wooden coffee table, he saw a thick red photo-album that was opened at page one; its color photographs were still too far away, though, for his eyes to focus, inviting a closer look. He picked up the album without thinking and set it down on his lap. He looked.

The photos were of a wedding, and Lyle could see Janet, dressed as a bridesmaid, in the background of many of the pictures. As he attentively paged through the album, he began to notice the figures that blocked Janet from the camera's lens, and he imagined himself there with her as her escort, meeting these people and asking them kindly to step aside.

"Excuse me, sir, but could you, just for a minute . . ."

"Why, hello there, young fella! Tell me what I can do you for? Drinks? Talk to the band? Tell them to play something from your century? Anything you say. Just name it. Only, don't tell the wife, you understand? She kind of keeps an eye on me from over there at the other end of the room. See her? The one who's pretending her feet don't hurt in her new shoes and won't dance because it might mess up her hair? Don't look! Just pretend like we've known each other for years—that ought to trick her. She just keeps thinking that I'll make a fool out of myself by having too much fun and that'll embarrass her. Can you figure that? But it's like I keep telling her, 'When you're wearing rented clothes, you're supposed to have fun. Like bowling, for example.' But she's still my wife and I love her. She's got her good points, you know? And if I could think of one right now, I'd tell you. I just can't be put on the spot like this. Women . . . can't live with 'em, can't live without 'em."

"It's the photographer, sir, he . . ."

"Darn sadist. Flashbulbs popping off in my eyes every time I turn around. Ought to make him wear a cowbell around his neck or something. Regular stand-up guys like us need to be protected. It is just beyond me how some people can be so obnoxious, you know what I mean? Uh-oh. My wife is looking at us. Don't look! Been nice talking to you, son. But I better get back before she gets suspicious. Don't take any wooden nickels, and if my wife asks you, you're Christian from the CYO, taking a poll of what successful businessmen like myself do to help the community. If she asks you for specifics, just make something up. Nothing too good, though, she already thinks I'm a God. Adios."

"Adios."

Lyle turned the page. "Hi."

"Hi."

"You're not family, are you? I can tell, but it's okay. I'm Jen. My real name's Jennifer Marie, but no one ever calls me that. You don't think my bangs are too long, do you? My mom says they are, but Uncle Sid doesn't. He likes them. Where do you know Uncle Sid from?"

"Uncle Sid?"

"Yes, silly. You were just talking to him. Everyone calls him Sid the Squid because of his long skinny arms and the way he plasters his hair down with that slippery junk. Mom says we're supposed to humor him, but I like him anyway. So where do you know him from?"

"I don't, actually. You see, the photographer is over there and Janet is over there and . . ."

"Oh, isn't Janet so lucky? She gets to wear that beautiful dress and gets to dance with everybody and anybody she wants. How old are you?"

"Excuse me?"

"Are you, like, in your twenties?"

"Well, yes, I am."

"Then will you dance with me, please? You just have to dance with me. Please? You just have to. All my friends will just die. Do you shave, too?"

A dreamy smile came to Lyle's face as he imagined a genuine excitement in the girl's voice. "I'll dance with you if you can tell me who that woman over there is. The one sitting at the table. Wearing the shiny gold sash."

"Oh, her. Sure. That's Janet's mom. She's my aunt, Helen, but she doesn't dance much because she has varicose veins. Mom says it's from all those years where she had to work standing up and that I should go to college and get an education so that nothing like that will happen to me. She's real nice—Aunt Helen, I mean. Every Christmas, she makes me cookies with my name on them—Jen, not Jennifer Marie, because that's too long —and invites the whole family over for dinner, even Uncle Sid, who my mom says is a bad influence on me. Sometimes she even lets him carve the turkey—I think because he always brings his own carving knife and Aunt Helen is just being nice by letting him. One year, he accidentally cut my sister Angeline's fingers as she was reaching for the drumstick, and my mom wanted to have him arrested, but Aunt Helen just said, 'Accidents will happen,' and everything went back to normal. She always knows just what to say."

Just then, something clicked, and Lyle felt himself becoming carried away with silliness and felt that the time was inappropriate for a game of "let's pretend." The picture of the woman seated at the table reminded him all too much of his recently departed mother and the manner in which she had recently departed: packing up in the middle of the night and leaving to that retirement community in Arizona, leaving nothing behind but a note that said, "You're on your own now, son." He remembered how alone he felt that day and how he didn't exactly know what his first move should have been, to clean his room or watch a little TV. And then he imagined that the woman in the picture could hear the wedding band playing some kind of tune, and she was listening like the song was just for her, and that there would be nothing but silence in Janet's apartment—no band, no background music like in in the movies to tell him when the good parts were coming up. There would be nothing but his imagination and the plasticy fwap of the album's pages being closed atop one another. Still, he tried to keep a good thought and continued turning pages.

He saw two small children, girls, wearing first-communion-like white dresses, looking bored at the reception; they were probably flower girls, he thought, and sat at a table, overdressed, like once-animate baggage now left at the outermost edge of an adults-only sandbox. He imagined he would walk over to them and show them how he could make twisty balloon animals, then tell them unfunny knock-knock jokes that they would laugh hysterically at anyway. Someone's mother would call him "a gem." Behind the girls and seated at the next table, the man wearing the tuxedo, collar loosened and tie untied, pink, and draped around his neck like a papal vestment, relaxed with an entourage of smiles. On his face was the boy-I-think-I-drank-too-much smile, the I'm-glad-I-can-sit-down-and-catch-my-breath smile, the amusing how-am-I-ever-going-to-be-able-to-pay-for-this smile; and, perhaps the brightest, most charismatic, my-God-how-beautiful-she-looks-today smile. It was an interpretation that warmed Lyle, and he allowed himself a moment to bask in that warmth—but only for a brief moment, lest he feel himself getting sappy and on the verge of a solitary, irrational tear. He turned back to page one.

In one smooth motion, Lyle then returned the photo album to the exact spot on the table where he had found it. Locking his fingers together behind his head, he eased himself back into the sofa, unsure as to whether or not he should put up his feet. A deep sigh came out of his mouth as if by accident, and he wondered what to do next: if he should continue to look for his clothes or not. I'm a waiter . . . Or, an ex-waiter . . . Maybe I'll just wait, was the first thing to come to his mind.

Minutes passed in half real time as Lyle's well-practiced waiter's skills attended professionally to the silence. Moments were served with recollections and imaginations of Janet that consumed time, ravenous, filling his heart and soul and ego to a sumptuous bloat. That the festive rush of imagining thoughts would then suddenly rise like an arrow to its apex surprised him, and he felt breathless for a moment, pleased, and only then did he allow himself to feel a little giddy, a little glorious. Do people know about things like this? Does this kind of thing really happen? Speckman logic almost immediately deduced yes.

Time passed.

Rational practical thoughts now filed into Lyle's brain, and he felt the need to formulate a plan. The next time he saw Janet would be the second time, a time on her part for the confirmation or categorical denial of the first meeting—a time to clear the air. He wondered what to wear. He wondered if he dare wear cologne and run the risk of all too obviously trying to impress her. He tried to remember all the different colognes Nick always wore, and the names of each, knowing that to pick one for smell alone could have disastrous results in the face of the inevitable "What's that you're wearing?" An all too provocative name might suggest to her that he had expectations about the evening, presupposing the date in favor of an anticipated hopeful conclusion. Decisions, decisions.

More logistical problems such as where to go and what to do seemed trivial to him, to the major social coup he was about to pull off: being seen in public with a woman not his mother—a real date. Lyle's mind perused imaginary scripted conversations, introductions that would attempt to show to others how exactly run-of-the-mill, yet suave and confident, his dating mannerisms were. Tonight he'd be ready. He'd show them, he thought. He'd show them all. But exactly where would he show them? What place? Different places, different conversations. Different introductions. The sudden surprise lack of triviality overcame him, and his scripted conversations faded, instants before he could commit any of them to memory. He had inadvertently served up a blank slate, a new time to think.

The tinny clanking of the mail slot in Janet's door being closed then interrupted Lyle and proved a well-timed, and, perhaps, much-needed diversion. Within a fraction of a second, at what seemed the first of several sharp and then quickly dissipating tones, he turned to see that a colorful, red-white-and-blue flyer had been shot through the slot and floated in the air over the kitchen tiles, hanging for a second before scissoring to the floor and a graceful landing. Lyle got up off the sofa and walked into the kitchen. He picked up the flyer. It read:

### CELEBRATION*

8:00PM Tonight!    July 7th    Town Square!
Witness the unveiling!
See the statue! "The Patriot"
Keynote Speaker: Ald. Peabody
Topic: "Indecision: The Fulcrum of Communism"
Fireworks to follow
*Attendance mandatory

Lyle smiled glowingly and felt like jumping up and down. For in his hands, he felt, he held a most divine intervention, as if a postage-paid letter had been heaven sent special delivery, somehow nicely, neatly putting all aspects of his immediate future down in writing. How convenient. Plans had been made, wonderful plans. The entire town would see him escort Janet to the celebration, and it would be tonight.

A cool Speckman swagger ushered Lyle back toward the sofa, and he dropped the flyer on the table beside the photo album. The slick flyer slipped off the table, though, and whisked itself under the sofa. Lyle dropped to his hands and knees and, as he reached for it, spied a small black book like a secret only half hidden under a thin dusty cover. A curious Speckman mitt grabbed the book and he stood up, leaving the flyer behind, itself an inefficient tag-team partner.

The book's cover had no title or name, and Lyle began to wonder whether or not it was one of 'those' books, the kind that Nick always kept in his back pocket and said was worth more than all his gold chains put together. Lyle remembered seeing Nick writing in his book one day at work, short sentences notated with stars, and the way Nick reacted when he discovered he was being watched, like a big game hunter mugging for the camera after a much-sought-after kill. That grin was memorable and gave the book a quality of buried treasure, the loss of which would no doubt send its rightful owner into a delirious panic. Had another man been here, he thought, and lost the book during a night of . . . ? He couldn't even think the next word. Trembling hands snapped the book open, and Lyle read.

> Grossman, Leo:
> Competent. Efficient. Sturdy. A well-oiled machine with relatively few breakdowns. Tendency to bark out commands, though. But I kind of liked that part. Fun.

"Whew!" Lyle exclaimed, relieved. That the book contained no stars relaxed him, and the surprise of a familiar name made him feel less an intruder, a snoop. As quickly as it came, the fear of thumbing through pages of women's names and descriptions was gone, replaced by a casual reading of cute comments neatly printed beside the names of what must have been dozens of men. "MEN'S NAMES!" Lyle's realization came only after he naively made it to 'S.' 'Sp' to be exact.

> Sparelli, Nick:
> Very proud of his chest hair (singular). But I loved the eyebrows. Also, wouldn't pay off on the arm wrestling bet. Says he slipped.

This was not a good sign, he felt. His only small consolation came from the fact that there was no entry marked, "Speckman, Lyle." And even that consolation was short-lived when Speckman fingers remembered his bruised forehead, a bruised forehead that belonged, in Janet's eyes, to a Mr. Death Ray Drake. Now, though, he didn't have strength or the stomach to page backward to "D." Those names, all those names began spinning about his head, and he could see them as if in orbit around him, all seemingly led by Nick Sparelli and maniacal laughter. It made him dizzy.

The idea of sharing a woman with Nick hit Lyle like an armor-piercing shell from the blast of a Sherman tank, or the fiery, merciless destruction of the ignorant and innocent alike by another Sherman, him on a death march, down, long ago in the South. Lyle felt that fire within him and it left him shivering, an ice fire to confuse his already too-taxed mind, and the strength fading, escaping from the muscles of his arms and legs as if in fear of contamination from something evil, something foreign and wrong. He fell to the floor like an unhuman and feelingless thing, a vacant look, staring, wide-eyed, eyeball to carpet fiber. Lyle did not feel well.

"It's the quiet ones. You've got to watch out for the quiet ones," Nick always said.

Maybe he was right, Lyle thought. Maybe a lot of strange things. He even found himself wishing that he and Nick had been better friends; right now he felt closer to him than ever before. He even remembered Nick saying something about a talk show he saw where women kept men as sex slaves and how it happened to him once during a fishing trip in the Yukon. He said the woman had stolen his clothes, and everything.

But there was still something inside of Lyle that refused to believe that Janet was any kind of a creature akin to the wildebeest that abducted Nick in the Yukon, something that denied the facts, the most incriminating of which were the book and the fact that he indeed had woken up in her bed the very next day after meeting her. He didn't even know her last name. What would Caesar do? Or Alexander? Or Napoleon? At that moment, he feared himself a weak link in the quartet and demanded action—any action. But preferably manly, take-charge kind of stuff.

He got up, incensed, almost possessed with an energy that came out of nowhere, yet seemed strong and driving and positive. A new plan was in the works.

Lyle knew he must find the truth. Truth about women. Truth about Janet.

He would seek it, he thought, in the manner of all great men, leaders—boldly, firmly, and with a certain degree of stealth. He felt that last part a bit of a safety feature, but rationalized it was for the good of the plan as a whole.

The impending celebration seemed a prime locale for maneuvers, he figured, and he couldn't wait to send his plan into action. He sprinted into Janet's bedroom, ambition first, and flung himself into her closet. Eager Speckman arms and legs fitted themselves into one of Janet's house dresses, a roomy floral print, as Lyle smiled wryly at his cleverness. He pulled a scarf, satiny green with frilly edges and filled with miniature replicas of the Eiffel Tower, from an adjacent hanger and tied it about his head, careful to tuck each hair under its new cover.

Yes, he thought, this would allow him to move freely among the women of the town, in hopes that a false sense of security and, perhaps, a momentary indiscretion, would give one of them and Janet away and bring to light some solid evidence of widespread promiscuity, evidence other than that which had been offered to him daily by Nick at Grossman's: "One night stands rule." He often wondered about the bias of Nick's statement, albeit secretly. More important, he felt, was that he was now in disguise and Phase One of the plan was complete.

"Phase Two."

Lyle could see it so clearly now. All that remained was to find his way back to TBNL and Grossman's, hop on his bicycle and ride into town, making sure to stay out of sight until the celebration began. The idea of riding his bicycle on deflated tires, on the rims, little black book still in hand, seemed to him a minor discomfort that must be endured in the name of secrecy, in the name of sacrifice, in the name of the plan, amen. Common sense also told him not to hitchhike or to call a cab for fear of drawing attention to himself.

"I am off!" he cried.

Lyle rushed out of her bedroom and bee-lined a path out the door. He found himself in the hallway of her apartment building, lobby doors ahead at the end of the hall and the sunshine of the day looking like a white new world beyond, outside. He ran toward the light, the clip-clop of Speckman oxfords pounding rhythmically against the tiled floor.

# Chapter 4

"And in conclusion, I'd like to say . . ."

"Did you want tuna or ham, or what?" Deb shouted in the direction of the alderman, the proximity of the phone to her mouth having no bearing on the decibel level of her voice. It was now at its attention-getting, eardrum-penetrating best.

"And in conclusion, I'd only like to say . . ."

"Lester!"

"I'd like to say, in conclusion . . ."

"Lester I. Peabody, you tell me what you want for lunch this instant or you go hungry!"

Alderman Peabody was staring out his office window into Town Square as he practiced his speech, emphasis on major points coming in the form of well-crafted arm movements and alternatively raised eyebrows. He turned from his office window to look at Deb; she was seated at her desk, tethered by a curly phone cord.

The arm and hand that were raised only seconds ago in his most triumphant political posture now relaxed by his side, tugging playfully at the loose fibers of his long, grey waistcoat, the tails of which hung about his knees. The coat was much too warm for the midsummer heat, but filled his aldermanic heart with a sense of propriety, loyalty, and history.

Long ago, he had seen a well-worn photo of his grandfather,

the Honorable Nero A. Peabody, taken during what looked like an oppressively hot summer celebration, wearing a similar coat, and from that day forth, he vowed to keep his appearance in line with the Peabody tradition forever. Last year, on his forty-fifth birthday, he felt the epitome of his lifelong ambition: the mutton-chop sideburns he had labored to grow since puberty had finally grown in, and the paunch he was developing was now looking positively portly, an attribute, he reasoned, of all successful men of re-election. His dark black hair had begun to turn grey in a salt-and-pepper fashion, and his serious dark eyes and affable smile proved a nice complement to each other. Whenever possible, he stood with both thumbs tucked smartly and evenly under his lapels, an image, it seemed, designed and crafted by Peabody himself to promote competency, and may have worked if not for one small detail: the alderman invariably wore his shoes on the wrong feet, often complaining about the skill level of shoemakers worldwide, remarking, "They just don't make them like they used to." This day, he wore loafers. He knew that registered voters often noticed the inconsistency but let it pass, sometimes hearing them say amongst themselves, "It's just a phase," or "Doesn't he look just like his father?" Such familial comparisons actually pleased Peabody, since in all aspects he considered himself a "chip off the old block."

"Well," Deb continued, "which is it?"

"What are my choices again?"

"Tuna or ham."

"I'll have the usual, Miss, Miss . . ." Peabody's deep official voice trailed off into mumbles and then silence as he turned to look back out the window. He pulled a white linen handkerchief with his initials on it from his coat pocket and began to clear a smudge on the glass.

"He'll have a bologna and ketchup sandwich cut in four pieces, using only soft white bread. And make sure that the edges crinkle together when cut with the knife, that's important. He likes that. And a glass of grape juice." Deb paused, only halfheartedly listening to the voice at the other end of the line repeat the order. "I don't know why, but that's what he wants. Just send it over and don't be too bashful with the ketchup like last time, or I'll make sure he does something about it." Deb slammed down the phone. "Moron."

The alderman was not listening closely. He continued to rub the smudge on the glass with his handkerchief. The feverish effort produced rapid, squeaky sounds until he was satisfied with the result.

"Today is . . . Today . . . Today is a glorious day!" Lester suddenly proclaimed, as he turned toward Deb. He sported an ebullient smile.

"Yes, Lester, glorious. Look, I told O'Connell himself . . ."

"O'Connell? Fine man. Fine, fine man. What this country needs are more outstanding citizens like that O'Connell fellow. Honest. Level headed. He knew Dad, you know."

"You might say he had his number," she said out of the side of her mouth.

"How's that?"

"I said, 'I'm sure he did.'"

"Right. Very popular man, my father. Strong. Forthright. A born leader. Sat tall in the mayor's chair, too. It's in the Peabody blood, you know, that instinctive knowledge to forge ahead."

"Yes, forge."

"Like a man with a gift for true foresight."

"20/20."

"And to be called away, mystically summoned as it were in his prime—along with the rest of the respected politicos of our fair town, his public service brethren—to that, that most inexplicable of emergencies. It was a day for us as dark as a total eclipse. A fateful day for us all . . ." The alderman struck a reflective pose. "The first indelible marks of redevelopment etched ten years ago this very day. I remember the moment I knew they were gone, and in that instant, the imagined images of their departure became fixtures in my mind, the decorum of their sudden exit, and it was as if I were seeing their stoic likenesses carved into a long wooden tableau, following the orderliness of their mission, their calling. Each step moving them closer to their destiny. I was just a lad then, barely old enough to run for president. But I guess that Dad knew that I was ready to step in and take charge, to handle things in the face of the worst and most unexpected financial crisis in the history of our soon-to-be megalopolis, to judiciously lead and comfort the townspeople in their time of need. To protect them from, from . . . things. Yes. To be calm. To be the eye of the storm. To be . . . To be . . . To be or not to be . . . a Peabody."

"You are a Peabody, Les."

"Yes, I say proudly, I am. And I'm sure that when Dad and the rest of the fellows come back—or even write, for that matter—they'll be proud of me. Don't you think the redevelopment projects are coming along nicely?"

"Love that road, Les."

\* \* \* \* \*

Janet stood on the front steps of the Chamber of Commerce building and took several deep breaths. From her previous visits to Peabody's office, she had learned that proper breathing techniques must be used in the climb to the third floor, lest she become winded and forced to rest along the way. The imitation marble steps had worn all the way down to the plywood about the time of the elder Peabody's disappearance, and they constantly creaked and made cracking sounds even without the weight of a user to encourage them. Best to keep moving, she thought, onward and upward.

One last deep breath and she was off. Using a nifty skip-hop step, she dashed into the building, a courageous look of trepidation on her face. She sped past the elevator, a sign hanging from a string over its buttons and saying: "THIS WORKS FINE," and hit the first step of the stairwell at full stride. She often wondered if the elevator was slated for redevelopment. Or if it already had been.

When Janet reached the third floor, a relieved and grateful smile came to her face, as if in partial payment for her safe passage to the summit. She stood in the corridor in front of the alderman's office, looking through the large glass windows that stood on either side of the door and that acted as partition to the hallway. Through the window, she could see Alderman Peabody looking out toward Town Square, his left and right arm alternately rising and falling with inaudible salient points; she could only catch glimpses of his mouth moving, as an apparently less interested Deb fanned herself with past, present, and future copies of The Town Annual Report, all in various stages of incompletion.

"Am I early?" Janet said, opening the door only far enough to stick her head through.

Deb looked at Janet standing in the doorway and shook her head.

"Why hello, Jane!" Peabody said in an honest and friendly manner as he heard Janet and saw her enter. "How very nice to see you again. Come in, come in. How very nice to see you on such a fine, fine day. A day that, one other day, we'll all be able to tell our very old friends about remembering. A day of revelry, a day of community, a day of peace and goodwill, a day of . . . celebration."

"I'm off to lunch, Les." Deb pushed herself back from her desk. "If I see O'Connell, I'll try and remember to threaten him about the ketchup thing."

Peabody started to chuckle and said, "An international incident will not be required, Miss, Miss . . ."

Janet watched as Deb got out from behind her desk and put on her sunglasses; she was not listening to Peabody. Deb straightened her leopard-spotted halter top, a gift, Janet knew, from a former associate who claimed to have personally hunted and killed the animal in deepest, darkest Africa. Her long red hair fell wildly about her bare shoulders, and her soft, cottony Bermuda shorts contributed to a natural coolness that Janet always felt Deb had. That coolness made Janet think of the story Deb told her of her thirty-third birthday party, held last month at O'Connell's, where Deb stood up on the bar and patrons dropped gifts at her feet. Most knew all the words to "Happy Birthday," she said.

"Lester, if anyone calls for me, just tell them I'll be back around two or three or four. Heck, just have them call me at O'Connell's."

"O'Connell's, right. Fine man, that O'Connell."

"Now, I put the rest of your notes in the usual place."

"Notes, right. Which notes?"

"Pay attention, Lester. Your speech."

"My speech, right. Which usual place?"

"On the bookshelf."

"Right. In the safe."

"You don't have a safe, Lester."

"Well, then, make a note of it. I'll add it into the redevelopment projects. I should have a safe for my important things. Dad had one."

"Your dad had a lot of things."

"I could use his usual safe place."

"Lester, you don't know where it is. That is why you have your own usual place."

"Right . . . Which is?"

Deb sighed. "Your hollowed-out version of *The Body Politic,* right next to *Treasure Island* and *Around the World in Eighty Days.*"

"Of course, how mindless of me. Isn't she a gem?" he directed to Janet. "I don't know what I'd do without her. What with all the first-class, top-level, executive-type duties I possess, to say nothing of the enormous burden and responsibility of my position as sole member of the governing class . . . But don't get me wrong—'tis a burden I bear with courage, with pride, with, with . . . honour."

Janet curtsied.

"Don't encourage him," Deb said quietly as she grabbed Janet by the arm and led her out of the office. "Come on, I'll race you down the stairs."

The workmen were just unloading the statue in the square for the celebration that evening when the women came out of the building. From where they stood on the street, they could see Peabody, face pressed firmly against the glass of his office window, carefully overseeing the placement of the statue with erratic, semiphore-like hand gestures.

The target was a newly poured square of concrete beside the specially erected "celebration podium" as the workmen apparently surmised, and a long white sheet was draped over the statue to enhance the drama of the unveiling.

Janet noted the alderman's child-like eagerness. She watched his blur of hand motion, his heaving chest a byproduct of erratic breathing patterns in the alderman, the glass fogging up and hindering quick and proper placement of the monument.

"His father was a heavy breather, too," Deb said.

"Why doesn't he just open the window?"

"He can't. About the time he got the idea for the redevelopment projects, he decided to paint the whole building white. He said it would be good for the morale of the voting populace, or some such nonsense. Well, anyway, his nephew, Ed, painted all the windows shut."

"That's too bad. I bet it gets really hot in there."

"It's not so bad. Besides, like Les always says, 'This unfortunate incident has earmarked our future for central air conditioning.' He's a scream."

The women took off in the direction of O'Connell's, one block away, past the vacant lot and directly opposite the Chamber of Commerce. A two-story brick complex the entire block long, the Hall of Records, was the only other building of prominence in sight, itself adjacent to both O'Connell's and the Chamber of Commerce, almost as if connecting the two like mortar to brick, labor to management.

"Celebration tonight?" Janet asked in a lilting hopeful voice. The words "Ray Drake" were on the tip of her tongue. "I saw the truck from the granite place when I was coming in."

"Couldn't you tell from Les? I always love it when Lester uses his official voice. He seems so much less, less . . . political."

Janet covered a giggle. "I think he's nice," she said.

"He is nice. More than that, even. I think he's genuinely nice. And great to work for—a lot like his father in that way. I can even see some family resemblance."

"Maybe around the eyes, I've heard."

"Now don't start with the eye thing. Every election, I heard his father tell the same lame joke about having two glass eyes, and about how he would pledge to take them out and leave them on his desk when he left the office for the day so that 'Peabody eyes will always be open for community affairs.' Every election, same dumb line and still he got elected. Come to think of it, though, people always did stare at him funny, at the way his eyes moved."

"People stare at Les."

"Only when he's walking. Almost nobody ever looks at him when he's saying anything."

"I think I've noticed that. But I still think he's nice. I can't say about his father, though. I've only seen him in pictures."

"Les looks pretty good in pictures, too."

The women stopped on the sidewalk in front of the vacant lot. They were looking at a large plywood sign that had been sunk in the dirt on two wooden posts and that said:

ANOTHER FINE REDEVELOPMENT PROJECT
FUTURE SITE

Included was a profile of the Alderman beside the words, "Building is Good."

"He looks almost profound there," Janet said.

"Well . . . Just as Ed was about to take the picture, Les turned to spit out his bubble gum. Ed didn't have any more film."

"Oh." Janet paused. "Good resolution. What is he going to build here?"

"He didn't say, exactly. With Lester, sometimes there's only a hint of an idea that escapes into the atmosphere. Understanding him can be like trying to decipher smoke signals. The other day he marched me out to this very spot and turned me around to face the square like he wanted me to notice something. Well, the first thing I see in the Town Square, right in front of the Hall of Records, is that crazy blond Italian guy chasing that waitress, Stella, from O'Connell's around that monster tree. What that woman sees in that man . . ."

"Did he catch her?"

"He never catches her. He must be slow."

"I can't believe that's what Lester wanted you to see."

"I don't think he noticed. I think he wanted me to say something about the sign and the vacant lot."

"Why do you say that?"

"Because he asked me, 'What do you think about the sign and the vacant lot? Can you see the possibilities?'"

"Oh."

"I was very direct. It's the best policy in situations like this. I told him I thought the sign was nice and who wouldn't love a good possibility, and that the photo of him made him look very official."

"It is a good photo."

"Then he stuck his fingers under his lapels and said . . . wait a minute," Deb stopped, her mind redirected. She reached in her pants pocket and pulled out two index cards. She read aloud from the first card: "But a soon-to-be redeveloped vacant lot. An emptiness that cries out for a presence, that alone cries out for I, Peabody to hear. A vacancy no longer void of future, but soon to be filled with bustling commerce, skyscrapers, or bulldozers and dump trucks, at least. Something with promise! Maybe a little league field. Hear the crack of the bat! Youngsters rounding the bases! Head first slides into home! Clouds of dust! But a brand new something. A splendid something new, a splendid something grand. Something new from something else. Something that was not there before. A . . . redevelopment."

"Why did you write that down on a little card?" Janet asked.

"*I* don't actually take dictation. Lester, on the other hand, is quite the stenographer . . . No kidding. Word for word, he wrote it down in his best penmanship, right down to the annotations. I don't think he got to rehearse it much, though. He does like to be prepared. Look right here," she said, pointing to the small notation at the bottom of the card, "'Attempt Number One.' He always gives me a copy on an index card and tells me what version of his speech it is. Usually I only get to see the threes and fours. He's not too proud of the ones. He says they need to mature from tiny acorns to mighty oaks."

"I've heard him speak. Shade is a way off."

"He keeps practicing, though. Every day in front of that giant mirror in his office. I think he's getting better."

"I guess."

"Speeches are important to Les. He keeps copies of his favorites with him at all times, just like his father did, and he hands them out like baseball cards to the kids. His father told him it was a good way to flaunt the literacy of high government office. Look, here's another one," Deb said, as she handed Janet the second card.

Janet read aloud:

> It is not the critic who counts, nor the man who points out how the strong man stumbled, or where the doer of deeds could have done them better. The credit belongs to the man who is actually in the arena; whose face is marred by dust and sweat and blood; who strives valiantly; who errs

and comes short again and again; who knows the great enthusiasms, the great devotions, and spends himself in a worthy cause; Who, at the best, knows in the end the triumph of high achievement; and who, at the worst, at least fails while daring greatly, so that his place shall never be with those timid souls who know neither victory nor defeat.

-President Theodore Roosevelt
-Speech at the Sorbonne
-Paris, France April 23, 1910
4 stars

"It's hard for Lester, though, to sound too official," Deb began. "What with the shoes and the changing voice, and all. I told you, he's a scream. I never know what's going to come out of him."

"I had a teacher like that when I was in high school," Janet said. "Mr. Finch, the history teacher. He'd be telling us all about these great generals and great commanders of giant armies, and it was as if he thought he was right there, living in the moment, when his voice would crack and squeak and some of the kids would laugh. The class was never the same after one of those squeaks. It made him blush. I thought he was a good teacher, though. I learned a lot."

"Ingrid Gloobniecht," Deb said slowly.

"Who is that?"

"Mrs. Gloobniecht was my Mr. Finch. She was my spelling teacher back when they used to hold classes on the first floor of the Hall of Records. They don't anymore—not since all the government people and teachers left. They just closed the whole building down. No one knows what happened to most of them. Not even Gloobniecht."

"Isn't that odd?"

"I don't know. She was this old crone of a bag of bones that really spooked everybody anyway. Combat boots, and all. She used to rap our knuckles with a yardstick whenever we spelled a word wrong."

"That's awful! How does that remind you of my Mr. Finch?"

"We all learned a lot, honest. I learned how to spell, and Bobby R. learned to come to school in boxing gloves."

"He did not," Janet said incredulously.

"Sure, he did. He's doing great now. Last I heard, he was fighting for the title in Venezuela. He said he owed it all to Mrs. G., too. Peabody had me send him a flyer."

"For tonight?"

"Yes. I don't know if he'll show, or not. He was really pretty messed up over the Gloobniecht thing when he was a kid. Never did learn how to tie his shoes."

"And no one knows what happened to her?"

"No, not really. A lot of rumors, though. Someone told me she joined the Peace Corps and was sent to some God-awful third world country, but was killed in her sleep by a band of juvenile thugs with bloody knuckles. They left a note claiming responsibility, but no one could read it, so their government just dropped the whole thing. Now, late at night, people say the ghost of Gloobniecht roams the Hall of Records, searching for answers about why Les' dad and all the other government people left."

"And this is what you believe happened?"

"Now, I didn't say that. I just said someone told me. A friend. People tell me lots of things. I ask questions and people tell me things."

"A close friend? Would a close friend tell you a story like that?"

"A friend. Just a friend. We should leave it at that."

"It just seems that a story like that would raise a little curiosity."

"Jane, dear, you are a bright, wonderful girl, but you haven't been in town all that long, and you just have to realize that here we take some things at face value. Like that very first day I walked into Eat and saw you pulling on the collar of your uniform and I said to myself, 'Deb, this is a girl who could benefit from your experience in all matters worldly.' Okay? Besides, you didn't look like you were having any fun there all by yourself. You shouldn't be sentenced behind that counter, you know. Doesn't anybody ever come into that place?"

"Sometimes," Janet said. As she walked, her mind flashed back to that first night Deb walked into Eat and the way that she seemed to command the empty space around her to somehow be brighter, greater than it was. The way she first said "hello" was filled with the magnificence and exuberance of something far away and exotic, as if she just came from the bullfights and an audience with El Cordobes himself and now wished to share the experience. Her smile offered friendship with no strings attached in a manner Janet recognized from her schooldays as "confidently chancey," like the way a classmate would show up in a new hairdo or be the first to assume a fashion risk on self-confidence alone. In this case, however, to suggest, even to herself, that an act was being put on for peer approval seemed inappropriate. More than inappropriate—simply wrong. The energy level of the café seemed truly heightened and, for a moment, she felt the jealousy of desiring that which another human being possessed. Yes, there was indeed face value. Then she remembered pouring Deb a cup of coffee and wondering about herself, about the hope that somewhere, maybe deep inside of her, there was an adventuresome free spirit. And then she remembered last evening. "Someone came in last night. A man."

"Really? Who? Anyone I know?"

"He just looked so kind, bookish even. A little like Mr. Finch."

"What was his name?"

Janet slowed her walk to the point where Deb noticed her uncertainty. All the way over to the office, flying up the steps of the Chamber of Commerce and before at MacNamara's, she readied herself for this moment of revelation, planning to work ever so nonchalantly the news of her excitement into the conversation. She envisioned herself, hair blowing slow-motion-like in the wind, as graceful—sexy even—long strides conquered the sidewalk beneath her feet. But now, the entrance to O'Connell's approaching rapidly, herself aware that she must confront the exact moment for which she prepared, she felt lost, as if the spirit of her courage chickened out at the last minute and departed via the imaginary wind that was to have tousled her hair. She looked over her shoulder, away from Deb, and exhaled, "Ray Drake."

"Did you say something? Are you okay?"

Janet caught her breath. "Ray Drake," she said plainly. She felt that an element of repetitiveness took away some of the impact of the words, causing them to flow, lifeless, from her mouth the second time around.

"Death Ray? What about him? Was that the guy who came in last night?"

"Yes."

"The clod. How some people get into a title match, I'll never know. Grunts and groans and kooky stares with those saucer-wide, googly eyes. Rumor has it, O'Connell was even giving two-to-one against the pin and seven-to-five against the submission hold. Missed that one. Death Ray, humpf. Who would have thought? I heard he looked more like Fay Wray in that match. But still . . . I guess he's kind of cute in a brutish, simian kind of way. Good gimmick, too, that stare and the way he always points and says: 'I . . . I . . . SEE YOU! NO ESCAPE FOR YOU!' Did he say that? Did he say anything?"

"Oh, we just talked about the weather and things. Then, later . . . "

"He talked? Really?" Deb seemed taken aback. "Usually he only gets to say that one line. Or else he just grunts. Or, maybe, that was just for the TV. You know how TV changes everything around, what with distortion and scripts, and all."

"He did mention something about that."

"Now I am impressed," Deb said, with a surprised look. She assumed a playful, accusatory tone and said, "And what, may I ask, did you have to do to turn Mr. Death into such a conversationalist? Mmm? A little submission hold of your own?"

Janet felt her face begin to turn a warming red. A possessed Deb skipped up the stairs to O'Connell's and opened the door wide, lighting a path from door to floor to bar and to just beyond, to O'Connell standing behind the taps, and to that miraculous gold front tooth of his that returned the light and punctuated his smile with a 'Hi, I'm glad you came' kind of wordlessness. Deb eased herself into the doorway, a silhouette, and posed. Janet stood outside on the first step, craning to see past Deb, first between and then around her legs.

Deb whispered over her shoulder, "O'C's a little dim and sometimes gets on my nerves when he doesn't do exactly as I say, but his powers of observation are usually flawless."

"Hark, is that the brightest shining star of the heavens I see standing in my doorway?" O'Connell beckoned.

"See what I mean?" Deb said. "Let's get a chair . . . slowly."

Deb led the way to a table reserved for her, round, wooden, and notched with the graffiti of idle lunch hours, days, evenings, and wild nights alike. Janet could only follow, and she sensed herself before the crowd eye even less a presence than Deb's shadow, at that moment outshone, dark and unseen when watched across the floorboards. Not even Janet's unfamiliarity with O'Connell's was enough to elicit a glance from the all-male crowd, and she remembered how different things were from years ago when, in some far away classroom, the children's eyes always managed to find the new kid in the class, the stranger to the neighborhood. Now, all remained as fixtures, as if the beamed ceilings that gave O'Connell's its rustic homey look were supported by patrons, their years of loyal service to the bar documented by photos on the wall, each patron proudly shown shaking hands with O'C himself. The smokeless room was a pleasant surprise to her, though, and a large display of Redevelopment Project informational pamphlets next to the doorway made her feel a little more at home, a little less a foreigner.

"Did you send over Lester's sandwich yet?" Deb squawked toward O'C as she sat.

"Heavens no, your ladyship. Praythee, I am only now corralling an extra hand to scrape the good ketchup out of the vat."

"Then you remembered? How sweet."

"Aye, thou dost not quickly forget an electronic tongue-lashing. My lobes doth sting from your prickly barbs."

"Sorry about that, I was working. And you can cut the comedy, please. I have a guest."

"Comedy? Nay, I only wish to serve." O'Connell stepped out from behind the bar and walked over to Deb and Janet's table. He handed the women two menus. "I only wish to serve you with the finest of offerings. You'll notice the specials at 50-1 and 100-1," he said, pointing. "Beneath the cheese sandwich and the curd loaf."

"I've never heard of them before," Deb said.

"Nor they you, your highness."

"But these names mean nothing to me."

"Oh, how you have broken a heart somewhere, I fear. Would you like me to give you a few moments?"

"Not necessary," Deb said, pointing to the menu. Her exquisitely manicured fingernail highlighted 'The O'Connell,' a delicate and finely marbled Delmonico, served pub style with Bavarian pretzel rods and a chilled lager brewed and bottled in Milwaukee.

A gold-toothed smile and O'Connell stepped away from the table. "Two regulars!" he called to the cook. "Stella! The round table!" he added with flair.

"Will you wait, already!" was the reply. Stella's response was from places or origins not immediately ascertainable. Her forceful diction, however, clearly conveyed to all that she believed herself overworked and under compensated, and that somehow, she felt the need to speak up, regardless of content or informational value.

Back at the round table, Deb continued to stare at her menu in a deliberate fashion. "So, what do you like?" she said.

"The Delmonico seems like a nice change of pace. I don't get much of an opportunity to eat food with its own special name. Sometimes cook accidentally lets the food catch on fire when he's making my dinner and he calls out all kinds of words I never heard before, and then he calls his ex-wife bad names. I know it's really not good for me, but I do so hate to offend cook by not eating. After all, he did prepare a meal for me and I should be thankful and sometimes I even say 'gracias.' But today is a definitely a steak day. You might say, a momentous occasion."

"How special can it be?" Deb said, staring at her menu. "O'Connell doesn't even have the decency to show me a name I recognize. Who is this guy? Carl the Mean? This guy belongs under the curd loaf. For that matter, O'Connell belongs under the curd loaf for these offerings."

"It's just that, well, when a day seems special to a person, somehow you should do something to set it apart from everything else. To remember it later on, don't you think so?"

Deb didn't answer. Her eyes were still fixed on the menu, puzzled amazement now only seconds away from claiming squatters rights on her face.

Janet asked, "Don't you think Ray is special?"

Deb set the menu down in front of her. "Ray Drake? Show me where you see Ray Drake on this menu. Drake, I would recognize. Look for yourself . . . Go ahead, look."

Janet's mind went blank for a second before she politely looked at the menu. What am I looking for? she thought, and for a moment, she actually felt nothing, as if even the simplicity of looking at a menu was beyond her, the words and pictures all blurring together in a meaningless lump. She felt her eyes cross before she finally pushed the menu back in front of Deb. "I'm not sure I know what you mean," she said.

"The specials? Which of the specials do you want? The 50-1 or the 100-1? I know they are both hard to pass up, but we really should make a decision even if we never did hear of either of them before. After all, an unknown favorite could make you just as much as a well-known underdog—or vice-versa—if you know what you're doing. But in wrestling, you've got to look hard at the names. And, in this case, it's not like we're talking about Death Ray Drake, is it?"

"But about Ray . . ."

"He's not on the card. So which is it? Murray the Terrible or Luscious Louie the Lizard Lip?"

Deb's attention was then not so uniquely diverted by a slap square on her back from a burly hand that landed with a crisp, clear, snapping sound. Deb let out a customary, "Yow!"

"And a yow-do-you-do, too!" he said. "How's my favorite Deb today? Tell me you're glad to see me and send a jillion volts of eeeeelectricity to charge my burnt out heart! Bzzz! Bzzz!"

"Hi, Mort," Deb said. "Mort, Jane. Jane, Mort."

Janet looked up at Mort, the corners of her mouth curled slightly upward in a manner she often reserved for conversations with patrons at Eat, conversations which all too seriously turned toward the existence of the Loch Ness Monster, Elvis sightings, or someone's cousin named Yeti. Mort's boyish face, large hands, lightning bolts tattooed on each finger, denim ensemble—jeans, jacket and cap—along with a pair of rubber, buckle-up boots seemed too much. Just too much.

"And hello to you, too, Jane. Allow me to introduce myself: Mort from Mort's Neon Tombstones. That glitter gas that glows forever! Don't go without gas, as I always say. How do you like me so far? Bzzz. Bzz."

"Well, I haven't thought . . ."

"Mort, you see, it's like this," Deb started with a smile.

"Say no more. Girl talk. Mort understands. I have to get back to O'C anyway. I'm getting eeeeelectric vibrations about this 50-1, this Murray person. Bzzz. Bzzz." And Mort zipped away quickly.

What just happened? Jane thought. How could that man be so odd? Was he acting? Was he serious? And what kind of person goes around buzzing? And why didn't Deb want to talk to him? He seemed nice enough. Odd, yes, but nice enough. "Deb," Janet asked shyly, "is that man, well, is he . . . does he feel okay?"

"He's fine. Why do you ask?"

"Well, he . . . buzzes."

"Rule No. 1: Men do strange things."

Janet thought about Rule No. 1 for a moment, half wondering about just exactly how far this 'male strangeness scale' stretched. "But should they actually make noises?" she asked, her rising tone giving away her embarrassment at asking the question.

"Noises, grunts, groans, squeaks, pips, screams, yelps, sighs, growls, tee-hees, ha-has, whines, whinnies, nays, brays, and even the occasional tally-ho. Not to mention, farts and belches. It's all perfectly normal."

"So, Mort is normal?"

"Perfectly."

"But you didn't want to talk to him. He seemed nice."

"Rule No. 2: The men in this town are all nice and they always have been. Not very free with information, but . . . Mort is just not for me, that's all. I need somebody special, somebody a little different, a truly devoted heart, someone who believes the sun rises and sets in my presence for all the ages, that's all. However, always remember Corollary Rule 2A: Smile and pretend you like all men. First impressions are not always on the money, and there is always the possibility that you could end up with someone who you thought was pure raw sewage at first. Best to keep a scorecard, of some kind. Which brings us to Rule No. 3: Never explain anything. To explain something to a man will lead him to believe that you have a rational, thinking brain, which may be more developed than his. And at this point, the man will panic and start a fight with you so he can go to the pub all alone . . . Which we don't want, because this is where all the action is, see? Now, which special do you want?"

Too fast. Everything is happening so fast, Janet thought. "Tell me how this works again. Murray the Lip or—?"

"No, no, no. Murray the Terrible or Luscious Louie the Lizard Lip. When Stella comes over, we tell her our order and she gives it to O'C."

"But O'C already knows our order. We're having the Delmonico's and beers. He said, 'Two regulars.'"

"No," Deb said smoothly. "Our *special order*, get it?" she added with wink of her eye. "The one we pick from above the curd loaf. The 50-1 or the 100-1. If we hit, at these odds, we can really clean up."

At that moment, it occurred to Janet what Deb was asking her to do, to bet money on the names of men she'd never seen before, for some contest of skill or luck or chance. A chance to double her fortune. Wager. Bet. Those two words to her carried connotations of ruffians who shot pool and smoked cigarettes and of squalid barrooms where lonely old men passed the time and their money between each other. She had not expected to gamble. To be honest, however, she had not expected Mort or Ray either. "I have to think," Janet said, pushing herself away from the table.

"What's to think? You just choose."

"But about winning and losing . . . How much can you win and how much can you lose? And how do you know how much to bet and whether or not to even take a chance? And for everything you win, doesn't that mean that someone else will suffer a painful loss? Are there no losers?"

Janet stood up, her mind offering unanswered question after unanswered question, her legs unable to move, to walk, or even to know if they were moving or standing still. The sounds of the barroom around her, snorts, giggles, chortles, hiccups, Stella's!, and even squeaky wooden floor squeaks all became a unified, nondescript sound, as if blending harmoniously together, balancing tittering highs and somber lows and creating that consummate level of mediocrity that always has room for one more voice, another average participant. Janet had never felt this plainness before until . . ." How much can I win again?" somehow came out of her mouth.

"Win? Oh, I've never won," said Deb. "But I'm no loser."

"Never?" Janet asked with a gasp. She again sat, quickly, pulling her chair close to Deb, her dish-watered hand covering her mouth in oh-my-gosh fashion. "Then why do you play?"

"Are you kidding?" Deb said. "At these odds! Besides, everybody plays. Come to think of it, though, I can't honestly remember the last time anybody won. But just look around. I mean, just everybody's here, and everybody plays. And we're no losers."

"But I don't understand how no one can win. Because if there are only two specials to bet on, it would seem to me that one special would appeal to a certain number of people, while the second special would appeal to an entirely different group of second people, so that no matter what happened, someone would always win."

"Jane, Jane, Jane, you just don't understand gambling. That's not the way O'C explained it to me at all. Not at all. There are odds and calculations, previous outcomes, likely results. Very complicated. Perhaps you should just pick one."

"But how? Exactly how? I don't understand how it works."

"Why don't you ask your new friend, Ray? Mmmm? I mean, since he actually speaks to you. I think I have his number here somewhere," Deb said. She reached for her back pocket.

Janet thought about Ray for a split sec . . . "NOOOO!"

Her scream, a towering yelp above the crowd, attracted the attention of all in O'Connell's, none with a more surprised look on their face than Deb.

"Okay," Deb said almost timidly. "If you feel that strongly about it."

"No, nothing like that," Janet said with a cheap smile, her voice trying to return to a conversational, let's-forget-all-about-what-happened-a-few-seconds-ago tone. "It's just that, well, I think I may know where to find him. That's all. Nothing out of the ordinary. Nothing strange or uncommon or out of the ordinary or undecent. Indecent, I mean. Definitely nothing indecent or out of the ordinary. Everything is perfectly normal and why wouldn't it be?"

"Okay," Deb said slowly. "Good, I think."

"Great. I'll go call him. On the phone. I'll call him on the phone by dialing the number of the place where he is. Yes, that's it. The number of the place where he is and where no one else knows he is."

"Oh, everyone knows where he is."

"NOBODY KNOWS!"

Glasses dipped, heads spun, eyes focused.

Deb reached over the table and grabbed Janet's hand. "Look," she said quietly. "There is no one on the face of this planet that enjoys turning a head more than myself. Lord knows that on occasion, I've even gone out of my way to do so. But you've got to learn to take it easy or, darling, you'll snap the heads right off of some of these guys."

"Snapping heads, right," Janet nodded nervously.

"Okay, now. So just call Ray and ask him about the bet for tonight. I'm sure he'll be happy to help you out." Deb paused, waiting for Janet to get up from the table. "Go on," she said. "The phone's over by the door. Behind the redevelopment mess."

Janet remained seated, lost in her own thoughts. She knew that this was one of life's point-of-no-return moments. She also knew that whatever actions she now took would be those she alone forced upon herself. She wanted to call Ray and even have him meet Deb, but this wasn't the way she envisioned it, not even close. There was another scenario somewhere inside of her that remained, out of sight for now, but hoping for a chance to come to life.

"What are you waiting for?" Deb asked. "Take a chance. Call him. That is, if you really know him."

"Of course I know him. Last night, he . . ."

"I know. I was only teasing. Why would you lie about meeting someone, right? Just go call him." Deb reached into her pants pocket and pulled out a small pencil and notebook. She opened at a blank page one. "Here, take these with you," she said, passing the items across the table under cupped hand. "Now, make sure you write down everything he says and be careful that no one else sees or hears you. Get the odds. Get the match. Get the sure-fire winner. And when you've got it all, bring me the dope."

"The dope?"

"Yes, the dope . The scoop. The info. The sure thing . . . Bring me the name of the winner."

"But I . . ."

"What?" Deb said, her voice still a whisper. "It's not cheating, if that's what you're thinking. It's really not. Cheating is when you, er . . . well, cheating is just something entirely different altogether. It requires sneaking around and at least one midnight rendezvous. Secrets, too. And, usually, gobs of missing money. Maybe, hopefully, a patsy with a heart of gold."

Janet remained motionless, staring at the pencil and notebook in her hand as if searching for some tangible written answer to magically appear.

"Greed?" Deb continued. "Is that it? Are you afraid we're being greedy? Well, let me tell you that we are not. Everyone in life gets their fair share, and so what if our fair share happens to be bigger than everyone else's? Sometimes that's just the way things are and we should learn to live with our own good fortune. No matter how fantastic it may be. It all evens out in the long run, anyway. Just ask O'Connell. Now go."

Janet got up without saying a word and marched in the direction of the phone. It was one of those mindless marches that simply take people from one place to another, totally oblivious to all other things in the universe, as if the mere difference of altering physical location would somehow obliterate each unpleasant element of the previous location and for that reason alone a person should step lively. Not even when she walked behind the redevelopment pamphlets did she bat an eye. She then looked at the receiver before realizing that she had no idea of what to say, of the way to begin. And then she stopped, her delicate hand unsure of exactly what to reach for.

# Chapter 5

"So there I was," Clancy began in his most eerie Irish tone, "face to face with the devil 'imself and me a'prayin' for the strength of Cuchulainn like an honest Catholic priest on a bingo night."

Clancy had acquired a small audience among the patrons at O'Connell's, each of whom already deftly decided upon a special and now wished to pursue other, more adventuresome, pursuits. Some whistled.

"I saw this evil once before on the outskirts of Tralee. So many years ago, it was," Clancy added.

Seeing the camera around Clancy's neck, one asked, "Did you get his picture, Clance?"

"'Twas not so lucky," Clancy said. "'Twas me luck I used t'escape with me life."

"What did he do?" the man asked quickly.

"Do? What did 'e do? Lad, 'e tried to stare me down, 'e did. Tried to stare the cold steel 'eart of Lucifer 'imself into me weary bones! That's what 'e did!" Clancy became quiet only long enough to make eye contact with each of those around him. He continued in a low, soft voice. "'is eyes were open wider than the Caves of Altamira! Blood red, they were, with a fire burnin' the eternal flames of hell and damnation right in the center! And then he come closer, closer, closer . . ."

"Don't let him touch you!" another yelled.

"Never!" Clancy yelled back. "'e stood before me and hissed a sound like that I never heard before, and then 'e grew and 'e grew and 'e grew. Inch by inch and foot by foot, the most evil, wickedest creature I e'er saw towered o'er me and sure if I didno' think I'd be swallowed whole and on me way to the good St. Patrick's merciful doorstep when—"

"How could a man grow?" interrupted the disbeliever.

Clancy looked the man straight in the eyes. A gathering without a disbeliever is an ill-formed crowd, he thought. "Aye, but this was no' a man," he said. "This was a . . . a creature." The crowd gasped collectively.

At that moment, Clancy saw that, from behind the bar, O'Connell had turned ear to the tale. "And 'ave you seen scale or fire of this beast, fair barkeep?"

"No," O'Connell said plainly. "But I think Sparelli might be here later."

The crowd around Clancy laughed heartily, and he didn't get the joke. He could only surmise the existence of a patron named Sparelli, a wonk, a misfit, perhaps a scamp or an easier absentee target still—a blowhard—until, strangely, a short, thin man with squinty eyes and dressed all in black suddenly appeared before the group. He looked to Clancy as if he was trying to appear older than his years, with wingtips and wool suit, an uneven and unnatural beard and a curious makeup applied to his face. He was more disguised than any living man Clancy ever saw before, and his face was pale and ashen in O'Connell's dim light. He was so stunned by the man's appearance, to the lengths this man would go to conceal his identity, that he couldn't begin to guess from where or whence he came, or for what tortured and labored purpose. He stood stunned and silent, waiting for the man to speak.

With a zombied stare into space and a voice pitched in such monotone as to dull the senses in a man's soul, the man in black spoke. "There is but one creature in this world . . . She of the book and switch . . . Now she seeks revenge." The man closed his eyes and dropped a celebration flyer to the floor.

"Through hallowed halls by night, she went,
In combat boots, this sad lament,
'Learn to spell, by God, I say,
Or face the ruler every day.'
Beware of Gloobniecht!!"

And with that, the man headed for the door, eyes squinted almost shut, bumping into Clancy and accidentally setting off the loud popping flash of his camera.

With the man gone, Mort then started the crowd off with a buzz, and the rest soon joined along in a subdued and prayerful way. Clancy tried to rub the sight back into his eyes, the unexpected flash causing a complete whiteout, a temporary blindness he tried to see the humor in.

"Who was that?" one man asked.

"The devil!" cried another above the crowd noise.

"'Twasn't," said Clancy.

"How can you be so sure?" said the disbeliever.

"'Cause I've seen the devil with me own two eyes, I 'ave, and 'twasn't him. You can ask my wife, you can. She's seen 'im, too. Thinks he's a fascist, she does," he said, as he continued to rub his eyes.

"But what do we do about Gloobniecht?" a panic-stricken man asked. "We're being warned! I know it! What will we do when she comes to the celebration to kill us all?!!"

"Let's form a posse," ballyhooed a man in a cowboy hat.

"It'll pass," gurgled the stockbroker, his trousers sharply pressed and a fresh shine on his Allen Edmonds.

"Let's just not be nice to her," said a man wearing a derby and claiming to be the voice of reason. He took another sip of his beer.

Clancy recognized the moment. The pot was stirring by another hand. When he had arrived for lunch that day, he had every intention of playfulness and mischief, of injecting the crowd with the loosest and most contorted facts of his morning's encounter with a genuine character, the fun of it, of rousing imaginations to the point of outburst, of a spirited debate to pass the time and stretch the mind, of once again drawing them all into his orbit. Now he acknowledged that a secret ingredient had been added, an ominous interloper whose dire prose had elevated the discourse beyond amusement and into some fearful place that Clancy knew he must lead them out of. A mild and controlled redirection was required, he felt, perhaps a project of some sort or the creation of an icon, something to rally round, anything to restore the belief that the future was not full of dire consequences, and that all would be well, sunshine and blue sky.

"You're all daft!" Clancy pleaded. "Simply daft! In all my days, I've not been frightened by the portent of spirits in the light of day, let alone by messengers wearing wingtips. Listen to man who knows that what's needed now more than ever is to slay this dark evil beast with the fire in 'is eyes and let the everlasting light of goodness and truth and solid Irish virtue back into our lives. 'Tis the flesh and blood demons that must be cast out, lads. Spirits have a mind of their own, their appearances as sudden and unpredictable as a Moorish fog. Never known one with the common decency to announce a return, either. Let's do the sane thing, lads. Think . . . Would there, by chance, be a good Catholic exorcist in town? Preferably one who knows his way around demons with fiery eyes and such?"

The crowd thought.

\* \* \* \* \*

From behind the Redevelopment display, Janet was trying to make sense of what she was hearing. Beasts and creatures and devils? Were there such things? She continued to listen.

\* \* \* \* \*

"Well, just one minute," chimed the disbeliever. "I, for one, am not going to put any faith into this ghost of Gloobniecht thing. Now we all know that she was put to death by that bloody-knuckled crowd from God-knows-where—and I'm not saying they were wrong, mind you—a long time ago. Now dead is dead and done is done and never shall the done dead be undone, or something like that. And as for Clancy's beast, well, I'll believe that one when the beast taps me on the shoulder and orders me to the front of the line in the Fool's Parade."

Clancy put his hands to his head. "Oh! Now you've gone and done it, lad. You've summoned that most evil one! You've challenged the Devil 'imself to appear at your side! I'd not turn 'round if I felt a tapping on my shoulder, if I were you. You haven't a clue you've brought wickedness and drought and plague and general nastiness and probably famine, too, upon us! Woe's us! Woe's us!" Clancy turned to O'Connell. "Tell them, fair barkeep, that the evil I speak of is nigh!"

"Evil is nigh," O'Connell repeated.

"AHA!" Clancy cried. "Confirmation from the fairest of the fair! Sure, but I would bet that he's a Kerry man, as well. And for ten thousand years has no Kerry man ever let a ticklish tongue speak an untrue word. Alas, if O'Connell says it, it must be true."

"Blarney," said the disbeliever.

"No," Clancy said, tilting his head to one side. "Blarney be too far inland. Though they've got a nice castle, the inlanders tend to breed liars like dandelions. 'Tis the Kerry man you can trust longer than the day is long. You see, lad, they live by the sea."

"Well, I live by my wits," said the disbeliever.

Clancy winked. "And wouldn't you know, they've been askin' for cutlasses and broadswords to aid in the defense all these years."

"Says you," snapped the disbeliever.

Clancy put his hand to his heart. "Alas, I am disarmed." He then skillfully fainted in the direction of Mort, the neon king catching him with ease and trying to prop him back on his feet.

"No dancing," O'Connell said.

Clancy opened one eye and looked at O'Connell. He jigged to his feet. "'Twas the dance of life 'e give me, O'C. The sturdy lad a throwin' 'imself right betwixt the path of me head to the floor. 'Twas the second time today I've been saved from death, no less." Clancy turned to Mort and put his arms around his shoulders. "Was a brave thing, lad. A very brave thing you've done for a frail and tired old Irishman, and I've got to tell you, you'll be in me prayers at night, and during the day, I'll be praising your name and wishing you prosperity in business and hoping you find the love of a good woman."

"Ah, it was nothing, Clance," Mort said.

Clancy's mouth dropped open. "And modest, to boot!" he said. "Will this man's goodness never end?"

The disbeliever smirked. "Clancy, you only fell backwards six inches, and Mort didn't even have to move to catch you."

"Ah, the mysteries of fate," Clancy said.

"But he didn't have to do anything!"

"'Tis the most courageous man who can trust his bravery to luck." Clancy dropped to one knee and bowed his head in front of Mort. "You're blessed, son," he said to him.

"No! No! No! No! No!" the disbeliever yelled, stomping his feet, his fists clenched and pounding up and down wildly.

"Now, don't be too jealous of the lad," Clancy said cheerily. "There's no time for jealousy with a devil in our midst."

"And Gloobniecht! Don't forget Gloobniecht!" the panic-stricken man added.

"Aye, lad, she's not forgotten," Clancy conceded. It became obvious to Clancy that the fun he expected to have at the expense of his morning customer was being shared, almost hijacked, usurped by the ominous stranger whose rhyme and mere mention of the name Gloobniecht roused emotions and sent imaginations off on their own course. Only the disbeliever was completely dismissive of ghosts and devils and things otherworldly; that much was expected. The others seemed certain of their contagion, especially the panic-stricken man. In the moment, however, even Clancy resigned to feeling a certain magnetism to the stranger—the monotone, the squinty eyes and the wingtips, the oddness.

His presence was so out of sorts, so beyond the latitude and boundaries of the free range narrative Clancy outlined in his mind, the day's sport, that he had no choice but to acknowledge that he, like the others, had been mysteriously drawn toward it. He! The realization brought a loud and sudden guffaw that drew no attention from the others. How unexpected the moment was for him. How positively unexpected! There was pure surprise in it! To be caught completely and naturally unaware, flat-footed! What a powerful force! To be swept off your flat feet! The proverbial and hackneyed shoe on the other foot! From out of the blue! It can happen to anyone! . . . Time for a breath.

Clancy thoroughly enjoyed the moment. He enjoyed being drawn in, the final destination tantalizingly unknown, and so did, he surmised, the others, whether they wanted to admit it, or not.

The direction was clearly new. Opportunity was knocking, the good and unpredictable fortune of it, he figured. If the celebration were to host an unwelcome visitor, so be it. If his brethren were to require a salve or a balm to remove the stinging fears of the unknown, it should be applied and served with care, from the delicate hands of a master, naturally. If they were to require a hero or a savior, someone to repel all unpleasantness and carry a mighty standard, someone whose bravery was either carefully crafted or indisputable in the face of a manly test, one should likewise be provided, with gusto, if possible. One should be made known, conjured even, he thought, his eyes drifting toward Mort.

Clancy proceeded, "Indeed, 'tis with her in mind, I put forth a proposition the likes of which could alter the lives of all men for all eternity. No small task, lads. A proposition the likes of which makes legends of otherwise normal men and hero worshippers of small children, molding their waif-like minds for all time. A proposition based on penultimate faith and the knowledge of a mighty unseen goodness. A proposition that will save our celebration and this fair town! In short men, I propose we rally 'round our strength, our tower, our blessed vanquisher and avenger, our undoubtedly most brave—and a man who is in the spelling business, no less. Friends, I give you—Mort, the Conqueror!"

"Hurrah! Hip, Hip Hoorah!"

The crowd cheered their new hero with "oles, bravos, and countless hurrahs" for almost a full minute until Deb walked over and put herself in the center of the crowd. She stood next to Clancy and Mort with her hands upon her hips, offering her most seductively nonchalant pose, obviously trying to intercept as much of the crowd's adulation as possible. Clancy recognized the principle from a traveling salesman who sold solar collectors and figured that, even if she could absorb a little of what the crowd was offering, the effort would have been well rewarded. Modern science applied, he figured. However, no sooner did she take her ground, than did the crowd stop cheering.

"They weren't cheering you," said the disbeliever.

"So, what's all the excitement about?" she said.

Clancy smiled and then explained to Deb with astounding recall the reason for the crowd's jubilation, the crowd nodding in all the appropriate places.

"You're kidding, right?" Deb replied. "Guys," she then addressed them, "you all know as well as I do what kind of guy Mort is . . ."

"Bzzz."

"Easy, Electro-boy. He's a big sweet guy with a heart of gold who puts the names of dead people up in lights. A commendable occupation, sure. And I know that he, more or less, works with dead people and that because of that, he should get first crack at this Gloobniecht ghost, but he's just not very scary, and I would hate to think about what would happen if he stood face-to-face with an actual creature." She turned to Mort. "Sorry, big fella."

Mort buzzed softly.

"What we need is a professional scary person. Someone experienced in the ways of intimidation. Someone bigger than life with an eye-popping stare that says something! We need massiveness . . . We need flying figure-four leg locks and secret choke holds! Maybe a foreign object, or two! . . . We need Death Ray Drake!"

97

"Carl the Mean," yelled one man.

"Get that Lizard Lip guy!" yelled another. "O'Connell told me he's got the world's greatest submission hold."

"Get a guy on a horse!" ballyhooed the man in the cowboy hat.

"Let me tell you about this really big gun I have at home," added the man in the NRA cap.

"Perhaps if we ignore it, it would just go away," said the man in the derby. He claimed to be the voice of reason and offered to prove it by continuing to sip his beer.

Clancy then eased himself away from Deb's side and moved into the heart of the crowd. Deb began to campaign vigorously for the appointment of Death Ray Drake as Town Avenger, citing numerous previous victories and the fact that he already had his own equipment: shoes, tights, championship belt, etc. He then noticed the primed assembly all nodding in what seemed to him a well-rehearsed unison, and he smiled. Once again, he had given way, politely stepped aside, the stew at a delicate simmer, this time in order for Deb to take center stage, for her to speak and be heard and, most of all, to be seen by all of those who before only dared to steal glances of her, the shy ones. Of her, he thought, patient and hopeful eyes may be watching, hopeful hearts may be wondering, if "she's the one."

That first time he came into O'Connell's, he noticed Deb, that bewitching red hair, the way surreptitious eyes followed her around the room, and he remembered himself as a young man in Limerick and how hopelessly invisible and wordless he had been. He remembered he too never knew just what to say about things, anything, and how he would have given the pot of gold at the end of the rainbow had someone provided a shortcut to an introduction, or a path to a conversation, or even a more certain way to coax a sentence from his silent thoughts.

Those silent moments now seemed foolish and so long ago, he felt. Maturity had brought with it a steamer trunk packed full to the brim with the wisdom aged from missed opportunities, popping at the rivets, begging him to share the wealth and lighten his load at the same time. He now felt it a noble project to draw attention to himself, a capable man of years and lively tales, like a comet blazing across the sky, and now his mission, to help the young lads, to mix things up, to be the uniter of kindred and not so kindred spirits, to stir embers and outbursts, to perhaps bring them to within an inch of their immaculate destiny, passions ignited!

And then he suddenly remembered Mrs. MacNamara and that glorious day long ago at the bank where he coolly said, "Change for your note, ma'am?" And for the first time in his life, he focused on the simple dullness of his words, the plainness. He couldn't help but realize that something spectacular had been born to an unscripted moment, to the most average of moments, and that it wouldn't have made any difference what he said to her on that particular day or the manner in which he said it—only that he said something. No matter it didn't begin spectacularly.

And this he knew from a single heartbeat that seemed to come to him from a far-away place, from a far-away moment he actually loved, and for a second, it took his breath away.

Clancy had to find a chair; he had to sit down. The sharp memory of that common morn had jolted him. He shivered like no other time at the realization. It was truly the uncertainty of the moment that gave it its passion, its life, he thought, and he smiled. Room enough for serendipity. Room enough, indeed.

Clancy now sat and watched and listened to those around Deb, a renewed appreciation for the less poetic or less creative or less inventive moments that passed. And he was dumbstruck. How's a person to know what's next?

"Tell us how to find Death Ray," said one.

"Let's get him fast," yelled another.

Just then the men became loud and louder still and more aggressive toward Deb, surrounding her as closely as they felt proper, all cheering uncontrollably, and all but one or two voicing approval of Deb's suggestion to engage the services of Death Ray Drake.

"I still want to see that Lizard Lip guy," one disappointed crowdster said to Clancy. His objection, however, soon proved to be the basest experience in futility and within moments he, too, was prepared to usher in Death Ray the Great. Some battles are not meant to be won, Clancy noted.

As Clancy watched, Deb then ascended to a position atop the bar, a location, he surmised, more proper for addressing the masses. 'Friends," she began in a commanding tone, "It just so happens that I've been on top of this situation from the beginning. I've had faith in all of you. I've had faith and trust that you would see the light exactly as I've shown it to you. Because, you know what? You're all just a bunch of big lugs, and I truly love all of you. You're all so sweet. And that's why I've taken the liberty of allowing my very best friend in the whole world to phone Death Ray and ask for his help. And there she is now!"

Clancy saw Deb point in the direction of the phone, a line of sight from his vantage point which traversed the Redevelopment Project pamphlet display Janet had been hiding behind, a line of sight he perceived as being like the greatest and grandest of spotlights coming from above. He saw the look on Janet's face, and it was as if she wanted to scream, but instead she just closed her eyes, a gesture Clancy identified as a feeble attempt at invisibility.

"Quick, everyone! To the phone!" The voice was indistinguishable, but came from the center of the crowd, the heart, and a dozen pair of legs as if belonging to a centipede with a dozen heads, then obediently shuffled in the direction of the phone, and Janet. The pitter-patter of excited crowd feet lingered even after they reached their destination.

Clancy watched as the crowd stood in front of Janet, her eyes still closed, and he knew what she now faced. He knew exactly what was in front of her. There would be eyes and stares and people would expect answers from her. People would quiz her. He knew she would have to face the music, whatever that meant, and he imagined all those in front of her playing musical instruments, all horribly out of tune and each playing a different song, as if to say to her, 'We know this sounds unpleasant, but don't be too surprised—you knew this was coming. We are the people you must face. We are the people who must know the truth. We are a band of merry truth-seekers and this is what we sound like.' She opened her eyes.

"Well . . . ? Will he do it?" said one.

"Well, that's not exactly clear," Janet said in a lilting voice.

"What do you mean?"

"I mean . . . he was out."

"Should we wait?"

"Waiting would be good," Janet said, for a moment relieved. Other ideas, however, were then graciously offered.

"Let's send him a telegram!"

"Sure!"

"No! What a dumb idea. Who said that?"

"Who cares who said it, let's just not do it. Let's write a letter, politely asking him to save us all."

"Now, if that's not the stupidest."

"It's not stupid. Letters are nice."

"We could send flowers . . . or candy."

"I'm sorry, now that is really the stupidest. We want to hire him, not date him."

"Yeah, who'd want to date him?" one said.

The others all laughed wildly. Janet tried to hide her face.

"Can you even believe Death Ray with a girl? She'd have to be unbreakable, or at least indestructible."

"She'd have to be blind."

"Or deaf."

"Or dumb."

"Or she'd have to be wonderful." Clancy interrupted them with a peaceful voice. "The kindest of hearts and the bringer of good fortune. Or someone you'd like to meet, perhaps. Maybe like someone you know. Oh, lads, that you all imagine this woman is grand! Her unbreakable spirit must give her the strength of 10,000 men; yet, still, she is blind to point out any weaknesses—and she is dumber still to speak of them. And her deaf ears have proven the most virtuous, to not let the cruelest and most unkind of words destroy or invade her tender, faithful heart. What a woman she must be, lads! Certainly a woman for a champion and not for clods such as we. For, alas, it is the champion who has the greatest of all things: the greatest, most persistent record; the greatest heart; and, pity the poor man, the greatest woes and fears and sadness. 'Tis simply his nature to possess the greatest of all things, good and bad. Being a champion, he could do no less. And this woman, this grand, grand, dear sweet woman, will comfort him in his sadness, offer the kindness in her heart always, and understand that the champion performs the most colossal of blunders with all the ease of the change of seasons, and is just as predictable. Because this woman, too, must be a champion. You see, somehow champions find each other and know they belong together, and it is as if the rest of the world is lost and floundering behind them, unaware that the view from the mountaintop truly goes on forever and ever and will never be lost. And what a view it is, men—blue sky and horizon, as far as the eye can see. We should all be so lucky. Would that someone thought that we were champions."

Clancy bowed his head and walked slowly to the door.

"Where are you going, Clancy?" one asked.

Clancy didn't turn around, but spoke just as he was raising a finger to his eye. "Something in me eye," he said. "Devil if it doesn't just come at the oddest times, too. Thirty-five years afflicted, I've been."

"Will you be coming back when it's better?"

"'Tis not the cure I'd be wanting, lads. 'Tis the strength of my eye's heart to endure that I pray for. I shall see you all later at the celebration. Good day."

"Bye, Clance," Mort said.

\* \* \* \* \*

Clancy was only a step out of O'Connell's when Janet proudly proclaimed, "I know exactly where Ray Drake is, and he's not where you think he is. He is in my apartment."

All again gasped collectively. It was the second group gasp of the afternoon, and some, especially the more creative-minded, were feeling a little winded. Some felt a tither. Others agog. Deb screamed, "All right!"

# Chapter 6

When Lyle ran out of Janet's apartment building and into the early morning sun en route to Grossman's, he felt invigorated, enthralled, enticed, and even strengthened to the point of possessing superhuman powers, simply by the notion and belief in a really good plan. His plan. Cleverness and ingenuity would feed his soul and create new ways for summoning the inner strength he was now sure he possessed. Feed the plan. No obstacle was too great to stand in the way of his objective. No obstacle was too great to stand in the way of his discovering the truth about Janet, and of his discovering the true meaning of the evening they spent together. Nothing could slow a man on a mission, he figured. Nothing except . . . tiredness.

Lyle had been running down TBNL for an awfully long time, and he was beginning to wonder if he was running in the wrong direction. His feet hurt. He was hot. And it was at this moment that Lyle began to wonder whether or not other plans of great men had fallen by the wayside in the face of the realities of life. Far less energy had been expended in the actual formulation of the plan, for example, than in the actions needed to carry it out. Could indecision and tired feet be the first real tests of character? Lyle immediately reasoned they could, and summarily modified his timetable to include a slower pace for clarity of thinking, and frequent rest stops for rejuvenation of body. And, on an extra positive note, he added that the housedress he was wearing provided him with a certain freeness of motion which he had heretofore never experienced, and he became genuinely impressed at the practicality of women's clothing. Credit where credit was due, he figured.

So here was Lyle, now walking down TBNL, content in believing he was definitely heading toward Grossman's and his bicycle, and more than pleased at the way in which he handled the nasty indecision problem he faced. Looking back, it was clear dispassionate thinking that led him to make a logical choice between his alternatives:

1. To continue running would have meant a risk of passing out and possible death due to heatstroke;
2. To slow the pace to a walk would allow an opportunity to catch one's breath, as well as continue forward operations; and
3. To stop would have meant certain death by starvation in a most unattractive locale (shoulder of nameless highway).

Clearly, the correct choices had been made.

Lyle also thought it funny that, in this particular instance, he learned the value of walking over the speed of running, somehow disproving the old adage that 'You must walk before you can run.' He realized, however, that he was a little off base in even making the connection between the adage and his present situation, but still felt a bit clever for making the connection, all the while hoping that it signaled the development of a wit or at least the ability to laugh at oneself— because walking also gave him more time to think about Janet. He knew he had to ask himself some tough questions.

Q. Does she really like me?

A. Of course she does. I'm nice. Hard working. Honest. And besides, why else would she have taken me to her apartment? Unless, of course, she takes everyone to her apartment, which would explain why I found that rather descriptive, most probably secretly encoded book describing all those, those . . .

Q. But how could that book belong to her?

A. It can't. No one who appeared so sweet and innocent could possibly be involved in anything like that. But, then again, if a person were to want to participate in that kind of behavior, they probably wouldn't want anyone to know about it and would then disguise themselves as the person least likely to be accused of being so that when the time came to really accuse someone of something like that, everyone would say 'Her? Oh, no. It's just not even possible. She's the last person on Earth who would do a thing like that. Clever.'

Q. Just what kind of fool does she think I am?

A. Obviously first class.

Q. How could I fall for that old trick and allow having all my clothes stolen at the same time?

A. Pass.

Q. But what if I'm wrong?

A. What if I'm right?

Q. But what if she was just as embarrassed as I was about last night and then couldn't bear to face me in the light of day?

A. Quite possible. That book is not hers.

Q. She really did smile at me, didn't she?

A. Of course she did. At the diner. And I smiled back. Proof positive that she likes me.

Q. But does she *really* like me?

A. How else could I have woken up in her bed this morning?

Q. But does she *really, really* like me, and am I still a . . . ?

A. No positive way to tell.

Q. Proceed with caution?

A. No doubt.

Lyle's hard-nosed, no-nonsense approach to self-interrogation aimed not only at discerning the truth, but also at the passage of time as he walked, was, even by his own standards, yielding few fruitful results. Step by step followed closely by question and answer were beginning to become the order for the day when Lyle heard faint, muffled sobs coming from a place nearby, just barely ahead. He looked and saw that, just off the roadway, there was a young man, dressed in a sharkskin grey suit, sitting beneath a tree and holding his head in his hands. Lyle decided to walk over.

The tree was large and tall and dark, and gave great shade, expanding outward for many, many, feet from its base. Thick roots were breaking through the ground near the spot where the man sat, and as Lyle approached him, he imagined how much they looked like long spindly fingers reaching to the edge of the shade, clutching and holding the ground and all else that ventured too close for a look. He stepped with caution.

"Are you all right?" Lyle asked.

The man didn't answer right away. "She doesn't love me anymore," he said, after a while.

"Who doesn't love you anymore?" Lyle continued.

"She doesn't."

Lyle stopped for a moment to think. The man was obviously very troubled, and Lyle wondered if further questioning would be wise, helpful, or even proper. Never before had he seen a man in a more lifeless, pathetic state. What is the right thing to do, he thought. And then Lyle thought of exactly where the man was, in isolation, literally left alone in some, most probably, self-induced no-man's-land to fight off whatever demons troubled him. Obviously, Lyle deduced, this man had no plan and could definitely benefit from his company.

"Can you tell me what happened?" Lyle started. "Maybe I can help."

"No one can help me. Go away."

"No, I won't go away," Lyle said firmly. "I'm a man with a plan and I'm here to help."

Obviously curious at the tone of Lyle's voice, the man in the sharksin grey suit took his hands away from his face. He wiped the tears from his eyes and then looked at Lyle. "Why are you wearing a dress?" he asked. There was more than a hint of idle curiosity in his voice.

Lyle stammered, "Well, you see . . ."

"My life is falling apart. Crashing around me in little tiny pieces that I may never be able to put back together again. And now you . . . What's your name?"

"Lyle."

"Lyle, go away."

"Wait."

"No, Lyle. Listen, she just doesn't love me anymore. She told me so. I heard the words that came out of her mouth, and I believe she meant them. She was beautiful, and smart, and witty, and charming. And she had the most miraculous blue eyes that she said I could call my own. She said they were just for me and that they would never look upon a face that they loved more than mine. And now she's gone."

Lyle watched and listened.

"We went everywhere together. We had fun and laughs and tender moments that we both said we would cherish forever. Once, in a park, I fashioned a necklace made from clover and we pretended they were pearls. She wore it the entire day, and wherever we went, people stared and laughed amongst themselves at the girl with the weeds around her neck, but we didn't care. They were the finest weeds I ever saw. And, to this day, whenever I see a field of clover, I picture myself tying thin green clover stalks around her throat. It was glorious."

Lyle continued to listen.

"And now I'm prepared to sit under this tree and mope and sob and generally feel sorry for myself for all eternity or some other really long amount of time, because I have now officially cast my lot with those who have lost at love. None, however, have lost as much as I. I am alone."

There was a long silence.

"You look like a wretch," Lyle said. "Except, maybe, for the suit."

"I am a martyr. Years from now, when my suffering has reached epic proportions, a statue will be erected in my honor. People will come from all the corners of the Earth to weep at my feet for their lost loves. People will wail. Their tears will flow and anoint my stone cold feet."

"Birds will crap on you."

"What's your point, Lyle?"

"Well, although I've never actually seen a wretch, I think you may be one—grey sharkskin suit aside. Just from all the things Mother Speckman used to tell me, you understand. And whenever Mother Speckman would tell me these stories about these wretches, she would offer me advice. She said it was the same advice that had been passed down the line, touching generation after generation. And I would now like to pass that advice on to you and make all things perfect, well, and good forever."

"And what advice would that be?"

"About wretches," she would say, "Don't be one."

The man pursed his lips. He stared at Lyle's face, the meekness of his features, and paused to take a deep breath. He took another. "Do you have a girl?" he asked.

"I . . . I don't know." Lyle almost said yes and he wondered why.

"Well, are you in love?"

"I don't believe so, no."

"But you had to think about whether or not you even had

a girl, right? And since I know that love makes you do strange things, and since you are wearing a dress, I just figured. From my own experience, you understand."

"Well, you see, I've just recently met someone and . . ."

"Oh, so there is a girl."

"Well, yes, but we don't really know each other very well, I think."

"So you just figured that you'd try on one of her dresses in an attempt to get to know her a little better, is that it?"

"No, of course not. This is a disguise."

"I see. So you've decided to spy on this girl you've just met?"

"I'm not spying. I just need to find out a few things."

"Look, Lyle, if you're going to go around spying on people, don't lie about it. Believe me when I say that you can get yourself in plenty of trouble without really doing anything at all. There is no reason to resort to spying and then lying about it."

"But you don't understand. This is different."

"That's what they all say. Besides, the only truly different situation is mine. Did I tell you what happened? She left me—"

"But you don't understand! She stole my clothes and left me and then I had to put on this dress and—"

"Don't rationalize, Lyle. It can only get you in more trouble."

"Me in trouble? I thought that you were the one in trouble. That's why I came over here to help. Remember, you were crying and sobbing and everything."

"I'm not the one in trouble, and I'm not the one wearing a dress."

"Stop! You're confusing me. I think you've tried to confuse me in the way that only a wretch can."

"No, not me. Believe me when I say that confusion has a way of showing up all by itself. It doesn't need an expert to help it find its way. Interruptions, on the other hand, operate on an entirely different principle. Now go away and leave me alone in misery. You'll be along again shortly, I'm sure."

"But I don't understand. Will everything be okay? I mean, if I leave you alone out here, won't you die?"

"Don't be an idiot. I'll leave when I'm hungry. Now go."

The man put his face back in his hands and once again began to sob. He looked exactly the same as when Lyle first saw him. There was no difference, none at all. And Lyle turned his back and walked toward TBNL.

# Chapter 7

"Quick, everyone! To Jane's!"

"To Jane's!"

"To Jane's!"

"Yee-ha!" Deb added.

The O'Connell's crowd quickly rallied around Janet, enveloped her, and ushered her out O'Connell's front door with all the grace and eloquence of a well-directed cattle stampede. Shoes were shuffling and dust was flying. Those who felt like hooting hooted. Those who felt like jumping jumped. Those who felt like following followed. And those who felt like watching watched. O'Connell watched.

"To Jane's!" they continued. "To Jane's!"

Together, all chanting, all jumping and hooting under the hot, midday sun, they sounded powerful, perhaps even a little invincible. There were even a few who sounded a bit delirious.

"To Jane's!" they continued. More cheers followed. More hoots followed the cheers. More people jumped. And more people became tired and winded.

"Just wait one minute," said the disbeliever. "Where are we going? Where are we all going? I mean, exactly?"

All stopped what they were doing and looked directly at Janet. She pointed at TBNL, indicating with a wave of her hand that she lived some distance from the center of town. She could manage no words.

"And just how are we all going to get there?" the disbeliever continued. "Surely, we all must go. Surely, we all must go because there is no way that any one person could face Death Ray. We must be certain he will be at the celebration."

"I can talk to him," Janet said quickly. It was a nervous response.

"No, I can't believe that's possible. All of us should go and speak to him. Or, at least, I should go and speak to him. A calmer head should make the suggestion."

"We could all take my bus," Mort said. "Bzzz."

"All of us?"

"Sure. It's right over there. Bzzz."

Mort's bus was parked right behind O'Connell's, off the road and out of sight from those within Town Square. He had been parking it there for some time now, Janet knew, ever since Deb told her Alderman Peabody had ticketed Mort for parking on the city streets, citing that he had been casting a pall upon the town by exposing passersby to the sight. Apparently Peabody felt that Mort's bus was not completely in keeping with the newness and freshness motif that he was trying to convey via redevelopment projects. Or he felt the need, as governing member of the town's executive branch, to take a more active role in town law enforcement. Either, or, for whatever reason, there it sat—forty-five feet of seldom-used-for business, school-bus-yellow, chewing-gum-stuck-under-the-seat transportation, the last remnant of the Hall of Records fleet. A string of red-and-green Christmas tree lights, always on, stretched lengthwise down both sides, the words 'Mort's Neon Tombstones' printed somewhat neatly beneath the windows. A giant ball of electrical tape occupied most of the back of the bus, in a place where the last three rows of seats used to be, as extension cords, copper wires, adaptor plugs, long and short metal rods, a box of wire coat hangers, and a set of golf clubs were all stacked neatly and in descending order of conductivity nearby. The words 'Caution: Electricity' were stenciled across the rear exit door in fluorescent red paint, words to the wise.

"I'll just make some room," Mort said, heading for the bus at a brisk pace. He pulled a pair of dark rubber gloves out of his back pocket and quickly put them on, each forming to the neon king's hands with a plucky popping sound, readying himself for a safe passage into that familiar, wondrous, but potentially hazardous environment. He entered without breaking stride.

Outside Janet listened to clutters and clanks, scrapes and scratches, squeaky metal-against-metal screeches, and tried to imagine what sort of reconfiguration was taking place before her. Janet heard some around her attest to spare parts being thrown out windows, but she could not be certain; movements inside the bus were a fleeting blur amidst a greenish-grey dust cloud. Others, however, argued loudly that any amount of progress should begin with a good destructive effort and encouraged more dust and more speed and more of whatever the others suspected was being thrown about. Deb swore she saw sparks.

And when that mysterious dust cloud settled, the clutters and clanks all gone, and all refocused their eyes, there sat

Mort smartly in the driver's seat, firmly buckled up for safety with gloved hands ten and two on the wheel, a nod of his head to the others indicating all systems were go and that boarding should begin.

"Hurrah!" they all cried, piling into the bus like so many clowns in a three-ring circus. "To Jane's! To Jane's!"

And with all packed safely inside, Mort revved the gas and spun once around Town Square, buzzing the Chamber of Commerce with a blast of the horn, the O'Connell's crowd— all but Janet—all hooting and hollering at the top of their lungs, Deb louder than most, her arms flailing, her hair flowing free out the window, all soon to be speeding down TBNL in search of their vanquisher, their conqueror, their salvation.

# Chapter 8

"Stella! The books! Where are the books?" O'Connell pulled his private chair out from behind the bar, a high-backed, hand-carved, regal-looking piece of furniture with velvety-green padding over the arms and seat and dragged it over to the round table. "And my visor! Don't forget my visor!" he added with a couple snaps of his fingers.

Stella, though, didn't answer, and O'Connell imagined her consumed with kitchen duties, her arms filled with glasses and plates, each stacked three high, the pockets of her apron overstuffed with pub orders, both special and otherwise, several unused steak knives clenched between her teeth with such a vengeance that it would have made Bluebeard himself proud of the effort and initiative. She was a gem.

When Stella came out of the kitchen, her arms were extended outward, the O'Connell Pub books resting peacefully atop a satiny pillow she offered in her hands. She stepped slowly and with circumstance, a combination of well-taught reverie and dubious practice, as O'C waited. Her presentation was again perfect: the well-measured steps, dutiful eyes focused front, precision of uniform in apron, nametag and order books. All aligned in a polished image, a model. And that face, that gloriously perfect face, acting stoic. She stepped in front of O'C. "The books."

"Thanks ever so kindly," O'C said, taking the ledger from the pillow and placing it before him. He opened at the mark. "And my visor? Did you remember my visor?"

Stella reached into the waistband of her apron and removed O'C's visor. A quick exhale upon its transparent green shade, a wipe from her handkerchief, and it was ready for action. She placed the visor upon O'C's head, and curtsied. "Your visor."

"And my extra sharp number two pencils?"

Stella reached into her apron. She removed two extra sharp pencils and placed them before O'C.

"Excellent. I may begin. The orders please."

Stella unloaded the pockets of her apron, slips of paper filled with orders of the day. She laid them out on the table in front of O'C. She heaped them in piles as O'C studied, his extra sharp number two pencil poised, at the ready. He began.

O'Connell plucked the first piece of paper from the tippiest top of the pile. "Pub order, *special*," he read aloud. It made him feel good. It always made him feel good. Sometimes, in his mind, the duty and diligence required in managing the books recalled memories of his father before him, he a respected, but long-departed, bookmaker in the old country. 'Good recordkeeping avoids misunderstandings,' his father would say. O'C had always agreed.

A small mark in a book, his father told him when he was young, was all that would be required, all that would be necessary to record the action. A simple notation to forever connect patron to hopeful victor, to monitor the hard-earned money cast into the unknown, the abyss, in the hope that a favorable outcome might produce a sporting gusher, a windfall of imaginary proportions. Or not. After all, his father said, a man who would put his money where his mouth was had already considered the possibility that a loss would put his funds on the first bus out of town, gone and only to be seen again in memory. That was the sport of it to these men his father said, to chance a parting of the ways with a few precious dollars, in the hopes their intuitions or superfluous research on the man in the ring were correct, and that some Herculean and bountiful spoils were within their earthly grasp.

Besides, he said, no one loses a bet the moment it's placed. Can't be done. The waiting for the outcome was positively priceless, the hopefulness and the dreaming, the dreams like balloons filled with the faintest breathes of hope. They would fill and fill and fill them until those balloons became so stout they would clutch them by the throat with white-knuckled grasps, so tight that their forearms shook, until they couldn't anymore, the results in, and they would have to let go, the hope rushing out, and the balloons flying helter-skelter through the air to land in completely unpredictable places. Nothing like it in the world.

O'Connell so loved the *special* orders, the highest odds. He always felt they brought him closer to his father and to his legacy. He only hoped that dearly departed Dad would grant him some form of creative absolution as it pertained to the specifics of his daily offerings. From time to time, he attempted to reconcile a minor detail that only he and Stella knew, that with the exception of Death Ray Drake, who was never on the card, each and every combatant whose bout appeared on a menu between the cheese curd and bologna loaf had been a carefully crafted figment of his imagination—an exceptionally high-risk, no-reward phantom, a bust.

He reached for another order. One by one, he separated the orders into two neat piles, one for pub orders regular, and one for special orders, a smile so wry making its way to the corners of his mouth. Commerce in action.

"Stella, please, a hand," O'C asked.

Her well-rehearsed hands knew just what to do. "Sure, Boss," she said. She sat at the table and grabbed a pile of orders. "Shall we begin with the pub orders, regular?" she said.

"As always," was O'C's reply.

"Pub order, regular, number one," Stella began, "man with derby claiming to be the voice of reason: One Delmonico, pretzel rods, chilled lager."

"Man with derby, one regular," O'C repeated, the point of his pencil inching down the lines of his ledger to the man's name. "Excellent," O'C said, making a small mark. "That's his third regular order of the week. And the special?"

Stella put down the stack of regular orders and searched the stack of special orders to find the man's request. "Man with derby claiming to be the voice of reason, 100-1 for $10."

"Cash or tab?" O'C asked. He knew the answer, but tradition dictated he ask, a tradition that was laid out long before him, taught to him first by his father, whose father before him, and all fathers before them, were taught long, long ago by the ancients, those warrior Celtic priests who claimed to have taken the cash action when the Gauls sacked Rome in 410 A.D. It was a simple lesson to learn and required only a modicum of memorization: Get the cash up front. Almost anyone could learn it.

"Cash." It was the expected answer.

He never tired of the response. He took pride in his history as told to him, the procedures of his profession carved long ago in stone tablets and carried on the backs of those same ancients, those same Celtic warrior priests he was told of in his youth. Monuments to good judgment, he felt. Precise documentation a prerequisite for an accurate ledger, lest mistakes be made. Carelessness was to be left to the undocumented, and to those for whom chance was a risky proposition. Care was to be applied when calculating odds, the Irish algorithms a unique combination of integers and human nature; if done correctly, both profit and entertainment were assured. He only wished he could remember exactly how it was done.

"Excellent. And the change?"

"$30 even."

"Excellent again." Having long ago forgotten the formulas for calculating odds, payouts, etc., it seemed far easier to use those magnificent ledger books to return all monies bet by patrons back to them at different times, thus assuring recurring food and beverage sales. Customers simply thought Stella couldn't make change. It seemed a fair and creative compromise —combining the traditional cash harvest with the somewhat backward-thinking repatriation of assets. After all, O'Connell knew the absolute impropriety of simply bamboozling funds from patron's pockets for phony-baloney contests of skill. It simply wasn't to be done without an equal and opposite benefit provided: The thrill of anticipation. It also made people hungry. Had they known, he was convinced they all would have seen it as nothing more than good, clean fun. One by one, each order was addressed. "And the tabs?"

"None today."

O'C had not expected any. Tradition dictated that tab customers fall into a very narrow band of clientele with well-defined characteristics: select members of law enforcement (the gregarious and myopic), as well as those with the capability to grant and return favors (members of the ruling class and their nephews). Not since the days of Lester's father, the Honorable Schuyler A. Peabody, had O'C taken any serious tab action.

The long column of marks in O'C's ledger were a quiet reminder of an old, departed friend whose tab had grown and grown and grown into a boisterous figure, his delivered lunches long ago eaten, his change ledger a long line of zeros. He hoped it was nothing he said.

"And Nick?"

"Curious appetite, that one. He makes little hearts out of the mashed potatoes."

"Do you think you should say something to him?"

"I don't know. The last time I called him tall, dark, and handsome, he dyed his hair jet black and started wearing a fake mustache. And then, when he started chasing me around that tree in the square and couldn't catch me, I suggested he needed better traction. Two days later, he's got metal cleats on the bottom of his boots, and he's tearing up the linoleum over at Grossman's."

"Wow, linoleum."

"Maybe I'll let him sit with me at the celebration."

"Watch out for the maniac."

# Chapter 9

When Lyle arrived at Grossman's, the familiar sight of his bicycle made him smile. Flat tires aside, it was a refreshing vision and leaned comfortably beside the back door, the waiters' entrance. He rang the bell on the handlebars once for good measure and prepared to resume his mission. He found it funny, though, that the restaurant and parking lot were completely empty, that there were no cooks or waiters preparing for the early dinner crowd, no patrons jockeying for the prime parking spot, the sound of their dented fenders and honking horns inexplicably absent until Lyle read the small handwritten sign taped to the front door. It read:

Closed for Celebration tonight.
Will open 1 hour earlier tomorrow. Free Parking.
The management

Of course, Lyle thought. All would be there. The wise would arrive early to stake their claim; the curious would arrive with ears pricked, their eyes poppingly wide open to watch a myriad of secret events revealed to them. The adventurous and opportunistic would arrive eagerly, filled with the most delirious expectations of securing the most advantageous vantage points and lines of sight. The common would simply arrive and mingle.

He would be on a mission: uncover the truth about Janet in particular, and women in general. It was only two things.

He hopped on his bike and continued on his way into town, down TBNL.

Each pedal advanced his mission, he reasoned, brought him closer to the truth about Janet and last evening, the cool summer breeze bristling the hair on his legs beneath his dress. There was no doubt in his mind; his path lay clearly before him.

As he rode, his eyes fixed laser-like ahead at the silvery ball atop the flagpole in the square, the end of TBNL. Ground zero. The celebration and the unveiling would take place there, as surely as the sun rises in the east and sets in the west.

His mind raced as never before, to his boyhood and the old oak, to the fact that only yesterday he had ridden his bicycle over this very same stretch of road without a sense of urgency or purpose. Wisdom must be sought, not offered, Mother Speckman used to say, words that held no meaning for him before today. He pedaled faster, the rims of his wheels grinding purposefully into the asphalt. Occasionally he ran his fingers over the bump on his head. The thoughts he was having were certainly out of the ordinary for him, and it did cross his mind that he might be mildly concussed.

He pressed on.

# Chapter 10

"Watch out!" Someone screamed from the back of the bus. A hard yank of the wheel by Mort sent the bus careening back into its rightful lane, narrowly avoiding the oncoming bicyclist by the merest of the margins, the bicyclist veering into the ditch and into some abnormally fuzzy cattails, as if pulled by magnetism.

"What was that?"

"Who was that?"

"Someone on the way to the celebration?"

"Let's not waste valuable time debating a tragedy that didn't happen," said the man in the derby claiming to be the voice of reason . . . "To Jane's!"

"To Jane's!"

"To Jane's!"

Mort never got off the gas.

# Chapter 11

As Lyle approached the square, the lack of persons or activity was of no consequence to him; he crossed that bridge successfully at Grossman's: All were preparing for the celebration. Hair was to be combed, outfits to be chosen, children to be instructed to be on their best behavior. An ordinary silence before him guarded by, he surmised, the granite statue of "The Patriot" before him, itself silent and covered by a bed sheet to preserve cleanliness, suspense, and dignity. Soon would be the unveiling.

Where to hide and begin the surveillance became the first objective. Yes: surveillance, organization, plan of attack, and conquest. This was a plan worthy of a member of the quartet —Caesar, Napoleon, Alexander, and Speckman. Let no detail be overlooked. Wheels were in motion. Too late to turn back. Full speed ahead. He pulled his bike to the rear of the House of Records.

Several times each month, while in the employ of Grossman's, Lyle was sent to the Hall of Records with deliveries—peanut butter and jelly sandwiches, fig newtons, apples with the skin cut off, etc.—precisely at midnight, with instructions to make delivery only at the rear of the building to the door marked, " No Admittance. Go Away." Per Grossman's instructions, he would ring the buzzer three times and leave.

Tonight he entered unannounced, empty-handed, and would not go away, the unlocked door a testament to Alderman Peabody's "Trust Me" Crime Prevention Program. Not so much as a knock, a buzz, or a yoo-hoo. Stealth Speckman in action. He was in place.

"Phase Three."

# Chapter 12

"Do you really think he'll do it?" Deb asked.

Janet paused, "Yes," she said, her voice void of the confidence the reply demanded. Janet could only hope. What had she gotten herself into this time? she wondered.

She thought back to last evening and the encounter she had with Ray, to the pleasantness she felt in their first awkward conversation, the unease of it, and all that followed during the evening, and to now, to whether she presumed too much, too fast, inventing a familiarity that wasn't really there. She felt that now, only seconds from her doorstep, that not enough time elapsed since their first meeting to ask a favor, let alone a favor offering Ray's professional skills. Oh, the impropriety of it all. How would she begin? she thought, 'Oh, by the way, Ray, there's this celebration in town tonight, and, well, the whole Town is convinced that there will be a bloody slaughter by a missing spelling teacher and that, well, would you come and make sure that nothing like that happens and that we all have a swell time?'

What would it look like to Ray? she thought, as she glanced about the bus, each seat filled with an O'Connell pubgoer, each cheering in their own way, shouts of 'Vanquisher! Conqueror! Savior!' being heard above her conversation with Deb, the neon king's buzzing and popping sounds punctuating the shouts and cheers like miniature lightning bolts in a verbal thunderstorm. Would she still stand out, she hoped, the sane one in a mob?

"Would you like me to go in with you?" Deb asked. "Just for moral support, you understand. I wouldn't think to bring up any of the recent unpleasantness surrounding his last bout. Did he mention . . ."

"No. Nothing like that. I think I should go in alone," she said.

"Wait one minute," started the disbeliever, his interruption testimony to his eavesdropping. "We're all going in. Strength in numbers, that sort of thing. I want to see his reaction with my own eyes."

All forward motion came to a sudden and screechy halt.

"Jane's!" Mort exclaimed. He brought his bus to a full and complete stop immediately in front of Janet's apartment building, the roar of the crowd settling at first into a mild din, followed shortly by silence. Many looked at their shoes.

"I'll be right back," Janet said, as she shot up from her seat and pushed her way through the still closed bus doors. They opened easily. None followed.

The sidewalk lay before her, a concrete aisle, and the last path to confrontation; each step she took chaperoned at a distance by a dozen pair of eyes from inside the bus. As she came closer, she wondered what she would say, or even how to begin. Perhaps a humorous comment on the whereabouts of his clothing, or a recap of the previous evening's events was appropriate. Perhaps a knowing smile and a manufactured bravado would mask her discomfort and inexperience in these matters. Perhaps things would take care of themselves. She opened the door to the building and entered the hallway.

Now, out of sight from those on the bus, Janet felt a curious sense of privacy and relief, as if completely convinced the path she was on was the correct one, that the confrontation with Ray was inevitable and that there was no need for a well-rehearsed conversation. With only feet to go before opening the door to her apartment, it was decided quite simply that the truth would have to do.

# Chapter 13

Ever since he was a boy, the Hall of Records had always been one of Lyle's favorite places. The pride he felt that day he marched through those great oak front doors to purchase his bicycle license, Speckman 2, was one of civic-mindedness and duty. Four crisp one dollar bills and his name printed on an official form and handed to a civil servant (a man who wore a shirt with an emblem on it) ensured his paid admission to the Hall.

Each form would be alphabetized and categorized before making its way into the proper file. Each file was dutifully stored behind heavy and ornate, exquisitely hand-carved oak doors. It was the work of diligent craftsmen generations ago, their skills daily on display, cut crisply in relief, a legacy of immigrant and ability, both having survived a long sea journey on a mighty-masted ship.

Lyle imagined the exponential volume of facts and records that needed to be kept: bicycle licenses, marriage licenses, change of address notifications, birth and death notices, the permanent record of every school child as kept by Mrs. Gloobniecht, work permits, redevelopment plans, drivers' licenses, auto accidents, dog bites, immigration, name changes, taxes, fines for jaywalking, etc. So many facts and so many requirements, and there they all sat, securely locked away in orderly file cabinets behind each and every magnificent door Lyle saw before him.

He wondered if anyone had looked at his form since that day so many years ago, and he wondered whatever became of the facts and records that were not kept since Alderman Peabody's father and all the other politicos had left. Surely there were facts and records that needed to be kept, new records to accompany the old.

It seemed improper to Lyle to pry or attempt to force open the door of an officially locked government office, but, he reasoned, sacrifices might be in order for the good of the plan. His plan did, after all, have several immutable and important requirements, not the least of which was an open window and line of sight to Town Square for surreptitious information gathering. Comfort was a secondary concern, followed not so closely by pencils, pens, paper, or a recording device of some sort for the taking of notes and, perhaps, posterity. Even Caesar had a scribe, he noted.

Impropriety aside, this, however, was clearly a time for action. It was, without a doubt, a time for action born of preparation, deliberation and boldness. Certainly no time for the meek. "Onward!" he cried, the manifestation of his bravado morphing instantaneously into the thought of a manly, full-speed-ahead bull rush and shoulder throw he would aim at the heart of the largest, most official-looking door before him. He triple calculated that maneuver would be necessary to reduce any behemoth, any mighty oaken barrier before him into splinters, until he noticed the most sudden of breezes and surprise of sunlight coming from behind him. Like a feather tickle to the nape of the neck, the unavoidable onset of curiosity, the pure serendipity of it, he lost his thought and was easily diverted. Lyle turned his head and noticed a door ajar, and the sunlight beyond. "Why, yes! The janitor's closet, of course!" he said. "How convenient."

Lyle had heard stories of the janitor's closet for years, of the devices kept there to mind unruly schoolchildren, the secret substances used for unknown purposes, and the collection of brooms, mops and plungers, some rumored to be from foreign countries, with bizarre writings and carvings on them. Some thought they had mystical powers. He recalled how Bobby R. broke in one time, skipping class, just to get a look at them, but became intoxicated by the smell of the mimeograph machine and passed out with his head on a can of turpentine. Best to use caution, he decided.

The window view of Town Square from the closet was more than adequate for Lyle's purposes, and he didn't seem to mind the confined space either. He glanced out the window at the statue in the square, the setting sun casting its shadow over twenty feet long. "Great men leave tall shadows," he said aloud.

All that remained was to wait attentively for the crowd to arrive and the celebration to begin. "Waiting," he said softly. He thought it ironic he might have developed a capacity for it.

He looked around and saw what appeared to be a mimeograph machine on a metal shelf. And, although he had never seen one before, the curious smell and the proximity of the device to several cans of turpentine allowed him to deduce and validate the Bobby R. story from years ago. Paint cans, varnishes, window cleaners, oily rags, various powders, tapes, towels, dustpans, and aprons all appeared stowed. Several brooms, yardsticks, and a tall plunger were leaning against the wall near the window. He picked up the plunger and ran his fingers over the words, 'Der Uber Looser Klemmen Co., Stuttgart, Germany' engraved in the handle. He returned it to its place.

Lyle took a seat against the wall and directly beneath the window. He sat Indian style, both legs crossed beneath him, in a manner designed to effect a military precision. Having no actual military experience, he logically concluded, the lessons learned in his two summers at Indian Guides camp would have to suffice. When the time was right, he would open the window, just a crack, and listen. For now, though, he sat, mind focused on the task at hand, each deep breath filling Speckman lungs with an odorous cocktail of mimeograph machine aroma, varnish, oily rags, flowery air fresheners, and dust. In a matter of moments, he nodded off . . .

*       *       *       *       *       *

*       PROCLAMATION              *

*       For the grandest of senses       *
        Come one and come all,
*       For pleasures abound           *
        At the Olfactory Ball

*       *       *       *       *       *

They had sent out the scents
With good taste and good sense,
And had rented a hall
For the Olfactory Ball

Each scent had arrived
On a hint of a breeze,
For the wind was their carriage
On the road through the trees

The footman cries out
"Miss Sweet Princess Rose!"
She draped in her fragrance,
As everyone knows

Soft, silent, and sweet,
She drew a crowd in the Hall,
But the night was still young,
For the belle of the ball

As jealous Miss Lilac,
Her fragrance untrue,
Held quiet while smirking,
She was planning a coup

She engaged Mr. Acrid,
That crude out-of-towner,
For his merciless cunning,
And vile cruel demeanor

That conniving Miss Lilac,
Had searched the dark land,
For soon would be chaos,
Just as she planned

She snuck to the back,
And unlocked a door,
Soon her guest would arrive,
And pollute the whole floor

Then he arrived,
And crashed through the Hall,
What a face-crinkling smell,
At the Olfactory Ball

It was crude Mr. Acrid,
The guests were aghast,
Grotesque as he billowed,
Consumed with a task

Quite matter-of-factly,
He surrounded Miss Rose,
His intentions immoral,
When he uttered his prose:

"Our two scents are one, I
have rubbed off on you,
You've been dulled and defused,
And now smell like a zoo."

Then he bellowed a bellow,
Himself now a dark cloud,
His mission accomplished,
He felt very proud

Miss Rose was in tears,
Her sweetness invaded,
She fled from the Hall,
At the Olfactory Ball

The footman cries out
"Lord Horatio Musk!"
A fine cloak of cologne,
He'd do what he must

He paraded the Hall,
His swagger unique,
"I shall restore order,"
Was all that he'd speak

A man of action, no less,
Acrid's future looked bleak,
'Tis a coward's effort,
To frighten the weak

Musk shooed away Acrid,
Along with his stench,
The villain now gone,
He'd search for the wench

Alas, poor Miss Lilac,
Her evil plan foiled,
Confronted by Musk,
She turned grey and spoiled

Lord Musk firmly in charge,
But absent Miss Rose,
His gallant heart broken,
A path true love knows.

# Chapter 14

Her delicate fingers commanded a grasp of the doorknob to her apartment, a firm turn of the key in the lock, that familiar click as the deadbolt slid decidedly away, returning to its cradle, permitting passage like a thousand uneventful times before. "Ray," she said. "It's Janet."

There was no answer.

"Ray?" she repeated, as she closed the door behind her. Again, there was no answer.

An even dozen patient steps to her bedroom threshold. "Ray?" she asked again, this time in an even more quizzical tone.

To her surprise, he was not there. She quickly spied the bedspread lying in a heap on the floor, the bed sheets mussed up into a furious ball, and, in a second, she hoped he had not left in a hurry. She opened her closet door, the empty space on the floor which only recently had been occupied by a pair of shiny men's oxfords the final confirmation. He was gone.

Where had he gone? she thought. What had she done? Perhaps he left a note.

A surgical attempt to reconstruct more closely the details of last evening ensued. Surely a clue was in the details, a reason, she hoped, whilst the image of Ray walking down TBNL wearing only his "World's Greatest Son" boxer shorts, a secret she planned to keep from those on the bus, looped endlessly through her mind. His entrance to Eat, the whiteness of his shirt, and the brilliant shine of his shoes, the boyish glee he took from spinning the stool next to him at the counter, encouraging it to spin faster and faster, each revolution amplifying his joy and his smile. Their simple conversation, in hindsight, seemed forced, but in that most natural and perfect of ways, like baby steps along an uncertain path, the prudent choice, each careful not to advance too quickly, lest one fall behind and create a distance between the other. It was only when the conversation turned to names, she recalled, did she notice a true unease in him, in fact, a tremor, the violent tapping of his toes which preceded his mad dash to the men's room and the ensuing thuds. "Yes," she said. "The thuds."

When she heard the first thud, she ran to the men's room and thrust the door fully ajar, its natural path curtly truncated by Lyle's forehead and the second of the thuds, a woody, firm sound.

That could be it, she thought for a second before quickly dismissing the idea. No way to be 100 percent certain. Perhaps the reason for his departure was unimportant, or unclear. Perhaps there was a simple explanation. Perhaps it was complex. Perhaps he surmised a sequence of particularly emasculating events that may have included a fireman's carry taught in a Girl Scout lifesaving class, parading his lifeless body through the parking lot in front of curious onlookers and wrestling fans. Far too embarrassing for the Inter-Time Zone champ. That could be it. I guess I'll just have to ask him when I see him, she concluded, as she headed back to the bus.

# Chapter 15

"Will you look over there," Clancy said. He pointed in the direction of Alderman Peabody's stage and to several young men setting up folding chairs in front of the podium. "Would you rather we sat there?"

"No, thank you."

"We'd have a fine look at Alderman Peabody when he gives his speech."

"No, thank you."

"Right up front, we could sit. He could look right at us."

"Not necessary."

"Be a fine show of patriotism, it would."

"I'm fine right here, I said."

"We could have the first look at the statue. After the unveiling."

"I've a fair idea that statue is made of stone. 'Twill be here tomorrow, as well, or the day after."

Clancy conceded the logic. "That it would. Fine piece of stone like that should last thirty-five years."

"If it's lucky," Mrs. MacNamara said. "If it's lucky."

"Park bench, it is," Clancy said. He fidgeted in his seat. "Lots of leg room. Good for seeing the comings and watching the goings. Grand idea. Did we have park benches in Ireland?"

"Yes, dear."

"And we never sat on them?"

"I did. I sat on them all the time. But if it makes you feel any better, I watched the comings and saw the goings for many, many years. Some days I fed the pigeons. They'll eat whatever you throw them, you know."

"'Twas I who never sat on them?"

"Yes, dear. They didn't have them at the bank."

"No, they did not," Clancy said matter-of-factly.

"Perhaps you could have O'Connell put one in at the pub. What do you think?"

"I'll have a chat about it," Clancy said.

He turned his attention back to the eager young men in front of Alderman Peabody's podium, the spring in their step vibrant, smiles on their faces as they joked among one another, and the sound of the wooden seats popping open one after the other, row by row, lingering in the early evening air.

One young man was tying red, white and blue balloons to several of the chairs at the end of each row. This was not work. Clancy recognized it in an instant. He watched from his park bench as the townspeople began to arrive for the celebration. They came from all directions, from each corner of Town Square, and assembled.

"Who would that be over there?" Mrs. MacNamara said. "The lad with the boxing gloves around his neck surrounded by all the pretty young girls."

"I've not seen him before. But I believe he may be the ex-pat pugilist the lads speak of. Venezuela, I believe. Would you like me to be certain?"

"Not necessary," Mrs. MacNamara said. "But it's no trouble. I'd be back in a wink."

"That's quite all right. Not necessary."

"Are you sure?"

"Quite, thank you. I prefer to watch from here. Nothing quite like the view from a park bench for perspective."

"Okay," Clancy said. He smiled and gave Mrs. MacNamara a gentle pat on the knee. "Perspective, it is."

\* \* \* \* \*

Bobby R. had made the journey all the way from Venezuela after his last title defense and looked quite splendid, sporty in fact. His strong, square-jawed young face showed none of the ill effects of his profession; it remained unmarked and unbruised after his most recent encounter, just as it had after each and every fight he had had to this day. His full, toothy, white smile beamed with the confidence of a true young champion, obviously extra proud of his recent step up in class from lightweight to welterweight. Not the least bit bashful of his efforts, he proudly tied the strings of his boxing gloves together in a crafty slipknot and hung them about his shoulders, his large silver-and-black leather title belt conspicuously displayed buckled about his waist. Today he wore penny loafers, a nice touch of class.

"Are you really the champion?" asked the first young girl.

"Numero uno," Bobby R. replied. "Look right here," he said, pointing to the inscription on his belt. It read, 'Republica Bolivariana de Venezuela Campeon de Maracaibo.' "I couldn't say it if it wasn't true. And are you a fan of the sweet science?

Do you have an interest in the manly art of self-defense?" he said as he struck a combative pose.

"I sure do," the young girl said. "I think there are about a zillion things I'd like to know about you."

"And how may I be of assistance? Clarification on the Marquis de Queensbury rules? An historical recount of the most thrilling victories of the last century? Terms and definitions? Jab, hook, uppercut?" He cautiously looked over his shoulder. "Low blow?" he added, lowering his voice. "Fancy footwork? The Rope-a-Dope? Ask away. Anything. Anything you can think of."

She stared dreamily into his eyes. "Is your hair naturally curly?" the girl asked.

"Why, yes, it is. Sometimes, in between rounds, my corner man soaks my head with a sponge."

"That's very nice. And those biceps," she said in a breathy tone. "I bet you can lift a thousand pounds. I bet you could even lift me."

"No, a thousand pounds would require pure weight training. It's better for a boxer to have lightning-quick reflexes than pure brute strength. It's all about instincts, you see. And my reflexes and instincts are flawless. Simply flawless. Sometimes I can even tell what an opponent is going to do within the next two seconds! It's like telepathy."

"You don't say."

"No, I can. In a precise instant, my superior skills can evaluate a situation and steer me toward the absolute correct course of action. That way I can quickly move out of the way before absorbing the full force of my opponent's blows."

The young girl twirled her hair in her fingers and drew small circles in the grass with her foot. "Is there a Mrs. Champion of Mercedes?" she asked.

"I'm not sure I understand . . ."

"Have you ever been knocked out?" asked the second girl.

"I can say proudly, never. In fact, the local townspeople have a nickname for me, 'Cabeza de Piedra.' It means 'Head of Stone.' I'm told it's quite an honor."

"And you've never lost?" asked the third girl. "You must be the strongest, bravest man alive."

"And the handsomest," added the first girl.

"My strength and skills come from hard work and from lessons learned long ago. My bravery comes from heart," he said.

"But doesn't it hurt to get punched at all?" added the fourth girl. "To be hit over and over and over in the same place? I would think that would be torture."

At that moment, the word "torture" resonated with Bobby and took him back to his youth and to all those misspelled words and to the countless raps across his knuckles with a yardstick he endured. He recalled that first day that he couldn't take it anymore and his decision to wear boxing gloves to class to evade the pain, the first step toward the crown. "You're only hurting yourself," his teacher said. He recalled that he had no idea what she meant, and, in fact, thought she was dead wrong, since each successive rap across his knuckles could barely be felt. In fact, he felt he should thank her. In his mind, he adapted and flourished and followed a path that led to the crown, to the adulation of the townspeople of Maracaibo cheering his nickname, and to an unblemished record, not a single defeat.

"Torture . . ." he started. "That's something else entirely. For example, I can remember trying to spell champion. Now that was torture." Bobby stared off into space and squinted one eye, "C-H-A-M-P-E-O-N. How's that?"

Each of the girls traded cross-eyed looks. "He sure is pretty," they whispered.

Meanwhile, a lone figure began circling noticeably around them, his hand clutching at his shirt directly above the breast pocket, a fierce white-knuckled grasp. "MacNamara Cleaners! MacNamara Cleaners! MacNamara Cleaners!" he screamed at the girls.

"Are you insane!" the gang of four snapped back in unison.

"What? Nick Sparelli knows what's what. MacNamara Cleaners! MacNamara Cleaners! MacNamara Cleaners!" he continued.

"Is that man bothering you?" Bobby R. asked.

"Who are you?" Nick interrupted.

It took less than a flash of a second for Bobby R. to undo the slipknot tying his gloves together. In another half-second, Bobby fitted both hands snugly into his gloves and, before anyone could count to three, delivered a left jab squarely into Nick's midsection. Nick responded with a wheezing sound as all the air in his body exited through his nose and mouth. He started to double over in pain as a right uppercut to his jaw from Bobby straightened his back, loosened three teeth, and bloodied his nose all at once. Nick then fell to the ground in a heap. "Ooooh," he said.

\* \* \* \* \*

"Did you see that, Mum?" Clancy said in an elevated tone.

"Aye, that I did," his wife said. "Heard it, as well. It seems our maniac from this morning has found himself in a bit of a spot."

"It seems. It also seems he's taken to screaming our name all over Town Square. Would you know anything about that?"

"Now, Clancy, you know as well as I that you can't predict what a maniac is going to do from moment to moment. He could have just as easily screamed 'O'Connell's Pub' or 'Saints preserve us!' I say it is our own good fortune that he thought of us."

"I see. To be fair, though, he's really not much of a maniac, is he?"

"How do you mean?"

"I mean, he's really just a bit of an eejit. And, in fairness, I do believe he'll grow out of it. You can already see some of the blonde roots."

"'Tis a long road, I'm afraid."

"That it is. May the lad be blessed with a guide or a keen sense of direction."

\* \* \* \* \*

Nick managed to crawl on all fours to the last row of folding chairs. He pulled himself up to take a seat and tilted his head back in an attempt to stop the nosebleed. Several

148

drops of blood had fallen to dot and speckle his shirt directly on top of the pasta sauce stain he had been clutching for luck. Nick heard several bystanders comment among themselves that the coloring and design somewhat resembled a reddish-brown Jackson Pollack painting, and wasn't Nick lucky that the shirt was already ruined before he bled all over it. Nick, though, stared skyward, attempting to catch his breath, as the throbbing of his mouth incubated a fat lip.

"Hi, Nick," Stella said softly.

Nick hoped Stella didn't see him take the blow. He also hoped she wasn't forced to wait the three minutes for him to bring himself to a seated position before walking over.

"Herro," Nick said without looking at her.

"Do you mind if I sit next to you?" she asked.

"No."

"I saw you walking over there when you were calling for the MacNamaras, and I didn't know if you knew they were sitting right over there on the park bench." Stella pointed and exchanged a quick, friendly wave with Mrs. MacNamara. She mouthed the word 'Hi.' "Here, let me help you with that," she said. Stella took a spare bar towel from her apron and covered Nick's face. She applied pressure to his nose. "That should stop it. I've seen a few of these before, you know. They really bleed a lot. Sometimes it looks like all the blood in your head is about to run out. Best to sit and coagulate for a minute. We can take care of the shirt later."

"Uh-huh," Nick said from under the towel. Every few seconds Nick alternated pushing at the back of his teeth with his tongue to see if they were still loose, and trying to touch his lip to see if it still hurt —they were, and it did. He was, however, thankful to Stella for providing assistance, especially the towel which, in his mind, kept the busybodies and curiosity seekers from pointing and laughing at him as they walked by to take their seats. Periodically he heard snickers and the giggles of what seemed to be schoolchildren coming from close proximity, but he had no way to prove they were laughing at him and instead chose to believe they were not. And he thought of Stella. He could feel Stella's presence next to him, a closeness he never before felt during any of the dinners or lunchtime romps around the old oak. This was different. He was not in pursuit. "Why are you being so nice to me?" he asked through the towel, his right hand moving toward the stain.

"You were bleeding, I had a towel. It seemed like a good match at the time."

Nick took the answer at face value and decided it was best not to comment. Stella was seated next to him tonight, and that was all that mattered, not the comments people made when he had dyed his hair or darkened his mustache, not the hours he spent alone on a Saturday night, drawing in his tattoo with indelible ink pens, not the recent punch to the gut and embarrassing bloody mess. Not even the sounds of children's snickers and laughs, which he heard only moments ago and which now mysteriously vanished, mattered. He remembered himself as a boy and thought it most odd that the children would abandon such an easy target. It was as if they were a school of brightly colored tropical fish, all swimming together in unison, capriciously changing direction as one, and now scattered, frightened by perceived danger.

A curious Nick maneuvered one eye to look out over the top of the towel.

"Hi, Ray," Stella said with a small wave.

Nick tensed.

Nick watched as Death Ray Drake joined the celebration and took a seat several rows in front of them, about halfway to the stage. Several seats on either side of Ray, as well as front and back, were still open and provided a buffer zone to the champ. He and his massive frame stared ahead quietly, patiently waiting for the celebration to begin, the townspeople filling in the seats around him, all but the buffer zone. A small, stray kitten jumped up onto the seat next to Ray, and he picked it up and put it in his lap. He stroked its head and ears and smiled, a soft purr the peaceful retort.

"I guess that's Death Ray?" Nick asked.

"Yes," Stella said. "Just a few rows in front of us. Would you like me to ask him to move? I will if you think he'll be in the way. He is rather large."

"No, no, no," Nick quickly spoke. "It's okay."

Stella took her hand away from Nick's nose and brushed the hair back from in front of her face. Nick felt a question coming, perhaps about why that man had punched him and about why he was yelling for the MacNamaras. He hoped she would decide against it. He hoped she would just forget all about it. He hoped she would say anything else, like the small talk she made when taking his orders at O'Connell's, the way she wouldn't let him fret over which of the special orders to take, or the playful way she once called him tall, dark, and handsome. Anything at all. Anything would be better than a question that would force him to explain a punch to the gut and a punch to the nose. People don't get punched for no reason; she'd know that, he thought. She'd know. She'd know it was something that was said, or something that was done, some offensive thing that couldn't be undone. Then, in the reflective moment that followed, Stella's comforting hand unmistakably withdrawn from his face, he hoped for forgiveness, for his actions, for everything he might have done to be deserving of blows. He hoped for a new start and he knew he had no right to ask. It frightened him, until the silence broke.

"What should we talk about?" she said.

Nick didn't know how to react, to begin again, but took the towel from his face nonetheless. He felt it was a good first step. Summoning words, however, proved more difficult and what came out of his mouth next were a series of unintelligible mumbles that left Stella with a confused look on her face.

"Excuse me?" she said.

Nick was about to attempt a second effort when Mort's school bus, horn honking and lights flickering, zipped into the square and screeched to a halt directly in front of the Chamber of Commerce building. Nick felt it an untimely diversion, and both he and Stella watched as the doors flew open and Deb and Janet disembarked, followed closely by Mort and the O'Connell crowd, loud and argumentative, a collective pack. Clancy acknowledged the O'Connell crew with a salute from his park bench and watched as they headed to within earshot of Nick and Stella.

"I knew he wouldn't even be there. I bet she doesn't even know him," started the disbeliever. "What a wild goose chase."

"What do we do now?" the panic-stricken man whined. "The celebration is about to begin!"

"Please don't whine," said the man in the derby claiming to be the voice of reason. "We still have Mort."

"Bzzzzzz."

"But does he know about maniacs? Insane school teachers?" the panic-stricken man continued.

"Don't listen to them, Jane," Deb began. "I believe you. It happens all the time."

"But I . . ."

"I know," Deb said, as she skipped off in the general direction of Bobby R. "Time to see what this guy knows. See ya."

\* \* \* \* \*

As Janet got closer and closer to Nick and Stella, she could hear the buzzing growing louder behind her, and not just from Mort. The chatter among the group became more frantic with each step, their now-sotto-voce tones caught in an endlessly unproductive loop of 'You go ask him, I'm not going to ask him, Why do I have to ask him, You go ask him, It was my idea—You go ask him, I'm not going to ask him.' Janet stopped abruptly and turned around to face the group. "I told you I would have asked him, but he was gone," she said plainly.

"We know," the group said. "Look." Each of the men stood steadfast, their right arms outstretched, their pointed index fingers zeroing in like laser beams on the back of the shiny bald pate of Mr. Death Ray Drake seated in the crowd. "It's Death Ray," they exhaled.

Janet asked "Where?" but there could be no mistake. From her line of sight, it was crystal clear that the huge-ish man the group pointed to with such a high degree of certainty bore absolutely no resemblance whatsoever to the spindly wisp of a person she had cleaned up after and tucked smartly into bed the night before, and in a second, she knew that he had lied, whatever his name was. "Oh, my goodness," she said, covering her mouth with her hand.

"Well, go ask him," prodded the disbeliever.

"Hurry!" added the panic-stricken man. "It's about to begin!"

But Janet didn't answer. Instead of advancing toward Nick and Stella and the assembled crowd to take her place, she mindfully retreated at half pace to the old oak, away from the masses. She leaned against the mighty tree for support, and thought.

"I knew she wouldn't," said the disbeliever. "I knew it all the time."

Mort let out a subdued buzz and stood with the others. They didn't know what to do.

\* \* \* \* \*

Back in the Chamber of Commerce, Alderman Lester I. Peabody took one last look into what his father called "The Grand Mayoral Mirror," six feet tall and gilded with gold leaf at the edges, a flea market purchase during election week. It was time. The speech he practiced in his every spare moment, along with accompanying pregnant pauses, tonal inflections, finger points, and arm movements, was neatly printed on index cards and positioned in his vest pocket. He gave the pocket a couple of pats for luck and began to walk down the three flights of stairs toward Town Square. With each step, he summoned the strength to focus on his tasks: The fireworks display, twelve five-foot tall cannons each stamped with the word "DANGER," followed by long lines of Chinese characters, each aligned, side-by-side, behind the speaker's podium. Each must be individually checked for safety; children were present. When the time was right, he would be the one to light the fuse. Careful ascension to the podium (there would be no one else to help him) and the introduction of the evening's events—the weather, thank-yous, dignitaries, small joke, etc. would follow. Next, the unveiling, followed by applause. The speech, "Indecision: The Fulcrum of Communism," would go off as rehearsed. And, finally, light the fuse and enjoy the sights and sounds of the celebration.

Yes, he thought, focus was the key. He had the vision some time ago—The Redevelopment Plan. Now all that was needed was a good, old-fashioned introduction of folks, a nonthreatening way for friends, neighbors, acquaintances, and even strangers to meet and foster good feelings of brotherhood, camaraderie, and patriotism. Grassroots nation-building, he felt.

As he exited the building, he saw that Mort once again parked his bus on the city streets, this time directly in front of the Chamber of Commerce, despite several warnings and citations to the contrary. And, even though he was certain that the red and green flashing lights running down the side of the bus would present a distraction to the townspeople and divert their attention from the finer points of his speech, he decided to let it go. He figured that this was not the time to show the heavy hand of the executive branch. Rather, in the spirit of the event, special dispensation would be made and no ticket would be given. Surely, word would spread as to his fairness, and he would continue to be known as a reasonable man.

Peabody continued toward the podium and his fireworks inspection. One by one, he examined the cannons and their contents, closely following the safety checklist in the instructions. Roman candles, starbursts, twizzers, zingers, and sonic booms were all ready to go. He was by no means an expert in the subject, having had only the briefest of tutorials from the vendor who set up a tent in the vacant lot prior to the Fourth of July. He said anyone could do it if you just followed the instructions. The vendor's straightforward simplicity pleased him and reminded him of lessons learned on the campaign trail with his father. During those stumps, constituents would come up to his father and mention that politics were far too complicated for them to understand. 'Have no fear,' he would say. 'Simple' is my middle name.

Peabody stepped up to the podium amid a soft, controlled applause from the crowd. He tapped the microphone twice for good measure and removed the index cards from his vest pocket. He read card one: INTRODUCTION (Extemporaneous).

"Good evening, fine citizens of our fair town. Isn't this a beautiful evening for our celebration!" He pointed to a gentleman in the front row and mouthed the word 'Hi'. "I'd like to thank all of you for coming this evening to take part in this historic occasion. And I'd like to offer special thanks to international boxing sensation, and native son, Bobby R! Take a bow, Bobby! All the way from Venezuela!" Bobby waved as the crowd offered polite applause. "*Mi casa es su casa* as long as the furniture doesn't get broken." Peabody forced a tiny laugh and turned to card number two. It read: THE UNVEILING (also extemporaneous). "I would now like to turn your attention to one of the reasons we are gathered here this evening. This statue, this granite symbol of the sacrifices made by our forefathers in the name of progress and patriotism, will serve as a reminder to us all of those who have gone before us, those who have forged a path, those who have blazed a trail where none had existed before for the express purpose of advancing the causes of our fair town and this great nation. We owe a debt of gratitude for having been shown the way, and we bear the responsibility of continuing the tradition. Without further ado, I give you, 'The Patriot'!"

Peabody pulled the sheet off the statue with a flick of his wrist. The sheet made a snapping sound as if to say "Ole!" as the crowd clapped in an orderly fashion. Peabody stared intently at the statue and was pleased. The stonecutter had performed exactly as instructed: He had managed to sculpt the facial features in a nondescript way so as to give the piece an everyman quality, and he avoided the temptation to make this Patriot look like those in the history books—musket, tri-cornered hat, and fife. In this instance, Peabody chose to exercise executive authority, and instructed the sculptor to dress the statue in a long topcoat, a personal homage to his family's long line of public servants. In all other ways, it looked quite ordinary.

Peabody turned over card number three. It read: SPEECH—INDECISION: THE FULCRUM OF COMMUNISM (To be read as written). He motioned the crowd to settle down and began. "We have chosen to become a brave and passionate populace . . ."

\* \* \* \* \*

From inside the Hall of Records janitor's closet, Lyle began to stir. The noxious fumes that had provided the catalyst for his nap several hours earlier gave way to a brand of physical discomfort with which Lyle was not familiar. He had developed a crick in his neck from sleeping with his chin pinned to his chest, and his plan to sit Indian style had apparently caused a complete loss of circulation to his right leg. He tried to stretch his neck and arms when he noticed the darkness in the room and heard the muffled sounds of Alderman Peabody over the loudspeakers. "No," he moaned. "I'm missing it!" He tried to stand for a look out the window but was hobbled by the cramps in his leg. He pulled his dress up and tried a quick massage of his leg, but, alas, no use. He tried to hop on one foot and attempt to shake the other to consciousness, but that didn't work either. And then, in a moment of desperation, he reached for the tall plunger in the corner—Der Uber Looser Kleemmen Co. Stuttgart, Germany—and pounded the rubber end repeatedly into his foot, screaming, "Wake up! Wake up!" Not only did this not have the desired effect, but it sent a horrifically tight cramp up his leg which lodged in the back of his thigh, causing Lyle to scream, "Aargh!" and rush out of the closet. He limped down the hall as best he could and out the front doors into Town Square. He hobbled on one-and-a-half legs, his head and neck cocked to one side, making him look like the Hunchback of Notre Dame, his frilly Eiffel Tower scarf falling to cover his eyes, while he chopped hysterically at his foot with the plunger.

The panic-stricken man was the first to spot Lyle and felt a perverse comfort in knowing that his worst fears were about to come true. "LOOK!" he screamed. "IT'S GLOOBNIECHT!! AND SHE'S GOT AN AX!!"

Lyle couldn't see what was happening in front of him but relied upon his powers of deduction and observation to make sense of the cacophony of sounds he was hearing. Apparently, he reasoned, the missing schoolteacher, Mrs. Gloobniecht, had returned from places unknown, bent upon chopping down the old oak. Townspeople were naturally thrown into a state of chaos, as evidenced by the thrashing of wooden chairs, the popping of balloons, and the screech of an alley cat. Lyle, however, was still on a mission, and proudly proclaimed, "Phase Four! Phase Four!"

The panic-stricken man, barely within earshot but filled with a doomsayer's glory, repeated Lyle's comments as "FACE HORROR! FACE HORROR! She says we have to FACE HORROR!"

"Let's get her!" yelled a voice in the crowd. An angry mob formed faster than anyone wanted to admit and surrounded Lyle, smothering him.

Word spread quickly through the crowd that Gloobniecht was surrounded and punishment was about to be meted out when Bobby R. heard the news. A tear formed in the corner of his eye and his upper lip began to quiver. "I'll save you, Mrs. G!" he cried, as he sprinted into the fray, fists flying in the darkness and finding their mark.

Lyle fell to the ground, his dress and scarf ripped off his body, the shreds being torn apart by the mob, the little black book sent flying. He crawled through someone's legs and decided to head for the cover of the old oak. As he limped along in his boxer shorts, he could hear the mob behind him, and the argument that developed about whether Gloobniecht was a spirit, a ghost, an apparition, or beaten to dust.

And then he saw Janet.

She looked him in the eye with absolutely no animosity, no preconceived notions, no ill will, and Lyle couldn't understand. Completely absent from the look in her eyes was real anger. There was not an element of detest, or furiousness at being so obviously deceived. There was no sense an outburst of real temper was to follow, either. Only a pair of soft brown eyes staring clearly back at him as if to examine his very soul, eyes an embarrassed Lyle tried to a avert, as he fumbled for what to say. She held her ground, and very deliberately, in a calm and precise way, said, "Please explain."

"My name is Lyle Speckman and I . . . I don't know what to say next. And I'd very much like to start over. Is that possible?"

"No, Lyle. We can't start over. No one can ever start over. History is a stone that rolls downhill. We can only continue."

"Then I'd like to continue. You see, I've been on this mission, and I really don't know anything yet."

Lyle watched Janet as she seemed to process his answer. She crossed her arms and pursed her lips, her puppy-dog eyes soft and intense at the same time. She stared at Lyle for what seemed an interminable length of time, so long that Lyle squirmed a tiny bit, gulped, and looked down at his shoes. After a while more, she eased a smile. "Are there other strange things that you do?" she said.

"I'm not sure. But we could talk about it," he said. Lyle decided he would walk around the tree in an attempt at casualness and some playful gamesmanship, when he tripped over the fat ring bologna-like tires of a bicycle that had been leaning on the other side. He fell to the ground on his back, staring up into the tree, the license plate "Speckman 1" landing across his bare chest. He focused on a silhouette about eight feet above him, sitting on a thick branch.

"Hello, Mother," he said.

"Hello, son," she replied, as she pulled some abnormally fuzzy cattails from her hair. "Where are your pants?"

"I've met a girl, mother."

"Yes, son, I see. But you really should wear pants."

"Hello, Mrs. Speckman," Janet said with a cute wave, as Lyle pulled himself up from the ground.

\* \* \* \* \*

At the speaker's podium, Alderman Peabody put the last of his index cards back in his vest. He took a handkerchief from his pocket and pridefully wiped the brow of the statue, turned and lit the fuses for the fireworks, and watched with the town as the night sky filled with spectacle. And from inside the Hall of Records, with the brightest aisle of view, a pair of eyes watched. "Attaboy," he whispered.

# Part II

# Chapter 16

Hizzoner Schuyler A. Peabody awoke and rubbed the sleep from his eyes with a swipe from the back of his hand. He had spent the night on the floor, curled up in a ball beneath the still open second floor Hall of Records window; his faithful aide, Jenkins, lay still asleep under a heavy woven Indian blanket only feet away. The sights and the sounds of last evening's celebration were still fresh in his mind: the fireworks and the fisticuffs, the applause and the popping balloons, the mingling. No recollection, however, resonated more clearly, or with a greater sense of familial pride, than Lester's speech:

"We have chosen to become a brave and passionate populace . . ."

He couldn't get past the first few words. He noted immediately they were index card worthy. He hoped he was still part of the "We." Ten years had passed, in his mind a flyspeck of historical time, since the sequence of events he came to refer to as "The Great Undoing." While Jenkins slept, he was flooded with the memories of those days, astounded by the clarity of his recollections . . .

"Jenkins! Have you seen this?" the mayor questioned as he waved the National Geographic in the air. "It's absolutely, positively one of the best political opportunities of a lifetime. I may even go so far as to say an opportunity for political immortality. To be remembered for all eternity as one of the greats. To be the subject of schoolchildren's essays, and the topic of long, drawn-out think tank articles. I think I'm excited. Here, take a look," he said, as he handed the magazine to Jenkins.

"Papua New Guinea Tribesman to Erect Telescope," he read.

"No, not that. Page back." The mayor stood, hands behind his back, as he looked out his office window, the midday sky, the perfect blueness of it, an empty canvas for his imagination.

"Mt. Rushmore: A Perspective in Granite," he read aloud.

"Yes, that's it. Read on."

Jenkins adjusted his thin, wire-framed spectacles and continued reading to himself, at times interjecting a "hmmm" or an "ah, yes." Several pages of crisp color photos accompanied the article, taken from all angles and some taken from great distances. There was even a black-and-white photo showing men hanging from leather harnesses, hammers and chisels in hand, their faces covered in dust. "It seems to be quite an informative article detailing the history of the monument," he said.

"And?"

Jenkins continued to read. "And there are a number of facts and figures pertinent to the monument: elevation above sea level, size of each man's features, number of workmen used, and so on. There is even a humorous anecdote about a

Calvin Coolidge visit before construction, about him learning how to fish. It seems, at night, the townspeople would net off both ends of the stream in front of the lodge where he was staying and truck in large trout while he was sleeping . . ."

"Yes, yes, yes, the facts," he interrupted. "Thousands greeted him as he got off the train in Rapid City. Their cheers echoing throughout the Black Hills of South Dakota! I believe the First Lady brought her pet raccoon."

"It's said he gave quite a speech some time later at the dedication."

"The raccoon?"

"Wouldn't that be a sight? No, the President."

"The President, of course." The mayor calmly took the magazine from Jenkins. He paged back to the color photos, the prominent images of Washington, Jefferson, Roosevelt, and Lincoln, sixty feet tall if they were an inch, staring firmly back at him. He ran his fingers across their faces, paused the same amount of time at each one, his eyes half closed as if reading Braille. "But do you see the opportunity, Jenkins?"

"Certainly not as clearly as you, sir," was the well-measured response.

"Well said, Jenkins. Well said. In honor of your clear thinking, I shall elaborate to save time and move things along." He handed the magazine back to Jenkins. "Move down to the part about Sarah B. Anthony."

"Susan B. Anthony, sir."

"Yes, her. Move down."

Jenkins quickly scanned for the pertinent passages. "Here it is," he began. "I'm summarizing, of course."

"Naturally."

"In 1937, Susan B. Anthony was proposed to be the fifth face on the monument. It appears Congress would not appropriate funds."

"Quite right!" the mayor exclaimed. He was almost giddy, his voice pitched. "Right there! Right there!" he said pointing next to Lincoln's head. "She was to going to go right there!"

"Yes, sir, but without funding, there was no project."

"Congress has an almost miraculous method of finding funding for projects they want, Jenkins. I can only speculate, nay, conclude, that other, perhaps more dubious, reasons lie beneath the surface."

"Perhaps the Congressional Record, sir."

"Our purposes do not require that level of detail, Jenkins." The mayor assumed an official tone, one often reserved for lengthy summations of delicate political points in which he had already made up his mind, executive branch heavy-handedness, or ordering lunch.

"Will we be resurrecting the effort to bring Susan B. to the monument?" Jenkins interest was piqued. "Perhaps as homage to her lifelong courageous fights against slavery, or the evils of the drink? Or perhaps as an eternal reminder of the impassioned speeches she delivered while crisscrossing the country, often without any regard for her own desires, on behalf of women's rights, would be more appropriate. An homage to her devotion." He sighed. "She never married, you know."

"I should say not. That woman already has her face on a coin and, I believe, a stamp. She's held no elective office that I know of, and now she wishes to forever be a part of the national skyline, 10,000 years in granite? Vanity, thy name is woman. I'd be willing to bet that if she gets her way, before long, she'll want to have a turnpike named after her."

"I believe the woman is deceased, sir."

"Damn her persistence!"

"Yes, sir. Damn her. How are you proposing we proceed?"

The mayor began to pace; it was a well-worn path. He rubbed his bald head, stroked his pointy chin with his thumb and index finger, closed one eye, and stared at the ceiling in thought. It only took moments. "I believe that should be fairly obvious," he declared. "A suitable substitute should be proffered."

"Yes, sir. A substitute."

"Somebody from the political arena."

"Political, yes."

"Somebody with no skeletons in the closet."

"No arms, no legs, no backbones."

"Somebody possessing a most noble visage."

"Noblesse oblige."

"Somebody . . . Dare I say, a Peabody."

"You may, sir."

"Washington, Jefferson, Roosevelt, Lincoln, and Peabody."

"Yes, sir."

The mayor flashed a broad, inaugural smile. He patted his aide on the back. "Jenkins, I knew I could count on you." He lowered his voice to a whisper and focused deliberately on his aide's face. He used his most serious stare. "Let us begin."

Jenkins bowed his head. Next to 'Got a second' or 'Jenkins, come quick! I need you!' no words did more to convey to him the volume of tasks or effort which were about to be required. "At your service," he replied.

"Excellent!"

"Shall I ask Deb to come in? She could take notes."

"No, no, no," the mayor added quickly with a wave of his hand. "Let's not burden her with any undue anticipation. Besides, she's probably at lunch. I don't expect her back for several hours."

"Shall I notify the aldermen?"

"When the time is right. Best to take the bull by the horns and jump right in. Jenkins, take a letter."

"Yes, sir. To whom?" Jenkins took a seat in the mayor's chair and readied himself for transcription. He pulled a piece of unlined paper from the top drawer of the desk and dipped the mayor's ceremonial quill in ink. It was made of long, exotic Hungarian pheasant feathers and tickled at his nose as he wrote.

"To the people in charge of Mt. Rushmore, Sirs . . ."

"I believe, sir," Jenkins interrupted, "the National Park Service is in charge of Mt. Rushmore."

"Right. To the National Park Service, Sirs . . ."

"Yes, sir. It is a division of the Department of the Interior. Created, I believe, by Woodrow Wilson."

"Very good. As follows:

Sirs,

It has recently come to my attention that a vacancy exists on Mt. Rushmore immediately next to Abraham Lincoln. Furthermore, it is my understanding that this vacancy exists due to the unsuitable circumstances surrounding Susan B. Anthony (I have it on good authority she had been arrested, but I digress). I, for one, applaud your wise choice. After all, what woman wants to spend the rest of eternity being remembered as having a nose 20 ft long and a mouth 18 ft wide? I'd say you did her a favor. Not to mention that hair. Even Jefferson had the good sense to wear a wig (but I digress further). Enclosed please find a list of my qualifications as a public servant, as well as several photos of myself. Please feel free to select the one which you believe best compliments the other honorees. In addition, lest you believe I am simply some crackpot dashing off letters willy-nilly to government agencies, I have attached a check for $50,000 made payable to the National Park Service, Monument Division, a down payment, as I am eager to see this project underway.

Respectfully,

Schuyler A. Peabody, Mayor

"There. That should do nicely. Round up that nephew of Lester's and have him snap some photos to send along. Draft a list of my qualifications for review, and off we go. Things are about to happen."

"Yes, sir, I understand. Will the usual list of qualifications suffice?"

"Yes, with only minor additions." The mayor paused. "Try to think 'federal.'"

"'Federal,' yes, sir." Jenkins returned the ceremonial quill to its holder and blew softly across the letter to dry the ink.

The mayor watched Jenkins brush the pheasant feathers from his face as he blew, in smooth and well-measured breathes, as if each word required the exact amount of fresh air to achieve proper dryness. He also noted a familiar calmness in Jenkins, a calculated and concentrated ease, as if he were weighing his next words carefully, the pro and the con, the dutiful and the insubordinate. Perhaps Jenkins hoped for a precise moment of inspiration, a guiding light to shine and illuminate an apt script, before he spoke. There was no carelessness in him. The mayor felt the moment passing, until . . .

"About the check." dribbled out of Jenkins' mouth.

"Yes?"

"Do you believe this would be an appropriate time to convene a meeting with the aldermen? I could develop some sort of consensus as to the long-range wisdom and viability of such an expenditure."

"Jenkins," he began. He answered quickly and his tone indicated he prepared for the question in advance. "Democracy is not a simple machine. It is composed of cogs and gears and from time to time requires a spot of oil or a dab of grease. It is not a perpetual motion machine, but, rather, one which needs an occasional nudge to set it upon its course. Today we have set upon a new course, my steady hand firmly on the tiller."

"Yes, sir. I see," was the polite response.

Hizzoner was taken aback by his vivid recall, the verbatim nature of it, the product of enumerable replays, and he turned to look at the sleeping Jenkins. "Yes, I see," he clearly remembered Jenkins saying. Had he, in fact, seen? he wondered. It perplexed him that he did not know for sure whether his intelligent young friend had spoken those words with resignation or with purpose. And while there was never a moment where he had cause to doubt his aide's devotion to duty or loyalty of service, it took the constant jack hammering of the past within his brain to carve out a new and perhaps profound thought: Devotion is for the deserved. It was beginning to make sense to him: the long hours Jenkins spent in and around the office, running errands, offering to help Deb make copies or get the lunch, officiating at the meetings of Aldermen. Jenkins was in awe of him; his proximity to leadership was overwhelming. It made even more sense to him as he recalled the second letter some weeks later . . .

Hizzoner had begun that day in the most innocuous and familiar of ways: thumbing through his carefully labeled and meticulously organized collection of political speeches, each index card highlighted in the upper right hand corner with stars indicating its perceived historical importance, five stars being perfection—theme, vision, tone, passion, and memorability. It passed the time as he waited for the mail. Hizzoner loved to get mail—the bills and the advertisements, some socks from the mail order—it didn't matter. To him, it was an almost daily reminder of the useful intersection of the government and the public.

"I have the mail, sir," Jenkins said as he walked into the mayor's office. "I noticed Deb was out when I came in, so I thought I'd run back down and bring it up. Some of those stairs are becoming a little treacherous."

"Yes, we'll get right on that. Anything interesting in the mail?" he said, focusing on the bundled package Jenkins was carrying.

"There is a package which, I believe, is from your brother, a postcard from O'Connell's Pub announcing 'Las Vegas Night for Preferred Customers,' and a slim envelope marked 'Confidential: Town Bank Statement.'"

"A package from my brother?"

"Yes, sir. The return address clearly says 'Hiram I. Peabody, Actor.'"

"Fancy that. Let's open it."

"Yes, sir." Jenkins set the postcard and bank statement down on top of the mayor's desk and began to untie the string from around the package as the mayor watched.

Some time ago, the mayor recalled, he had told Jenkins about Hiram, his younger brother by a year, his only sibling. He told him of that evening years ago when Hiram confronted their father, the Honorable Nero A. Peabody, and told him of his decision to not enter politics, the family business, and instead to pursue his dream of becoming an actor, having fallen in love with the greasepaint and the footlights while participating in a college theatrical production, *Finian's Rainbow*. He told Jenkins how heated that discussion became, how Hiram agreed to move out of town so as not to disgrace the Peabody name, as he defied his father and proudly proclaimed, "I choose to act!" and stormed off on foot into the night.

"What is it?" the mayor asked.

Jenkins opened the box. "It appears to be a suit of clothes, sir, and a long black beard. There is also a note." He handed the black suit and beard to the mayor. Indicating the note, Jenkins asked, "May I?"

"Please," the mayor responded. The suit was well worn, and he wondered why his brother would forward it to him. He didn't know what to make of the beard and set it on the desk.

Jenkins read,

Dearest brother,

I hope this letter finds you well. I apologize for the infrequent communication; however, I hope this will make up for it. Are you still fond of historical figures? If so, please enjoy this genuine suit of clothes worn by none other than Abraham Lincoln (the beard is a construction of mine, but required to complete the illusion). I discovered it in an antique shop while on the road, and have no good reason to doubt its authenticity. May it bring you pleasure.

Tally Ho,

Hi.

The mayor's eyes bulged, Christmas-morning wide, as visions of log cabins, books being read by candlelight, and preliminary drafts of the Gettysburg address raced into his mind. "Abraham Lincoln! Abraham Lincoln!" the mayor exclaimed as he pressed the suit coat across his chest. He moved to in front of the mirror. "Do you know what this is, Jenkins? Do you know what this means?"

"Yes, sir. I believe it to mean that at one time a former U.S. president wore those clothes."

"Providence, Jenkins! This is Providence!" he said with a raised right hand, his index finger pointing skyward. "I am certain to take my rightful place next to Abraham Lincoln in due course! In due course!"

Jenkins watched the mayor preen in front of the mirror, first with the coat across his chest, then with the pants held to his waist. The pants stopped two inches short of the mayor's ankles and Jenkins made a curious face, as he knew the mayor's height to be five foot eight, nine inches tops. "Sir," he started, "I seem to recall Abraham Lincoln as a much taller man. Shouldn't he have had longer trousers?"

"Don't be naïve, Jenkins. No man is born six foot six inches tall. This is obviously a suit of Abraham Lincoln's younger years."

"Of course, sir. How slow of me."

The mayor draped the pants across the back of his office chair and reached for the beard. It was of theatrical quality, and its softness suggested it could have been made of real human hair, the fine strands intricately woven around a thin metal frame to give it shape and structure, a sleek wire protruding from each end to be curled around the ears. He held the beard to his face and tied each wire to an ear, adjusting for snugness. He again stepped to the mirror. He stood on his tiptoes and alternated views of his profile. "Jenkins, my index cards, if you please."

"Yes, sir." Jenkins handed the box of cards to the mayor. The mayor pulled a card from the "L" section.

The mayor read aloud:

> Let us strive to deserve, as far as mortals may, the continued care of Divine Providence, trusting that, in future national emergencies, He will not fail to provide us the instruments of safety and security.

Abraham Lincoln     July 6, 1852
Springfield, IL
Eulogy on Henry Clay
2 stars

"Very touching and appropriate, sir."

"I thought so, yes. Very apropos vis-à-vis our current situation."

"Shall we open the rest of the mail?" Jenkins picked up the bank statement and offered it to the mayor.

"Certainly." The mayor opened the envelope. He stroked his beard with one hand as he evaluated the statement. He looked it over twice. "Great news, Jenkins. The National Park Service has cashed our check. I can only conclude that our project is continuing apace."

Jenkins swallowed hard. "Perhaps now would be an appropriate time to convene the aldermen. I could sketch some broad strokes, perhaps a chart or a graph. I could include a public opinion poll . . ."

"Nonsense! We now have Providence on our side."

"Providence, yes, sir." Jenkins watched the mayor in front of the mirror. He continued to stroke his beard with one hand; the other he waved slowly back and forth behind his back.

"Do you see me, Jenkins? Do you see what I'm doing? Hand on the tiller, son. Hand on the tiller."

"Yes, sir. Hand on the tiller. You are firmly in charge."

The mayor abruptly turned from the mirror. "Jenkins, take a letter."

"Yes, sir." Jenkins scurried and again sat at the mayor's desk. He once again readied pen and ink.

"Ready, sir."

"To the National Park Service, as follows:

Sirs,

Have received confirmation you are in receipt of Project funds. I trust things are proceeding smoothly. I have the fullest faith and confidence in your ability to bring this endeavor to its rightful and historic conclusion. To that end, I vow not to hover over the day-to-day minutiae of your operation; rather, I trust in your good judgment. If you would be so kind, from time to time, to snap a photo of your progress and forward to me, it would be greatly appreciated. Enclosed please find an additional check for $25,000 in fervent hope you truly understand the gratefulness on my part.

Yours humbly,

Schuyler A. Peabody, Mayor

"There, that should do nicely. Is there anything you think I should add? Anything else?" The mayor was being facetious. He was fishing for a comment about the check.

"No, sir."

"No additional need to consider the aldermen?"

"No, sir, not at this time. I was mentally preparing some remarks, but now it is my understanding, as you have guided me, that we have Providence. Besides, I believe the amount of this check should exhaust almost all town funds. It may very well be Providence which, at this particular moment, puts me at a loss for how to proceed."

"Quite possible," he added with a nod.

Hizzoner recalled with fondness Jenkins' quick acceptance of Providence. Duty, devotion, and loyalty were always the minimum qualifications for a competent aide, but a kindred spirit, a like-minded free thinker, a confidante in matters coincidental, was more than any humble duly elected public servant would have expected. Jenkins was a real team player. He was an asset not to be squandered. And several weeks after that second letter had been sent, he recalled how much more would be asked of him . . .

"Jenkins! Have you gotten the mail?"

"Yes, sir. Nothing from the National Park Service."

"Perhaps a manila envelope marked 'Fragile: Photographs?'"

"No, sir, nothing like that. I do believe, however, we should address the continued correspondence from the bank. I've been fielding several calls, as well. And some of the aldermen are questioning why their postage allowance has been eliminated."

"Just toss the notice on the pile with the rest of them. Better yet, see if we can reuse any of the stamps. I hear steam sometimes works."

"Yes, sir, steam. Moist hot air, it is."

\* \* \* \* \*

The mayor's office became quite unfocused waiting for a response from the National Park Service. A pile of bank notices marked "Urgent: Please respond" were stacked, many of them unopened, next to the bust of Benjamin Franklin on the credenza. Official town business, petitions, zoning ordinances, and requests for appearances at various fundraising outings drew no executive attention and were scattered on top of his desk. Even the Abraham Lincoln suit and beard seemed a bit forgotten; they hung from a hook mounted to the back of his office door. Deb didn't seem to notice any difference and never said a word.

The mayor stood in front of his office window overlooking Town Square. The perfect blue midday July sky that had appeared before him three months ago and captivated his imagination gave way to a gray mid-October afternoon, the leaves of the old oak having curled and turned a pale brown, falling with the cool breeze.

"Jenkins, I've been thinking."

"Yes, sir."

"Perhaps I've made an error in judgment. Perhaps I've been too hands off with these National Park Service people. They are, after all, government employees and used to a certain amount of guidance and prodding. I may have jumped the gun when I proposed I keep my distance and not hold their feet to the fire. Without a tight hold on the reins, who knows what could happen? Their opinion of me could have been affected, and we can't have that at this delicate time. I wouldn't want them to think I was prone to lax oversight."

"No, sir. I do not believe that is the case."

"No?"

"No."

The mayor thought for a few moments. He tapped his foot. He searched for the right words. "What do you think it could be? Democrats?"

Jenkins answered in a direct tone. "I believe you may have caught them off guard, sir. I'll guess they were ill prepared to act quickly upon your suggestion, thus a delay in correspondence. Or they could be forming some type of task force. Either way, I believe their response is forthcoming."

The mayor processed his aide's answer. He picked up his box of index cards from the desk and held them to his heart. He let out a heavy sigh and rubbed his forehead and eyebrows with one hand as Jenkins fiddled with the pile of bank notices. After a short while, a curious look came over the mayor's face, and he walked calmly toward the Abraham Lincoln suit. He caressed the lapels and smiled. "Jenkins, what do you know about South Dakota?"

"South Dakota, sir?"

"Yes, its history, people, that sort of thing. The Black Hills."

"Well," he began, "Let me think. Originally known as the Dakota Territory, North and South Dakota were named after the Lakota and Dakota Sioux Indian tribes. Gold was found in the Black Hills in the late 1800s by, I believe, General George Armstrong Custer, prompting the movement of the Sioux to reservations."

"*The* General George Armstrong Custer?"

"Yes, sir. There are many intersections of famous individuals with the Dakotas. For example, they were explored by Lewis and Clark, partly at the behest of Thomas Jefferson; even some larger-than-life figures such as Wild Bill Hickok and Sitting Bull have a connection to South Dakota."

"Larger than life," the mayor said in a far away tone. "Like Mount Rushmore."

"Yes, sir, I guess you could say that." Jenkins took note of the dreamy look in the mayor's eyes. It seemed he weighed his next words very carefully, as he took the extra precaution of clearing his throat, loudly, twice, which could have been to draw the mayor's attention, before he spoke. "It is also my understanding there is a very different perspective on the monument by the Sioux people, many of whom may be direct descendants of Wounded Knee survivors."

"Indians? Are you saying the Black Hills aren't safe?"

"By no means, sir. The Black Hills are quite safe. I mention it only as part of the historical record and to acknowledge the Sioux viewpoint."

"Excellent and noted. I believe our course is set. Jenkins, take a letter."

"Yes, sir," he said in a plain voice. Jenkins once again took a seat in the mayor's chair and readied quill and ink. He moved a bit more slowly than in his previous stenographic efforts, flexed his writing hand two or three times, and attempted to shoo the Hungarian pheasant feathers from his face with several short quick breaths. "Ready, sir."

"To the National Park Service, as follows:

Sirs,

Not to be a busybody, and please pardon the interruption, but I've observed no progress, as of this late date, toward the sculpting of my features into your fine granite. Be that as it may, I am willing to accept part of the responsibility for what could be perceived as lax oversight on my end. I wish to state firmly and for the record that my supervisory skills are and always have been top notch. As proof, I am lending my aide, Jenkins, to this project temporarily. In the true spirit of the history of the monument, I am sending him by train to Rapid City, arriving much like Calvin Coolidge (sans raccoon). Treat him well. Furthermore, as I have become a bit of an expert on South Dakota, its people, history and culture, as well as its storied past where larger than life figures are concerned, I have chosen to honor your state in the following manner: Jenkins will arrive in the garb of none other than Abraham Lincoln (he will not be wearing a hat, but should stand out in a crowd nonetheless: short, blonde, spectacles, dark suit and beard) whom I believe to be a friend of the Sioux. He was called Honest Abe, you know. In addition, I have authorized Jenkins to present you with an envelope containing $714.00 in cash to be used as you see fit.

Your Partner In History,
Schuyler A. Peabody, Mayor"

As the mayor finished dictating, he looked out of the corner of his eye in the general direction of Jenkins. He went to well-practiced lengths to avoid looking directly at him. He folded his hands behind his back and attempted to whistle, the mayoral lips moving the air but creating no sound. He prepared his response.

Jenkins never blinked. "I am to wear the Lincoln suit to Rapid City, sir?"

"That is the plan, yes."

"And carry an envelope of cash for delivery?"

"Correct again. Preferably to a senior official of some sort, you know the type. Budgets on these things always become unpredictable. They appreciate a little wiggle room."

Jenkins stared at the letter in his hands. He did not look at the mayor. "How long am I to be gone?"

"Well, let's see." The mayor counted off on his fingers. "Go to Rapid City, find right-thinking official, oversee initial phase of sculpting, document event for posterity, report on your progress. I'm guessing eight, maybe ten, hours."

"And the cash, sir? The $714?"

"Say no more. I didn't want to worry you, Jenkins, and I certainly didn't want to heap any unnecessary pressure on your capable shoulders as it relates to the success of your efforts, but it appears the town may be in a bit of a financial pickle. Somehow there is a discrepancy."

"A discrepancy, sir?"

"Jenkins, these things happen. Suffice it to say that $714 is all that remains of our Town Emergency Fund. And I should thank Providence for that." The mayor walked to the credenza and the bust of Benjamin Franklin. He tilted the bust at the neck to reveal a hollowed-out head and a small wad of bills. He put them in an envelope and handed them to Jenkins. "Jenkins . . . I can see it now . . . A tall billboard on that magnificent empty road into town proclaiming 'Home of Schuyler A. Peabody The Fifth Face.' Tourism dollars will flow and fill our coffers, civic pride will swell, history will have been served." The mayor took the Lincoln suit from the hook on the back of the door and headed toward Jenkins. "Let's see how she fits."

Hizzoner recalled slipping the arms of his aide into the Lincoln topcoat, the fastening of the beard, and the stoic manner in which Jenkins stood in front of the mayoral mirror, wordless, readying himself for his mission. It was a prideful moment. Now, as he stood over the sleeping Jenkins, with only the empty room to hear, he whispered, "Capital effort, Jenkins. Capital effort."

# Chapter 17

Jenkins sat on the train by himself, staring out the window in an uncharacteristically forlorn way, waiting for the departure to Rapid City. He was certain that everyone else on the train, as well as those outside leering at him through the train window, some pointing fingers, were trying to place the familiar, bespectacled face beneath the obviously fake beard. Some did double takes. He wished it was dark.

The conductor yelled, "All aboard!" and the train began to nudge forward. The train whistle blew, and Jenkins could hear and feel the sounds of the heavy steel wheels beginning to turn against the track. He knew he was officially on his way, headed for South Dakota and a mostly unannounced visit with someone from the National Park Service. Jenkins was about to relax and try to enjoy the trip when his last look out the window noticed an angry mob of six men, their collars unbuttoned and their ties undone, moving decidedly as one and on the quick step toward the Chamber of Commerce building. He immediately recognized the identical dress and invariability of march as belonging to six of the seven aldermen, and he hoped he had not been seen. The mayor's son, Lester, was, not surprisingly, absent from this group; nepotism and foul play had been suspected by some in his recent election victory, leaving only the smallest of avenues available for camaraderie or political alliance building.

The conductor walked down the aisle and stopped in front of Jenkins. "Ticket please," he requested. Jenkins handed the ticket to the conductor, who punched a small hole in the upper-right-hand corner. "Aren't you a little old for trick-or-treat?" he said, as he returned the ticket to Jenkins. "You should find a girl, son."

Jenkins took the ticket, nodded a thank you, and tried not to feel too embarrassed. It was hard.

Just outside of town, and as the train picked up speed in the open plain, Jenkins listened to the melodic click-click, click-click, click-click of the train wheels against the track and stared out into the day and at the prairie grass and at the wild stallions in the distance at full gallop, as he tried to take his mind off the comments from the conductor. Find a girl, he said. It was not like he wasn't trying. He remembered the lecture his father gave him when he went off to college, that there would be plenty of time for girls and that college was a time for preparing for your future and getting good grades that would lead to a respectable, honorable occupation, and how he couldn't wait to ignore that advice. He remembered how he couldn't wait to rush into his first college classroom, a freshman in a thousand ways, in hopes of a fateful and spontaneous attraction. And then he remembered the disappointment of seeing the mostly male class in economics or political science, and that all the really pretty girls would be in the classes he didn't have, like art history or film or drama. Those girls did weird things to their hair and were exciting and fun and different, and some of them even smoked, he remembered. Apparently they didn't get lectures from their fathers, he figured.

Find a girl, the conductor said. He said it so simply, as if to imply it were a lost item, a key, a book, or a shoe. As hard as Jenkins tried, he couldn't shake those words. Mile after uneventful mile the time passed, yet he couldn't stop replaying the words in his mind. The staccato rhythm of the wheels against the track seemed to drive those three little words deeper into his brain, his conscious efforts to forget having the decidedly opposite effect.

He felt he never would forget them, nor the memory of the conductor's face, that look of disdain, until somehow, without notice, he recalled that first day he walked into Mayor Peabody's office.

The day after his college graduation, diploma in hand, Jenkins answered this ad:

"Wanted: Savvy Political Aide willing to be Right Hand Man to major political figure. Must possess knowledge of the various branches of government. Go-getters preferred. Qualified applicants apply in person only to Schuyler A. Peabody, Mayor."

He raced up the stairs of the Chamber of Commerce building and opened the door to the mayor's office, his cheeks flushed.

"Hiya, handsome," Deb said. She was seated at her desk. "You want to be president, too?" Deb opened her desk drawer to reveal a stack of blank job application forms two inches high. She took application number #002 from the top. As she prepared to hand the form to Jenkins, she noticed the document in his hands, the elegant cursive strokes across the top, the bold, important look of it. Her face began to scowl and she took on a defensive tone. "What have you got there?" she said. "It's not a subpoena, is it?"

"I've come about the ad," Jenkins said in an uncomfortable way, offering Deb a look at his diploma.

"Why, of course you have," Deb said, a warm and brilliant white smile returning to her face. She placed the application form in his hand. "Two's the charm," she said with a wink.

Jenkins' memory of that day brought a smile to his face and, for the first time since the train left the station, he felt himself ease back into his seat. That bewitching red hair of Deb's was best recollected with eyes closed, he felt, and as he closed his eyes, he softly exhaled, scratched beneath his beard, and remembered with fondness that first meeting, the pure-as-heaven white sparkle in her smile, the forever-azure sky in her eyes, the way she called him handsome and the way she even winked at him. He even recalled that when she handed him the job application form, the tip of her fingernail almost touched his wrist in an inviting way, and how he hoped he would get that job.

"Next stop, Rapid City," the conductor announced, as he walked deliberately down the aisle. "Rapid City, next stop," he repeated.

# Chapter 18

Hizzoner sat back in the mayoral chair and welcomed a peaceful moment. He envisioned his faithful charge stepping off the train platform in Rapid City to throngs of well wishers, their red-white-and-blue streamers, balloons and ribbons flying through a snow globe-like sky of confetti. A brass band led by a celebrity of some sort would encourage starry-eyed high school musicians playing John Phillip Souza or "The Star Spangled Banner" to welcome his envoy. Hands would be shaken and smiles would be broad. Politics would be the order of the day and history would be made.

The mayor smiled in a supremely confident manner. Jenkins was on his way and all would be well. Perhaps a rousing speech to commemorate his return would be appropriate, he thought, as he reached for the box of index cards on his desk. He carefully thumbed through the cards, hoping to be inspired by something in the "Return of a Conquering Hero" vein when he was interrupted by a rather firm knock on his door.

"Come in," he said plainly.

The door swung smartly open and in moved the aldermen. They formed a semi-circle around the mayor's desk and tried to speak in unison. "We are the 'Gang of Six,'" they offered in inexact fashion.

"Who?" Hizzoner asked.

"Now, don't try to distract us! On the walk over, through Town Square, we all agreed in principle that we would be called the 'Gang of Six.' It was a unanimous vote with no dissenters, punctuated with the occasional fist pump and rebel yell. We feel it is a bold attempt to attach a sense of seriousness and ferocity to our agenda. And we will not be distracted!"

"Oh. Hi, guys," the mayor responded.

"And we demand to know what's going on!" said the first.

"Where's that little fella?" added the second. "And Deb, where's Deb?"

"Yes, demand!" said the third.

A perplexed and slightly stunned mayor squirmed a tiny bit. "At your service, as always," he said. The mayor gestured easily with open arms. "You know my door is always open. And I am an open book."

"Something is fishy!" blurted one.

"I smell a rat!" said another.

"We weren't born yesterday, you know," still another added.

The mayor calmly interlocked the fingers of his hands and rested them on the ink blotter before him. He searched for his most innocuous voice. "Whatever could you mean, gentlemen? I know we've had our disagreements before as to matters political—as all men of opinion do—but rarely have I been confronted with such uncivil tones from such skilled orators, elected officials, and Kiwanis to boot! Certainly an avenue for more rational discourse exists, a path that we may walk together toward a common understanding. Perhaps some tea."

"None for me, thank you," said one automatically.

"We want to know what's going on!" interrupted another. "We don't want any tea. We don't want any cookies. We have suspicions!"

"You bet we do!" said another.

"And we don't have any postage, either. Where's that little fella that gets me the postage?"

"We are the 'Gang of Six!'" cried one.

The mayor began with a raised eyebrow. He looked each one directly in the eyes, maintaining an intense, breathless focus with each, as if to say to each of them, 'Are you the one? Is it you? Are you my accuser? We shall soon find out.'

"Suspicions, you say? Regarding . . . ?"

The aldermen suddenly and mysteriously traded nonconfrontational looks among themselves. It was as if the ad hoc committee they formed only moments ago, and that legislated an impromptu bravado, had mystically expired, vanished, evaporated, or sublimated into thin air, leaving in its wake an every-man-for-himself sensation that dried throats and melted resolve. Several pointed fingers, some at themselves in an unconvincing fashion, indicating who should begin. One stared at the ceiling, another at his shoes, while yet another attempted to summon the courage to speak with a quick gulp from a hip flask he produced with such speed and quickness that it would have drawn true envy from the second fastest gun in the Old West.

"You were mentioning you had suspicions," the mayor repeated. He waited for an answer, his pose stoic. He turned an ear toward them.

"Well . . . it's . . . like . . . this . . ." the alderman began, hoping each word he just spoke would somehow gain momentum on its own, concluding in a cohesive thought, or at the very least a declarative sentence.

"We've heard some things," continued another. "Rumblings, actually."

"More innuendo than rumblings, really," said a third.

"Probably outright lies," encouraged a fourth.

"We, all of us, decided it was best to discuss the situation," said the fifth.

"What sort of rumblings?" asked the mayor.

"Well, I can tell you that it's just the sort of thing that comes from malicious gossips."

"The worst sort of people."

"Who knows what these malcontents will say next?"

"Go on," the mayor said.

"In a nutshell—and I'm sure I'm way off base here . . ."

"Is the town broke?" blurted the Alderman with the hip flask. He added a hiccup for good measure. "Just asking."

"Broke? Why, not to my knowledge," the mayor stated in a firm and certain tone. He did his best to craft a concerned look on his face. "In fact, I'd suggest that it would take some first rate fiscal tomfoolery to drain our sufficiently funded municipal coffers right out from under the watchful dozen eyes of my budget committee hawks, my 'Gang of Six.' Wouldn't you think?"

The aldermen gasped.

"What sort of tattletale is spreading such nonsense?" the mayor asked defiantly.

"None other than Town Bank President J. Adam Snowden 'Jack' Smythe himself," came the quick response. "You see, I was on my way into the bank—on official business, of course —when Jack sees me and he says, 'How are things in the Chamber? Pity about the exhaustion of town funds. However, zero is a nice round number. Unforeseen expenditures, I imagine. Monuments and so forth. I hope this doesn't mean you'll be raising my taxes next year.' And off he went in a dash. Something about a Preferred Customer Night."

"And how did you respond?" the mayor asked firmly.

"Naturally, I denied the tax increase."

"Hear, hear. Bravo," offered each alderman. There were agreeing nods, as well, and for the briefest of moments self-congratulatory smiles on their faces.

The mayor was immediately inspired by the camaraderie of the aldermen, the effortless way in which they were quick to agree, the almost instantaneous way in which their emotions were capable of being swayed, reed-like in the wind, at a moment's notice and without a whit of actual thought, and, mostly, for that intrinsically perfect and most desperately desired political character trait known to modern man: the short memory. "Bravo," added the mayor. "I wouldn't give a second thought to Jack's comments."

"Jack's a boob," said one.

"No," the mayor continued, "I wouldn't give it a second thought. I'm sure it will all come out in the inquisition. I mean, the investigation."

"What investigation?" the aldermen asked in perfect unison, followed by a perfect silence.

"Why, the investigation into the missing funds, of course," replied the mayor. "An accusation has been made, floated as it were, right before my very desk and in front of duly elected witnesses. Why, I would be derelict in my duty to ignore it—regardless of the infinitesimally small likelihood of its truth. Let it never be said that Schuyler A. Peabody turned deaf ears and blind eyes to matters where propriety, virtue, and fiscal fitness are concerned. Naturally I'll be looking to you men for recommendations as to who shall sit on the panel. You know, in judgment."

"The panel?"

"Yes. It should go without saying that these must be individuals of the highest character, intelligent right down to their bootstraps, each possessing a dogged and rabid determination to ferret out the truth. In short, gentlemen, we are in desperate need of interrogators of the most ferocious variety, pit bulls at the pulpit."

"Interrogators?"

"Yes, interrogators. Perhaps ex-military."

The stunned group asked, "But who will they question?"

"I would imagine they would start with you," the mayor replied in his official voice.

"Us?" a shocked alderman replied. "Do you mean people will ask us questions?" A genuine look of terror overcame the aldermen. "But we didn't . . ."

"Try not to think of them as people," the mayor began. "It could only perpetuate and serve to foster the adversarial nature of the proceedings. Any names come to mind? Let's put on our thinking caps."

"But we don't want to be questioned!"

"Almost no one ever does," said the mayor. "Be that as it may, I feel we may have already embarked upon a course of action. May I suggest you refer to yourselves as the 'Gang of Six' as often as humanly possible. That should prevent the media from conjuring up some distasteful moniker of their own to run all over the newspapers. They have no respect for decency. Quite fiendish, actually."

"The newspapers, too?" they said in a whiny unison. The aldermen began to fidget.

"Why, yes. Investigations not covered in the public eye are talked about. Besides, the last thing we need is some hint of secrecy in the mayor's office. Politics is all about the truth and the manner in which we convey that to the voters." The mayor stared off into space and put his hand over his heart. "Propriety, propriety, propriety—at all times, propriety," he added.

The aldermen gulped collectively.

As Hizzoner watched, he surmised the prospect of appearing before a panel—even one of their own choosing—held no familiarity with the events and career path trajectory each alderman envisioned for himself. This he set upon quickly, as he watched nodding heads agree without any sort of bombastic discussion. They drew breath as brothers. They huddled together as closely as they could, bent at the waist with their arms around each other's shoulders, and debated their options in broken squeaky whispers. Hizzoner could overhear ideas relating to skill sets, previous work histories, foreign languages spoken, architecture and urban planning, all presented in an orderly fashion and without interruption.

And only when it seemed they were completely certain that all reasonable avenues had been explored, and that the full force of their collected wisdom and experience had been exhausted, did they become overwhelmed by a burdensome silence. One alderman dropped to a knee and pulled a large roadmap from inside the breast pocket of his coat. He unfolded it on the floor in front of his brethren. Seconds later they broke arms and stood to face the mayor.

"Your Honor, sir," the first began. He stood in his most professional posture, head stiffly back with a hand to his belt.

Hizzoner loved the pose every time he saw it. Once he had told the alderman it reminded him of a likeness of Patrick Henry he had seen in a chewing gum advertisement.

The first continued. "It brings us great pain, and it is with the most sincere of regrets, that we must officially inform you of our collective inability to participate in this worthy investigation."

"You don't say."

"I'm afraid it is true," he continued, the others all furiously nodding. "It seems the real reason we have come to see you today was to mention that we have been called away on a fact-finding mission of indeterminate length by persons who, at this very sensitive time, must remain anonymous, and we must leave at once, without so much as a parliamentary permission slip, lest the facts we seek remain uncovered."

"But what of your suspicions? Whom shall I investigate?"

"We have recently given this a great deal of thought in committee and can reach no other logical conclusion than to say, sadly and with all due respect . . . Lester."

"My son?" The mayor snapped to attention in his chair. "What could he possibly know of such matters? I am certain he knows nothing."

"We are certain that if such knowledge exists, it shall come out during the rightful and true course of the investigation. Furthermore, in our absence, we discharge our duties to him. He is free to answer all interrogatories regarding the office of alderman with our blessings. Please let him know that he shall have our vote of confidence with him at all times. Truth be told, we have been somewhat bashful with our support of Lester in the past; however, circumstances now permit clarity of thought and immediacy of spirit. To that end, wherever our quest shall lead, we will spread the word among the common folk as to his courage and honor in the face of persecution. May he be spared the hangman's noose. Viva Lester!"

The aldermen spun on their heels and headed for the door.

The mayor recognized the moment at hand. In a matter of two additional steps, the aldermen would be gone, spreading the word of Lester and of some fictitious panel to anyone they may meet. Reputations of a prominent storied political family were at stake. No time to lose. Detour needed ahead.

"Gentlemen," the mayor started in an uncertain and wavering voice. The aldermen were at the threshold. "I wish you Godspeed on your quest, and I beg your indulgence for one brief moment. It will not be necessary to proclaim Lester's many virtues among the masses—words of general kindness will suffice. For, I must admit, I have uncovered a fact of my own which must now see the inevitable light of day, a fact that may have bearing upon our issue at hand. It is not always known why things are done. Motives are not always evident, nor are outcomes always certain. There are, sometimes, surprises and bumps in the road that cloud one's clear vision of their destination, maybe even to the point of delusion. In fact, the difference between a delusion and an aspiration is sometimes the measure of success ultimately achieved, I would offer . . . My fellow public servants . . . It is with the heaviest of hearts I share . . . Jenkins is missing."

The aldermen exchanged double-take glances and walked out the door. "I'll bet he's got my postage," one whispered.

# Chapter 19

Jenkins stepped off the train in Rapid City to an empty train platform and wondered what to do next. He wondered exactly which direction to go. He had not expected anyone from the National Park Service to greet him, and in fact hoped they had forgotten all about the letters from Mayor Peabody. He hoped they simply cashed the checks, assuming they were gifts from a grateful community, and that they represented accumulated donations from well-wishers to help maintain an historic national treasure. Certainly, in his mind, patriotism had not gone out of fashion, and that would be a logical explanation for the communications and his costumed visit. To him, the next step was vividly clear: All that was to be required now was that he state the case for his presence to an official of the National Park Service (just in case they hadn't forgotten about the letters) in a calm and concise manner, then slip inconspicuously out of town to report back to the mayor—in a believable way—that his project had not been forgotten, and that it had only been unavoidably, and perhaps permanently, delayed. Simple.

Jenkins walked through the station and tried to blend in as he searched for anything that might give him the local address of the National Park Service. He looked through colorful brochures describing motor coach tours, helicopter excursions, old-fashioned steam engine trips, horseback riding through the prairie, and even Harley Davidson motorcycle rentals that all promised to offer 'once in a lifetime views of Mt. Rushmore and the Badlands.' He even looked at a giant map of South Dakota with a big red star on it that said, 'You are here,' but could not find the precise information he was looking for.

As Jenkins turned from the map, he saw that a small girl with pigtails was walking hand in hand with her mother and coming his way, the distracted mother attempting to navigate a path through hurried travelers and overly casual tourists alike, a firm grip on the child's hand and an overstuffed suitcase with a wobbly wheel in tow for good measure. Jenkins rationally decided there could be no harm in asking for directions and focused on the pair. With the first step he took toward them, the little girl saw him and pointed, her pigtails flopping as she jumped up and down with excitement.

"Look, Mommy! That man looks just like Abraham Lincoln with glasses! He looks just like the man on the mountain!"

The girl's mother tightened her grasp on the child's hand. "Keep walking, dear. Let's leave that man alone," she said as they passed him by.

"Maybe he's lost, Mommy. Can't we help Abraham Lincoln, Mommy? Please?"

"Just keep walking, dear. We don't talk to strange men in train stations. Haven't I taught you better than that? Come along, now." The mother quickened her pace, and added a tug or two on her daughter's arm for emphasis.

Jenkins, too, quickened his pace after them. "Excuse me, ma'am. Excuse me, please," he said with a wave of his hand.

The girl's mother looked over her shoulder toward Jenkins. He was continuing to approach. He was gaining on them. "Come on now, dear. Let's walk a little faster."

"But Mommy, he could be lost. Maybe we can help him find a policeman."

"Presidents don't get lost, dear. Keep walking. A little faster now," she said, as Jenkins was now only a handful of feet away.

Jenkins caught up to the pair and lightly tapped the mother on the shoulder from behind. "Excuse me," he began.

The woman then shrieked in a manner so shrill, a primal scream simultaneously capable of shattering glass and human will, that, for a moment, she let go of her daughter's hand. She reached in her pocket and, in a flash, pulled out a silver plated whistle, spun to face Jenkins, and with a well-trained determination and purpose, blew her whistle directly at him with all her force, stopping only intermittently to scream in an insane manner, "Help! Police! Somebody!"

Jenkins quickly deduced this was not the response he was hoping for, and that no useful information was forthcoming. He turned and ran as fast as he could, pushing aside businessmen, grandmothers, two catholic nuns, and a small group of Shriners assembling before some kind of memorial, as he moved toward the revolving doors and the street in front of him. He burst through them in a whirl and found himself on the sidewalk in front of the station. He began to walk away with a contrived nonchalance, deliberately refusing to look over his shoulder as a matter of good form. After all, only people who had reason to suspect they were being followed, hunted, or searched forever looked behind themselves in conspicuous ways, he reasoned. He even tried to whistle.

# Chapter 20

Hizzoner stared out his office window into Town Square and watched as the aldermen made their way out of town, a marching, huddled mass. With each step they took, he noticed them getting smaller before his eyes, and he wondered how long it would be before they were only a point in the distance, something completely indistinguishable on the horizon, a speck on the Earth. He couldn't say, for sure—yet he knew instinctively when to turn away, when he lost all but a casual focus, when he imagined himself too easily walking in their place or by their side, a confederate. Despite the tale of a missing Jenkins, it was obvious to him they feared a panel of inquisitors, that the perception of misdeeds would be cast upon them, he thought. They were not the ones to cast town funds into the abyss. He knew he was. He instinctively reached for his box of index cards. He pulled a card from the "J" section to read aloud:

> We have the wolf by the ears, and we can neither hold him, nor safely let him go. Justice is in one scale, and self-preservation in the other.
>
> Thomas Jefferson
> letter to John Holmes
> April 22, 1820    3 stars

He put the card back. He pulled the card before it and read aloud:

> The same prudence which in private life would forbid our paying our own money for unexplained projects, forbids it in the dispensation of the public moneys.
>
> Thomas Jefferson
> letter to Shelton Gilliam
> June 18, 1808     2 stars

"Forbids it in the dispensation of the public moneys," he repeated softly. He returned the card to its place with a heavy sigh, and as he passed by the mayoral mirror, he noticed a foreign look on his face staring back at him, the dullness of despair, which can only be seen and truly understood in reflection. He plopped himself unceremoniously into the mayoral chair. His body ached all over in indescribable ways, and he could feel a cold and sudden weariness overtake him as he mindlessly poked at the Hungarian pheasant feathers arching toward him from the penholder on his desk. Poke, poke, poke, he repeated for minutes, until he finally reached for the quill.

The mayor took a piece of paper from his desk and began to write:

Dear Lester,

It is with supreme regret that I must inform you of my decision to leave Town at once. I apologize for doing so in a letter; however, circumstances dictate a certain swiftness of action. I am certain you will understand. My destination is foreign to me, and I can only promise with the greatest degree of certainty that my return is assured once I have seen to several, as of yet unmentioned, redevelopments. In the interim, soldier on, as I know you will.

With Regards,

Schuyler A. Peabody, Mayor

Your Father

P.S. You may find that Town finances reflect a somewhat eccentric disarray, bordering on larceny to the untrained eye. I can assure you that this is nothing more than politics as usual, which will serve to challenge your sense of creativity. In addition, please note that I also challenge you with the highest of expectations until my return.

The mayor left the note on his desk, grabbed his index cards, and skulked out of his office and down the three flights of stairs to the street. And, at the precise moment when he was certain no one was looking, he darted next door into the Hall of Records, breathlessly closing the great oak doors behind him.

# Chapter 21

Jenkins continued down the sidewalk, having settled into a casual and inconspicuous saunter, when he felt an annoying little bonk on the back of his head. It was nothing really, he convinced himself, perhaps a windblown bit of debris or an errant nearsighted insect that lost its way. Until it happened again.

He took his hand and ran it over the back of his head, but felt nothing. As he kept walking, he took notice of the stillness of the October air, and listened for the buzz that accompanies all sorts and manner of flying things that swarm, but gathered no clue. And yet, despite all evidence to the contrary, he still refused to manage a look over his shoulder, one hundred percent resolute in his belief against actions that draw attention to oneself.

Bonk! Bonk! Bonk! Three then came in succession.

"Ow!" he cried out. "That one hurt!" He stopped abruptly and once again put his hand to the back of his head. He turned to look behind him.

Two small boys who could have been twins looked up at him, each with a bulging fistful of pebbles in one hand, some spilling out onto the sidewalk. Their straight, black hair fell almost into their eyes, and their golden brown complexion and dark eyes suggested a Native American ancestry.

"What do you think you're doing?" Jenkins asked in an incredulous tone.

"Go back! Go back, Abraham Lincoln!" the first boy said. He unloaded with a pebble that cracked Jenkins right in the middle of his forehead.

"Ow!" Jenkins yelled. "Stop that!"

"Go back!" yelled the second boy, as he whipped his pebble in the general direction of Jenkins' head.

The boy missed his mark, but before he could reload, Jenkins turned and set off on a full-blast kind of sprint down the sidewalk, every other step looking over his shoulder to see if he was putting any distance between himself and the boys. The boys gave chase with a perpetual and vicious energy, their short legs a furious blur of motion, their pitching arms unleashing a barrage of pebbles at the moving target.

For four full blocks, Jenkins raced at top speed, narrowly avoiding innocent bystanders and, on occasion, ducking to avoid a well-aimed salvo. Now spent and rubber-legged, he began to slow and wobble in a most unsteady way. Just ahead, in the middle of the sidewalk, a stout man in a white coat stood facing him, his arms outstretched as if about to catch the winded Jenkins, his knees flexed in an athletic posture, his moves mirroring the side-to-side sway of the obviously exhausted running man.

"Whoa! Whoa! Whoa there!" the man in the white coat directed. Momentum carried Jenkins into the arms of the man. He was stopped easily.

"They're chasing me," Jenkins said as he tried to catch his breath.

"It's okay. I'm pretty sure they'll stop now," the man said calmly, as he obliged to keep a limp Jenkins from falling to the ground. "They don't have any more stones."

Jenkins steadied himself and turned to see the boys standing at his side, their toothless smiles staring up at him, their empty hands, a small pile of pebbles on the sidewalk next to each boy's sneaker. "Hello, Uncle A," they said in a polite way.

"Run along, boys. We'll talk later . . . Maybe with your mother," the man in the white coat said. The boys scooted down the sidewalk.

"Do you . . . Do you know those hooligans?" Jenkins asked as he watched the boys run away.

"They're good boys. They just thought you came down from the mountain to kill them in their sleep, that's all. They're good boys."

"Who would tell them that? Who would say such a thing? Where would they get a preposterous idea like that?" Jenkins said, as he noticed the stencil on the window over the man's shoulder. It read: 'A. Black Elk, DDS.' It matched the red stitching over the man's breast pocket.

"Probably from an elder or a medicine man. I don't think my sister tells those kinds of stories. She's a good woman. The elders like to tell the story about Abraham Lincoln's spirit coming down from Mount Rushmore to seek revenge for his father being put to death in a Shawnee hatchet attack back in Illinois in the 1700s. It's all a lie, though. He was shot in Kentucky."

Jenkins smirked. "You seem certain."

"Common knowledge, really."

"And those boys?"

"They're my younger sister's kids. They're good boys. She drops them off sometimes when she has to go to work, or run an errand, or go to the doctor, or when she's expecting a repairman, or sometimes when she has a headache. They're good boys. I don't mind supervising them."

Jenkins touched his forehead where he was smacked with the stone and felt for blood.

"Good job."

"Looks like a lump. Come into my office and I'll take a look. I'm Dr. Black Elk."

"Jenkins."

Jenkins followed Dr. Black Elk into his office. The surroundings at once seemed a bit of an anachronism to Jenkins: a mahogany dental chair fitted with a red leather seat and head rest was positioned directly in front of the large office window to catch the day's light; a roll-top desk, its top up to reveal a collection of weathered and binding-tattered medical reference books (*Ailments and Maladies of the Plains Indian* caught his eye in particular); two mahogany, glass-enclosed cases on the wall filled with rather medieval-looking instruments, the names of each neatly written in script below each item—*toothkey with reversible fulcrum, gum lancet, pelican, extricating forceps, ivory handled scalers for manual calculus debridement, Lewis plugger;* a small Victorian sofa; a heavy woven Indian blanket folded for use as a pillow; and, sandwiched between what appeared to be generational photos of men, women, and children, a hand-written diploma which read quite simply:

## A. Black Elk
## Doctor of Dental Surgery

Jenkins recognized the stone throwing boys in the pictures.

"Have a seat," Dr. Black Elk said.

'It's probably okay," Jenkins said as he sat in the dental chair. "I don't feel any blood."

"Always a good sign," Dr. Black Elk said. "Now where did I put those glasses?"

"It's probably okay. I'm sure I'm fine."

Dr. Black Elk ruffled through several drawers of his desk, dislodging newspapers, fountain pens, old campaign buttons, three sets of yellowed dentures, and a set of skeleton keys, until he uncovered a slim leather case and removed his eyeglasses, a delicate pair of round, wire-rimmed bifocals. He rested them in a quite satisfactory fashion atop his prominent nose. "Here we go."

"Really, this is quite unnecessary. I'm really fine," Jenkins said.

"Nonsense. Already found the spectacles. They are an exact replica of those worn by Benjamin Franklin during the Second Continental Congress," he said, peering over the top of them. "They were a gift. Now, let's have a look."

Dr. Black Elk examined Jenkins's forehead, interjecting an occasional 'Ah-huh' or a 'hmmm' followed by an 'Ah, yes,' while Jenkins did his courteous best to avoid direct eye contact, choosing instead to look out the office window, past the stencil of the doctor's name and into the street.

"A. Black Elk," Jenkins read from the window. "What does the 'A' stand for?"

"Aristotle. My parents wanted me to be smart."

"Dentists are smart."

"Some of them are very smart . . . Some of the others, not so much. Tell me if this hurts," Dr. Black Elk said as he pressed his stubby thumb into the lump on Jenkins' forehead.

"Yow!" Jenkins let out.

"That would be affirmative," came the immediate reply. He continued without so much as a pause for breath, "You see, my father was Cherokee and my mother was Sioux. And when I was born, they had not yet picked a name for me. Being the first child, as you may suspect, my father's side of the family felt strongly about certain names, as did my mother's side of the family, but neither they nor my parents could reach an agreement. They were at an uncomfortable and unanticipated impasse. So, my parents, not wanting to offend either side of the family, and while I aged, decided to forego a traditional name in favor of something a little off the beaten path."

"But Aristotle?"

"My parents decided to approach the issue in a very logical fashion. They would start alphabetically and discuss the choices between themselves. Only they, too, could not reach an agreement. Several days of this went on, my parents unable to move past the letter 'A,' the discussions tedious amid growing frustrations, when a young Greek man passing through town heard them talking one day. He interrupted them, told them he was on his way into the Black Hills to seek his fortune digging for gold, but felt compelled to tell them the story of Aristotle. He told them Aristotle was a great philosopher, a student of Plato, and the teacher of Alexander the Great, and that his name in Greek meant 'the wisest of them all.' My parents knew their search was over."

"That's an interesting story."

"I feel more than fortunate. Had they met that young man one month later, my name could have been Heroditus."

"Neither snow nor rain nor gloom of night . . ."

'Yes, I am most familiar. The father of modern history. See what I would have had to put up with?"

"Yes, I see."

"Which brings us rather conveniently to your resemblance to an historical figure. I wouldn't even mention it except that I can see that the wire from your beard is causing some redness behind your ear. Does this hurt?" he said, as he tugged on the wire.

"Yow!"

"That would be affirmative," Dr. Black Elk said quickly. "Not that it's any business of mine how a person should dress, mind you. Why, there have been days myself when I woke up in the morning, and without so much as a midnight dream to guide me, felt the need to put on my rabbit fur cape. It's a fascinating piece, really, over one hundred years old and decorated with dyed porcupine quills. It was a gift. Most days, I just wear the smock, though . . . So, is there some kind of production in town?"

"Not that I'm aware, no."

"Some type of reenactment, perhaps?" Dr. Black Elk said as he alternated glances between the reddened ear and the lump on Jenkins' forehead.

"No, I don't believe so," Jenkins said matter-of-factly. He paused for a moment in anticipation of the next question. He could clearly see where this was going. He decided it was best to offer the next question himself. "So, what in the world am I doing dressed as Abraham Lincoln running down the streets of Rapid City, South Dakota?"

"Well, I'm not a busybody, but I do have children to look out for," Dr. Black Elk said, looking out over the top of his bifocals.

"Understood. My purpose here is harmless; in fact, civic in nature."

Jenkins went on to elaborate on the exact nature of his visit as he saw it, leaving out no detail. He was, after all, dying to tell somebody, anybody who might recognize his loyalty and devotion as noble just for a minute, anybody who'd respect the effort of it, silently, honorably, with no chance for Mayor Schuyler Peabody to ever hear. It also helped explain the suit.

He took pride in his ability to recount the events in the exact order in which they happened, almost as if he were reading them from a handwritten list, his memory on this issue so pristine. He also took great care to not embellish his role in the journey; rather, he did his level best to convey a bipartisan and impartial role in the retelling, right up until the part where the woman in the train station frightened the bejeesus out of him with her top-of-the-lungs protective mother shriek. On this point, he allowed himself temporary amnesia.

# Chapter 22

Hizzoner pressed his back against the great oak doors and stared ahead into the emptiness, expecting to see nothing, expecting to hear nothing, somehow certain of his solitude. He knew the aldermen had vacated and locked down their offices on the second floor prior to the march across Town Square as a precaution to their confrontation going badly (it had been a common practice), but he could only surmise as to what had become of the educators and the record-keepers, the first floor staff. Granted, he knew they were only a handful, but among them was Ingrid Gloobniecht, a bit of an icon, really, an impassioned educator whose reputation for enforcing the rules of grammar and punctuation were second only to her lifelong love of the truest form of orthography and the detest of phonics. For her to leave and abandon her post was a nonsequitur, the equivalent of winning the lottery the same day as being struck by lightning.

But there was no mistaking the stillness.

Hizzoner felt an uneasiness as though time and movement of all sorts stopped, the heaviness of the air seeming to press down on him, a cumbersome weight upon his chest pinning him like a sticky varnish to the door. He felt an inexplicable wordlessness encouraging him to join and become one with all that was inanimate in his field of view, the empty desks and the chairs and the bricks and the wood. To exhale too loudly and relieve the pressure on his chest would have seemed a violation, an effrontery to the soundless space. Be quiet then, his first thought. Try not to move, his second. That such silence and stillness would confront him in such a way, a way as direct and commanding as never before, surrounding and enveloping him like an overpowering invisible adversary, registered unforeseen and unimaginable shock for which he was unprepared to respond. This was new. This was nothingness. To be certainly alone, yet feel an indisputable interloper, made him question his own thoughts and interpretations of the present, as he suddenly did his mayoral best to fight the urge to cry.

As the discomfort of the moment ebbed, he retreated into his box of index cards. He removed one card and read softly aloud:

> I have been driven many times upon my knees by the overwhelming conviction that I had nowhere else to go. My wisdom and that of all about me is insufficient to meet the demands of the day.
>
> Abraham Lincoln
> after the Second Battle of Bull Run
> 4 Stars

He bowed his head in resignation and could only hope Jenkins would find him.

# Chapter 23

"The National Park Service, you say."

Dr. Black Elk listened in a polite way as Jenkins recounted the steps that had brought him to Black Elk's doorstep. He offered a curious, uneven smile when Jenkins told him of Mayor Peabody's plan for inclusion on Mt. Rushmore, yet smiled in a genuinely affable manner when Jenkins told him of the encounter with the train conductor. He even offered a disapproving look when Jenkins came to the part where he was beaned with a pebble in the middle of his forehead, and, in fact, attempted to interject a humorous moment by suggesting the pebbles the boys were throwing could have been remnants of the carving of Mt. Rushmore itself, tiny broken bits of history hurtling toward him like a meteor shower.

"Yes," Jenkins said. "Do you know where it is? Is it far?"

"I most certainly do," Dr. Black Elk said. The scrunched eyes and the shifting grin indicated he thought the question elementary. "Washington, D.C."

"No, not that office. Is there a local office? Is it within walking distance?"

"Today, it is most certainly not. Today is Columbus Day. All government offices closed in observation. It is, however, a Monday for me. The second this month, no less."

"Of course, Columbus Day," Jenkins said, exasperated.

"I should have known. How could I have not known?" He closed his eyes and put his hand to his forehead. He cringed a little as his fingers brushed over his new lump. Still, it was his best thinking man's pose.

"But to be precise, walking distance is a relative term . . ."

"How could I have forgotten Columbus Day?"

"Even according to the National Park Service, which oversees the National Trails System . . ."

"Every school kid knows Columbus Day . . ."

"Then there's the National Historic Trails . . ."

"In fourteen hundred and ninety-two, Columbus sailed the ocean blue . . ."

In an instant, Dr. Black Elk replied,

*"'In eighteen hundred and thirty-one,*
*the Choctaw march had just begun.'*

Or,

*'A thousand miles in thirty-eight,*
*step after step, the Cherokee fate.'"*

Dr. Black Elk smiled. "Never caught on with the schoolchildren. Probably too much dust and death. Too many tears. 'Columbus sailed the ocean blue' is far more cheerful, sunny, even."

Jenkins took his hand away from his forehead. "Are we talking about the same thing?" His curious look lingered, followed by half a pregnant pause.

"Columbus Day and nursery rhymes and paths taken a long time ago," Dr. Black Elk replied with a shrug. "And of schoolchildren, all I can say for sure is that their teeth will eventually fall out, just like my nephews'. They're good boys.

The wisdom teeth come much later on their own, after the skinned knees and the broken toys."

\* \* \* \* \*

Jenkins acknowledged the doctor with an agreeable nod and decided it was time to move on. With the government offices closed, the balance of his day was suddenly wide open, an unusual luxury that actually made him feel a bit directionless. It would be several more hours until he had to catch the train back to town, and he thought it best to spend it in no particular way, perhaps as a temporary vagabond in search of rare adventure (nothing too crazy). "I really should be leaving," Jenkins said. "Much to do."

"I know," the doctor replied. "There is no time like the present. Wait right here." Dr. Black Elk turned and went to the sofa and retrieved the blanket that had been folded in quarters and used as a pillow. He opened the large blanket to reveal its design, a single, eight-pointed star made of bright red and blue diamond-sized patches on a white background, a soaring eagle stitched into each corner. He stepped toward Jenkins and, with a flick of his wrists, twirled and flung the blanket into the air. It snapped and made a whooshing sound and landed perfectly atop Jenkins, the diamond point of a star fitting snugly beneath his chin.

Jenkins was stunned for a moment and didn't know what to say. He wiggled his feet instead. "That's quite a blanket," he said seconds later.

"It's a quilt," Dr. Black Elk replied.

"Yes, of course. That's quite a quilt, I meant to say. And a very colorful pattern."

"It is the morning star and was hand sewn by my sister. She's a good woman. She has great Star Knowledge and has sewn many quilts for birthdays and weddings and funerals. For quests, too. You see, as a young girl, she had seen the morning star rise into the sky and thought there could be nothing more beautiful on the face of the Earth. She would climb into the hills, to the highest spot, and watch that star all day, until it faded by the light of the sun. She never tired of the beauty. She never tired of climbing the hills. She never forgot the love she felt for the morning star, so far away. She never forgot. Then, one day, many years later, she married. She's a good woman. And it is my gift to you."

Jenkins felt a twinge of awkwardness come on. He felt that he had done nothing of note to warrant such a gift. He started to get up from the chair, careful to fold the quilt as neatly as before. "This is quite kind, but really not necessary. I couldn't accept such a gift, and from your own sister. I've done nothing but sit in your chair and recount my day. It is I who should be compensating you for your services."

"Nonsense. You've come a long way. You've shared your quest. I'd say that no one who shall sit in my chair today will have come farther. And you have farther to go, still. Steps to take. Nights to sleep. You will sleep under the quilt, and when you wake, the morning star will always be above you, its beauty and light a beacon in front of you, until you can grab it by the hand and feel it in your heart. I know about these things. Under your arm, it goes."

Jenkins reluctantly, but graciously accepted. "And my forehead . . ."

"It is a lump. It will fade."

"So there is no further treatment required? No bandages or ice packs? Have you any suggestions or advice for me as I make my way?"

Dr. Black Elk nodded slowly. "Yes, yes, I do. There are many small boys in town, good boys, boys full of promise with big ears and boundless imaginations for which nothing is impossible. If I were you, I would not buy a stovepipe hat."

# Chapter 24

Hizzoner debated with himself over when to wake the sleeping Jenkins, the whispers of "Capital effort" still lingering in the morning air like a dewy mist. He just conceded, after little personal debate, that his trip down memory lane was a bit of maudlin melodrama, yet a trip inspired to be taken by Lester's speech nonetheless—there was sure to be bravery and passion somewhere if he just looked hard enough for it. Not finding a particularly brave moment amid financial indiscretions, the desertions of his elected duties and his son —as well as the aspersions cast upon his faithful aide —he was positive the moment he was searching for must lie in his passions.

He recalled with a wry smile his assistant, Deb, a girl of twenty at the time, full of come-hither looks and a zesty bon vivants, and never too far from a stick of chewing gum, either. He surmised she was obviously drawn to him and his statesmanlike presence, but she was no match for his savoir faire, something she constantly attempted to conceal by pretending not to notice him whenever he walked by. Not even last summer, when he ordered a new personal accoutrement via mail order, 'The Commodore' (made from real human hair so the water won't bead off your head like a duck. Limited Warranty: for special occasions and wooing), and attempted to lose fifteen pounds, was her attitude toward him altered in the smallest way. He thought aloud, "Such is the curse of powerful men: We are unobtainable." Day after day, she answered the phone and combed her stunning red hair, went to lunch as long as she pleased, and made note after note in a small black book that she didn't think he saw. Pity the poor girl, her loss, her unimaginable loss, he thought.

Hizzoner could therefore reach the only logical, and, in retrospect, obvious conclusion, that the moments he searched for must be in front of him, imminent even.

"Jenkins! Jenkins! Time to wake up! A new day is before us!"

The mayor stood over Jenkins, the brilliant red-and-blue diamond patches that made up the morning star softly rippling as his aide stirred beneath the quilt.

\* \* \* \* \*

"Jenkins!"

A groggy Jenkins rolled to his side and opened one eye. "Yes, sir," he said in a sleepy voice. "Is it morning?"

"That it is, Jenkins! That it is! A new morning!"

The mayor's enthusiasm took Jenkins aback. "Is everything okay, sir? Has something happened? I mean . . . I mean, you seem . . . effused."

"Well, nothing as trite as being visited by three ghosts during the night, but you could say that I've been struck by a certain inspiration, yes."

"Will I be writing another letter, sir? I think I could probably find some paper in one of the other aldermen's offices, perhaps even an envelope. I'm afraid we're going to be on our own for the postage, though."

Jenkins got up off the floor and eased quickly into a morning stretch, back arched and arms reaching high over his head. He carefully folded his quilt and stowed it in its usual place, beneath a large map thumb tacked to the wall outlining the voyages of Magellan and inside a large vintage alligator suitcase that had been left behind by the previous occupant.

"Jenkins, I've been thinking. We've been here for ten years now. And while I prefer to think of our time spent together as ten consecutive sabbaticals for our diligent labors, in all that time, I don't believe I've ever formally given you your due for your efforts."

"Really, not necessary, sir."

"Now, now, Jenkins. Recognition is an important part of politics. Your efforts in Rapid City alone would have been enough for a meritorious citation. Why, your ability to convince the National Park Service people of the worthiness of our project will be legend! You must have had them eating out of your hand! And their fondness for you is obvious, to send you back home with their ceremonial Soaring Eagle Quilt of Agreement. If not for that damn sculptors' union refusing to play ball . . . Delays, delays, delays . . . Damn them!"

"Yes, sir. Damn them."

"Jenkins, had I a medal, I would pin it on you. I don't know why I didn't think of it before. It's not that I'm inconsiderate, you understand —I just wasn't thinking of you."

"Please, sir."

"No, no, Jenkins. I'm a brilliant enough man to know when I'm right. Your undying passions for government service are a badge you wear like a scarlet letter. They are for all to see. Your ability to assist me has been second to none, as well. I can't imagine having had anyone else run my errands or don my Lincoln suit. Your surreptitious trips in that suit to O'Connell's on reconnaissance missions are prima facie evidence of your bravery. Why, I've even caught you gazing wide-eyed out the window at our old office in the Chamber of Commerce, as if yearning passionately to be back where the action is."

"Yes, sir, yearning passionately."

"You're a good man, Jenkins. You're a good man to have at my side."

"Please, sir. I am only doing my job."

"Yes, I understand. And one day, you shall receive a just reward for your loyalty." The mayor's voice had begun to trail off; his attention had been divided. "It's a fine quality to have, Jenkins. A fine quality," he added softly.

"Thank you, sir. You are quite kind."

Hizzoner stood in front of the large map featuring the voyages of Magellan. He offered several casual glances at the map during his conversation with Jenkins, none more than a few seconds, really, but he now seemed completely engrossed with the journey's origin. He slowly traced the dotted line of Magellan's route with his finger, from Spain across the Atlantic and rounding Cape Horn into the Pacific Ocean.

Jenkins watched the mayor's very deliberate actions. There was no way he could quite know what to make of them. In the previous ten years, he referenced the map only in passing, occasionally remarking, 'Seems a bit of a bother to end a trip in the exact same place you started from.'

"Jenkins?"

"Yes, sir?"

Hizzoner was still focused on the dotted line. "Do you believe a journey of his type requires a brave captain? This circumnavigation?"

"Oh, yes, sir. Magellan's journey is quite well documented and shows numerous acts of bravery."

"And halfway through his voyage, do you believe that in his heart, he knew he would be successful, despite any misfortune or delay he may have encountered? That he knew he had to press on? That somehow, he knew he would return and triumphantly regale his well-wishers with passionate tales of the sea?"

"His commitment cannot be challenged. He was quite a brave man, sir."

The mayor turned from the map and focused on Jenkins. He seemed full of new energy. "Jenkins," he started, "it has suddenly become clear to me that we've made some mistakes, miscalculations, really. And these small errors in collective judgment these past ten years have slowed our ability to move forward."

"We have, sir?"

"Now, now, don't be too hard on yourself. I won't have it. Most likely these errors, and I shall not recount or attempt to recall them here, could not have been avoided. We have erred while daring greatly. We are members of a mighty club. Besides, I believe this will explain everything."

The mayor reached into his box of index cards and pulled a card from the 'W' section. He handed the card to Jenkins and he read aloud:

A man's intentions should be allowed in some respects to plead for his actions.

George Washington
letter to the Speaker of the House of Burgesses
December 1756    4 Stars

"I don't know how I could have said it any better than George Washington, the father of our country, a veteran of both Valley Forge and the crossing of the Delaware. Very photogenic man. He had wooden teeth, you know." The mayor stood at attention, his best posture. "Jenkins, time to press on. We have a journey to complete."

"A journey, sir?"

"The Chamber of Commerce awaits our triumphant return!" The mayor struck his most prominent pose: head back, chin out, one hand to a hip, the other raised high.

"Will we be leaving today, sir?" There was hopeful, yet cautious, expectance in Jenkins' voice.

"First things first, Jenkins. I noticed that we never received yesterday's delivery from Grossman's. Very unlike Grossman. The man is, after all, ex-military and a stickler for precision. Also, a fine patriot. It seems completely out of bounds that a man like that would forget my sandwich—yours, too. Best to investigate. I'd try O'Connell's."

'The Lincoln suit and beard again, sir?"

"I'm afraid we have no other choice. Run down to that janitor's closet and get some more of that pasty white stuff to smear all over your face. We can't take the chance of you being recognized until our triumphant return plans are complete."

"The sodium bicarbonate, sir? I think that's for putting out electrical fires."

"If that's what it was, yes. It seemed to obscure your identity quite well that last time."

"But, sir . . ." Jenkins fumbled for words, as if he could not think of an alternative in a timely fashion. "You know that I'm not one to complain, but the dust, sir. It gets in my eyes to the point where I can barely keep them open. And since you've suggested in the past —wisely so, I may add —that I not wear my glasses in town for further fear of being recognized, I'm afraid I wouldn't be able to see a hand before my face. Why, that last time I went to O'Connell's, as I left, I collided so fiercely into a man with a strange accent, he seemed to set off some sort of small explosive device. I am certain you understand —I wouldn't want to jeopardize the plan, sir."

"Poppycock, Jenkins. The stars are all aligning for us now. The bravery of Magellan has shown me the way. It is circumnavigation! To end where you have begun!" The mayor pointed to the map and the dotted line. "I am certain of it. I shall assume that, since we are ten years into our voyage, that we are more than halfway. I'd suspect that we are almost home. Enough time has passed."

"Are you referring to the statute of limitations, sir?"

"I am referring to the length of time required for an accomplishment of monumental scope: Rome, The Pyramids, Mt. Rushmore, circumnavigation. Acts of greatness, Jenkins."

"Can you really circumnavigate half a town block?"

"Not the point, Jenkins. You are missing it entirely."

"Yes, sir. I'll get the suit."

"You see, Jenkins, what great explorers like Vasco de Magellan . . ."

"Ferdinand," Jenkins interrupted. "It is Ferdinand Magellan."

"What great explorers like Ferdinand Magellan and I have in common is our unrelenting belief in our place in history. We were certain of our success before we achieved it—it propels us as gasoline. Very common among titans. Such success is to be found at the junction of the latitude of our bravery and the longitude of our passion. A child could find it if shown the way, Jenkins. Ours, of course, is most clearly evident in the successes we have achieved—or, in my case, about to achieve. Such greatness is timeless and not without considerable effort and hardships, however. He and I see eye to eye on this and I am supremely impressed with his genius! Such elegance in its simplicity—To go and to come back! We are as two peas in a pod."

"Sir, about Magellan's voyage . . ."

"It is now crystal clear. We shall arrange for some sort of small victory allowing us spoils of some kind. After all, conquering heroes are much better received if they don't come back empty handed. Naturally we will thank Lester for his efforts upon our return—I'm quite sure any financial unpleasantness would have seen the sunset ages ago; we'll jot down several bullet points from our adventures to entertain the masses —amusing anecdotes and such—I am sure there must be dozens, though they escape me now; we'll accept all accolades from well-wishers and registered voters; you shine my shoes and I'll cut your hair; and, finally, I shall enter the Chamber with the pomp and circumstance of a regal and victorious Magellan, fully prepared and reinvigorated to continue on as if we never left. The circle shall be complete. I will have circumnavigated!"

Jenkins attempted to interrupt the mayor before the revelation of his plan became too elaborate. He didn't have the heart now to tell him that Magellan never lived to see his journey completed. He couldn't bring it upon himself to offer that Magellan was impaled by spears as he attempted to wade ashore in the Philippines, his body hacked at mercilessly with knives and scimitars by the natives, his shredded lifeless body left in the shallow waters as his crew abandoned his side and retreated to the safety of their ship, defeated.

"Yes, sir. Good plan," Jenkins said.

"Very well, then. But first let's have some brunch. Off you go."

Jenkins begrudgingly put on the Lincoln suit and headed down the stairs in search of brunch. He, too, felt the missing sandwich delivery from Grossman a bit of a puzzle. Grossman had been quite reliable, having never missed a late night delivery in all the time they had spent in exile.

Jenkins recalled that first night he returned from Rapid City and joined the mayor in the Hall, the lateness of the hour, and the growing hunger he and the mayor felt. He recalled how pleased the mayor was to see him, the sense of relief, and the way he cavalierly discharged his aide with the task of procuring a late night snack, something tasteful and light, yet filling.

Jenkins recalled with amusement a thorough vetting of his only two culinary options: Grossman's and O'Connell's. He recalled how clever he felt when he remembered the stories Grossman would tell anyone within earshot of his days in the merchant marines, the swells and the storms, the barges toted and the bales lifted, the sea swagger, the discipline of a tightly run ship, the potatoes peeled, the briny sea air. And more clever still, of the note he slipped under Grossman's front door that night, which read:

ATTN: GALLEYMAN GROSSMAN

SOS   SOS   SOS   SOS   SOS   SOS

Mates in trouble. Chow needed. Until further notice, deliver nightly to Hall of Records. Midnight. Ring buzzer three times and go away. No questions.

THE COMMODORE

He hoped Grossman had not lost the faith.

# Chapter 25

"The carnage waged, roared on, and I pulled the lovely Mrs. MacNamara to the side, set her upon a nearby park bench for maximum safety, and thrust myself, a human shield, betwixt her and the melee, at no time giving any consideration to me own meager well-being, amid the thrashing and the screaming, dodging blows and praying the rosary that all malevolent spirits pass us by." Clancy took a breath. "Lads, I am spent."

"Clancy, we saw you," said the disbeliever. "You were feeding the pigeons."

The O'Connell regulars convened. It was high noon, the previous evening's events, the truths and the fictions, being openly debated by all. O'C moderated with his gold-toothed smile while he poured drinks and pondered the daily special, Mort buzzed, Nick and Stella pretended not to notice each other, Bobby R. relived each blow in slow motion, Deb listened, and a man in a sharkskin grey suit sat alone at a table, eating a sandwich.

"Aye, lad, the pigeons. Mother Nature's early warning system. An urban warrior's best friend. You'll notice they scattered at the first sign of trouble."

"Urban warrior's best friend, my foot."

"Aye, lad, an ancient and noble bird." Clancy looked the disbeliever in the eye; he put his hand on his shoulder. "I would not be drawing breath upon this Earth, nor in the company of such stalwart men such as yourselves, were it not for the sacrifices an' nobility of the teal-necked, feral squab."

The disbeliever shook his head. "Please stop. Are you trying to tell me that a pigeon saved your life?"

"My presence and my gratitude are surely proof enough."

"No, they're not. That's not proof. Proof is something that can be verified."

"Tell him, Clance," Mort said, a soft buzz trailing his words.

"Come on, tell him!" urged the others.

Clancy took the last slow sip from his beer as he leaned against the bar, and he knew all eyes were upon him, waiting for his next move. He smacked his lips and set the empty mug on the bar in front of O'C. He motioned for another. "Lads, you've left me no choice."

Mort pulled a stool away from the bar for Clancy and positioned him where all could see and hear plainly and without interference, even Nick and Stella who were trying to act nonchalant, and Deb who was trying to catch the attention of Bobby R. with a look and an occasional wink.

"Where to begin?" Clancy began.

"Some facts would be nice," said the disbeliever.

Clancy obliged with a nod and a clap of his hands. "Then it is facts you shall have. Names, dates, places of historical record shall not be omitted for brevity. It shall, however, require a wee bit longer recollection on my part. Pardon the tardiness of me effort as I close my eyes and allow the recollection time for the journey it must take from the caverns of my mind to the tip of my tongue."

"Sounds like pure crapola to me."

Clancy tilted his head slightly back and, with both lids firmly closed, rolled his eyes in small circles as his head wobbled back and forth, first clockwise and then counterclockwise. He would stop for a second, as if about to speak, only to resume the hypnotic and circular movements after a long, deep breath and silent exhale. Several patient moments later, and before the dizziness came upon him, he stopped, opened his eyes, and spoke in that eerie tone he preferred for drama. "'Twas the Siege of Limerick, lads, summer, and the year was 1651. The ancestral MacNamaras gathered, proud Catholics, fishermen, and lovers of life all, in the Limerick city square, which was not unlike our very own, having a Sunday picnic, no doubt, the laughter of small children and the cooing of the squab among the most pleasant sounds of the day. Historical point: Limerick of the day was surrounded on three sides by the river Abbey, by the river Shannon on the fourth; the Protestants cluttered about on the other side of the river Abbey, led by Oliver Cromwell himself, no less, doing God only knows what, but likely planning an advance as Protestants of that time were wont to do. And sure as I'm sitting here, this is the truth, lads— history knows no fiction. Now the river Abbey is a mighty body of water, 400 feet across, with a current so strong that any man who might think to swim across during cover of darkness for his nefarious purposes would be swept away without a trace, down into the river Shannon and then out to sea, his immortal soul lost forever, his eternal companions the wild salmon and the sea trout, his ghost unable to haunt a single mortal man, such is the magnificent power of this current."

"It's a magnificent power of something," said the disbeliever.

Clancy didn't slow. "'Twas a single bridge for the Protestants to cross into Limerick. 'Twas a single bridge to bear the foot traffic of Cromwell's army of 10,000 men strong, a single bridge of hand-hewn stone expertly laid across a dozen Roman arches for support. And when the first insurgent step trod upon that bridge, no sooner did that bevy of feral squab set wings to flutter in unison, they cooed a trumpeting sound as one, and the ancestral MacNamara men heeded the call, putting stout aside in a dash, ushering the women and children to the safety of their beds and their homes, and alerting all others that the time for defense was upon them. The siege was on."

The disbeliever paused, waiting for more. "That's it? That's the proof? That doesn't prove anything. You made that whole thing up."

"Verification is no further away than any competent 17th century Irish history text. Most probably in the footnotes."

"You weren't even there."

"Aye, lad. I am a direct descendant of Hayes MacNamara, survivor."

"That's preposterous."

"'Tisn't. Slaughter victims make poor patriarchs."

# Chapter 26

The disbeliever moved to the end of the bar at O'Connell's and sat by himself. He needed some alone time after listening to Clancy carry on and on about pigeons. He rested his elbows on the bar and put his head in his hands and attempted to lower his blood pressure through a breathing technique he had learned as a boy at summer camp: a big, deep inhale followed by a long slow exhale, repeat. Out with the bad thoughts, in with the good, was the simple explanation offered him at the time. It also helped the accompanying headaches go away.

He recognized that this technique was a bit of a production, but the alternative was completely unpalatable to him: to allow himself to be drawn in freely to the world of the gullible and the clueless. To offer no resistance to the inane drivel, the exorbitant claims, the irrational leaps of logic that he encountered daily seemed a clear violation of dispositive thinking. He would have none of it. His most infuriating reactions, however, were reserved for the comments that he considered to be at the pinnacle of implausibility, the Mt. Everest of the incredulous: the preposterous. For these, he had no patience; and for Clancy, he knew, he had none but the preposterous to offer.

As the disbeliever shook his head in his hands, he realized these actions were beginning to seem all too frequent and too familiar. It was getting old. He knew there was but one final conclusion to reach, a conclusion to salvage what remained of his once-princely argumentative skills, the last brittle bastions against a raging tide of lunacy: He would once and for all cut the cord to the outlandish and abandon all interactions with Clancy. The last straw had simply been broken. This episode would mark the end of the confrontations, the end of the rebuttals, the last debate. No longer would he feel the need to police the incongruent thoughts or the unsubstantiated claims— he would just let them go. The end of the line had unmistakably been reached. Never again. El fin. Finis. Finito. Admittedly, it was his personal Waterloo, but so be it. It was over. He had lost.

\* \* \* \* \*

Clancy stood at the other end of the bar amid a group of O'Connell regulars. The topic turned to Gloobniecht and whether the violent assault upon her likeness at the celebration had once and for all put an end to the rumors of her return.

The panic-stricken man's high-pitched voice carried with it a flailing sense of urgency directed at no one in particular and in no specific direction as he shot off, "She was coming right at me! She was screaming and yelling and swinging her ax! The air was full of death!"

"Now, now," said the man in the derby claiming to be the voice of reason, "for the record, there were no official ax murders at last evening's celebration. Some chairs were tipped over and, I believe, some balloons were popped. I may add, no ax was found."

"It was nearly a catastrophe," the panic-stricken man added in a calmer voice.

"Noted," said the man in the derby.

Others joined in.

"What I'd like to know is if she's coming back. I still can't spell and I think my knuckles have arthritis from all the wackings I took years ago in grade school. To this day, I can't use a yardstick without flashbacks."

"I'd say we taught her a lesson."

"Who invited her, anyway?"

"Who saw where she went?"

"First she's here; then she's not."

"It's witchcraft. Black magic, I say. Scared the clothes right off some poor sap. He was running around in his underwear."

"Did she leave any footprints? If there were no footprints, it proves she's a ghost!" The group then mumbled something about spooky sounds being heard in last evening's darkness. Some offered half-hearted imitations.

"I picked this up off the ground," offered a man holding up the scarf with the frilly edges and miniature replicas of the Eiffel Tower. "Maybe she went to Paris."

"Who said that?" Deb remarked in a condescending way. She had not been watching who was speaking. She scanned the group. "That is idiotic. That is positively idiotic."

Mort was standing tall next to Clancy, his denim ensemble playing off Clancy's boyish red hair in a complementary way. "What do you think, Clancy? Do you think she'll come back? Bzzz," he asked.

"Spirits live in the ether, lad. 'Tis a misbegotten place. Let us bow our heads."

Several adjacent heads bowed obediently and there was complete silence for almost four full seconds. As Clancy bowed his head, he noticed the emptiness of his beer mug and motioned O'C for another. He came quickly and drew a dark refill.

"What should I do with the scarf?" the man then asked, his head unbowed. He put the scarf on his head, the frilly edges dangling in front of his eyes. He bobbled his head from side to side and tried to make the fringe shake back and forth.

"Give me that," Deb said indignantly, as she snatched it from atop his head. She stuffed the scarf in her pocket. "Moron."

Clancy took a gulp of his beer and smacked his lips in a most refreshing way. It was clear to him that while Mort asked the question about Gloobniecht, the eyes and ears of all—all but one—were upon him. Another sip and a swallow later and he graciously offered, "Now, mind you, I've limited experience with American spirits, and how they may flit about. But in Ireland, aaah, in Ireland, lads, they are as welcome in the night as the darkness, and harder to grasp than the wind."

"Like neon!" Mort emitted.

"Aye, lad, only none as brave as you to tame them."

"Aw, Clance."

"Best we not jump ahead of ourselves, lads. 'Tis a time for logic."

"How so?"

"The Irish land is a mystical and ancient land, for sure, lads. From Malin Head to Mizen Head, she was sculpted by great ice and, in the wake of the Great Master, left such trinkets as the Wicklow Mountains and Macgillicuddy's Reeks to remember him by, each t'ousands of feet high, their noble peaks reaching fingers to God 'imself—the inspiration for Michaelangelo when he dabbled with paint so many years later, no less. 'Tis true. And these grand peaks, these mountains majesty, these that have risen from the lowlands and the bedrock and have ascended towards the heavens are home to some of these same spirits, just as the raised bogs of the Shannon Basin and the Belfast Loughs are home to others, the castles and the abbeys and the cliffs and the caves in the limestone home to others still —for each has a place and a home and a haunt and a purpose which we know not, yet belongs to them and to which they are devoted like no other. To decipher your American spirit now, we must examine where it dwells and what it dwells upon and what it is and what it is not."

"How do we do that?"

Clancy took the time to notice the disbeliever at the other end of the bar. It was only an instant of a glance, a blink, the brevity of a fraction of a second, so brief as to be almost immeasurable—yet he noticed the disbeliever had not raised his head or in any way turned his attention to the discussion. Clancy raised his voice slightly. "By elimination, lads! One by one, we shall recall the ancient logic; we shall apply the elements of the known and indisputable features of each class of spirit to our present encounter! May the Good Lord bless and pray for us, keep the d'vil at bay with our purity— for then we will know . . . I believe we shall start with the woodland creatures, eliminate the lot, as our encounter took place mid-town. And among them, I'd count off the sprites and the gnomes, the fairies and the leprechauns—pixies, too. Troublesome imps all, yet a wee bit of an embarrassment in the height department—their diminutive size more suited for the nooks and crannies of hollowed out logs and the dry stone walls of the countryside. Not a city-dweller among them. Just as well, though. I've always thought them a bit cowardly—they like to frighten the sheep, don't you know."

The man in the derby took a pencil from his pocket and took notes on a cocktail napkin. "Sprites, gnomes, fairies, leprechauns, pixies—out. They frighten sheep," he repeated as he wrote.

Clancy continued, "'Tis a city-dweller we seek, the likes of mischieviousness that enjoys four walls and a sturdy roof, a parlor room prankster who would just as soon spill a cup of sugar or snip a lock of your hair as you sleep . . . a hob-goblin, perhaps."

"They could swing an ax!" the panic-stricken man let out.

The group looked to Clancy for confirmation of ax-carrying ability. They awaited an indifferent shrug or an approving nod of a head.

"Now that you mention it," Clancy continued, "not a bit of a one has been known to carry tools of any kind at any time. On this, I'm most certain. You see, a man's tools are known for hard work—and they fear the contagion."

"Hob goblins—out," the man in the derby repeated as he wrote.

"They are also quite hairy," Clancy added in between gulps.

"Hairy, too," the man in the derby also repeated as he wrote.

Clancy took another quick look in the direction of the disbeliever. He still had not moved. He sat on that stool and stared straight ahead just as if he had been carved in that exact spot, not a flicker or a twitch. Clancy felt the need to raise his voice yet again. "Now a banshee, lads . . . From beyond, you can hear them!" For a moment, Clancy covered his ears and grimaced, a face-contorting scrunch. "Oh, the wails and the cries! I can almost hear them now! The screech and the shiver!" Clancy paused, posed and frozen, and waited for a group response that was not to come. He finally pulled a handkerchief from his back pocket and wiped his brow. He took a full deep breath and continued on. "Not as melodious as their sisters, the sirens of the sea, themselves calling out to voyagers and young seamen full of eager, lustful hearts. No, not at all. Aye, now, now, and I know what you think, that the sweet siren song that has been luring unsuspecting lads to crash their hopes upon the reefs and the rocks, turning mighty-masted ships into splinters since brave men put to sea is of no concern of ours—and fair to say, some had it coming— and you wouldn't be more right if you gaffed each drowning one from the Irish Sea and whistled along to the tune of 'A Drunken Sailor.' . . . But the banshee, lads, a creature of the night who announces her presence. Not a bashful one, she, and the bringer of the final darkness, too. Not a sweet siren sound there, no. To see her once, for a noble ear to suffer her wicked way, is to book your passage to the next world, all the while a look of horror struck upon your poor misfortunate face."

"She could swing an ax!" cried out the panic-stricken man. "Aye, lad, that she could! Twice or thrice or maybe more!"

"Then she could scream, 'Face Horror! Face Horror!' as she ran," the panic-stricken man added. His enthusiasm was mounting and evident to all, as he stood on his tiptoes and offered a tiny hop.

Clancy put his hand on the panic-stricken man's shoulder. It had a somewhat soothing effect on the man as the calm returned to him in an instant, leaving him flat-footed. "No, lad," Clancy said. "The banshee is a wailing harlot, her own mind too scrambled with the mischief of evil thoughts to take the time to fire warning shots of prose across the bow. I'd say the banshee is out."

"Banshee—out," repeated the man in the derby as he wrote.

A bewildered panic-stricken man fussed for a moment, then asked, "What, then?"

"Can be none other than the Favorite Son," Clancy said, an air of supreme conviction about him.

"Can the favorite son be a woman?" the panic-stricken man asked the man in the derby.

He was obviously confused. The man in the derby shrugged.

"'Tis a figure of speech," Clancy said. "An American favorite son, perhaps one of your own town come back to bask in the adoration and the tasks they knew well in life. In Ireland, though, and this I know to be true, the sainted favorite son would not be seen by so many as two at once (it cheapens the visit and mutes the effect), and his grand, triumphant return would be as gallant as a coronation, his otherworldliness borne upon the back of a white horse, a ballad in his heart, a noble lance at his side, the unforgettable visions of the haunted one left to become more than memory, and to not erode with the passing of time. 'Tis a tale to tell to virgin ears for generations to come."

"Okay," said the panic-stricken man. He pretended to understand.

Bobby R. was standing among the group and listened to Clancy with a champion's intensity, his boxing gloves bouncing off his chest as he bobbed and weaved with Clancy's every inflection. Clancy squared up to lock eyes with him and offered a pleasant smile and a quick wink. Clancy lowered his voice. "Lad, I admire your convictions. 'Twas no summer wedding full of tin whistles and Ceili bands I saw you dancing at last eve. And let no man say you don't step lively or that you gave an effort with half a heart, for these eyes know better. With fists flying like John L. Sullivan, you delivered a message of rightful defense without a single spoken word, yet was understood by all who felt the mighty blows—humbly, I can only say that the act of an honorable man stands out like an elephant in a tulip field. Admirable, son. 'Tis a pity there wasn't a more delightful reunion."

Bobby R. nodded a thank you.

"'Tis only one other possibility," Clancy proclaimed loudly to the group. "The lack of bagpipe music, the scruffy clothes, the laborers tool and the reckless, misguided way in which she trod upon our square uninvited . . . 'Twas probably a Scot — lost and too cheap to pay the piper or rent a proper horse."

At that moment, a man charged into the group surrounding Clancy. It was the disbeliever; he bolted off his stool and pushed others aside until he stood face-to-face with Clancy. He was beside himself in a huff, a single vein at his temple looking like the Nile River under his skin and throbbing so furiously and with such precise regularity that, had it made a sound, it could have been mistaken for a metronome keeping time for *The Flight of the Bumblebee.* He cried out, "A ghost too cheap to rent a horse? THAT'S PREPOSTEROUS!"

Clancy sported a broad smile. "Not for me to decide, lad. Were you thinking burrow, perhaps?"

# Chapter 27

From behind the bar, O'Connell watched as the disbeliever vaulted off his stool and headed for Clancy like he was magnetized. O'C flashed his gold-toothed smile in a familiar way and waited eagerly for the fireworks to start. It was his experience with human nature, however, that made the moment most enjoyable, most anticipatory, and that showed him time and again he had no reason to fear a confrontation between the two, no reason to suspect the episode would evolve into any kind of violent or disruptive force; in fact, on most days, he looked forward to it. To him, a little screaming, a little shouting, a little poke in a badger hole, a little bit of a something for people to watch was all in a day's work. After all, action is action. And action is good business.

"Stella!" O'Connell called out. "The Lunker Poster! Quick!"

Stella was at the other end of the bar, writing the daily specials on the menus. She immediately stopped what she was doing to retrieve the poster from O'Connell's office. The Lunker Lotto had been invented by O'Connell last year as a way to diversify his clientele's sporting blood, as well as extend an olive branch to a competitor and fellow innkeeper, the Lincoln Log Lodge. The cost was low (a cut of the day's receipts for canoe and fishing pole rental), and the benefit of an out-of-town friend was not to be underestimated. Even Vegas laid off-bets, he reasoned. All that was required was for O'Connell to recognize the precise moment at which to call the event, a completely unscientific judgment as to receptiveness of presumed participants and an unerring belief that their speculative spirits had been roused. A delicious cocktail of complimentary characters didn't hurt, either.

Stella came out of the office and handed O'C the poster. It had to be three feet high.

"Here you go," she said.

O'Connell took the poster and plotted a path to the saloon wall that best bisected Clancy's group. He whistled his way through the men like the Pied Piper and thumb tacked the poster to the wall. He added 'July 9th' with magic marker.

# O'Connell's 2nd Annual
# $50,000

## LUNKER LOTTO LUCK O'THE DRAW TOURNEY
## LAKE LULU
## WHEN: TOMORROW JULY 9th
## TIME: HIGH NOON    FREE ENTRY

(No Fish last Year? 2nd Chances Always Free At O'Connell's)

RULES:
1) Partners to be drawn at lakeside
2) 2 to a canoe
3) Each man to be given a numbered tag
4) Match your tag number to the specially tagged Blue Walleye and win $50,000!

DIRECTIONS:
1) Take TBNL north out of Town
2) When you come to the "T" (hwy LL), go the direction Horace Greeley would go
3) Stop when you see the sky blue water, flotilla of canoes, Lincoln Log Lodge

Mort started the crowd off with a buzz, and the topic of the moment switched with colossal ease from anything supernatural to who among them possessed the most fishing prowess, the largest pole, and what the victor would do with the winnings. There was no shortage of confidence in evidence. There was also no pair of ears that had not tuned in to the action, including the reddened ears of a short blond man in a scratchy beard and white, dusty face. He crouched beneath a wooden pub table in an attempt at being invisible and inconspicuous, his squinting eyes almost closed shut, and, as if in some Darwinian overcompensation, his wide open ears supremely attuned to every whisper and to every hushed syllable and spoken secret around him.

Stella watched patiently and waited for O'C to return to his spot behind the bar. "What would you do if someone caught that fish?" she said.

O'Connell returned a devilish grin. "I'd immediately have him flogged for being a brazen cheater and a charlatan. That fish has been extinct for almost two hundred years."

"And I thought it was going to be a silly answer."

"But understand, they won't care," O'Connell shot back, a cool detachment in his voice. "Look at them, full of spirit and opinion, full of energy and conviction."

"Full of liquor."

"The time of their lives has no discounted price tag. It requires no medal or validation."

"No, but I'd be willing to wager it requires . . ."

"Reasonably priced drinks and a pleasant locale to enjoy the camaraderie of one's brethren," O'Connell spoke up, finishing her sentence. "Granted, the map to happiness sometimes folds awkwardly, but there are seldom other requirements to follow it to its natural destination. It requires belly laughs and invective that makes your blood boil. It requires a pocketful of attitude and let the lint fall where it may, that's for sure.

Sometimes it requires you take a blind chance on your fellow man, that he'll be by your side to shoulder a burden or lighten a load, or to lend a sympathetic brotherly ear, or someone to share in that golden shining moment of victory, by the stars' early light." O'Connell paused as he noticed Stella watching Nick in the crowd; he was laughing and gesturing to the others as to the size of fish he was going to catch. "And sometimes it requires a solitary wink from a pretty girl across the room, a silent message that rings a gong deep in the heart of a young, fit man so loud to him that he'll carry the sound and the ringing and the excitement with him every step of his life, to his grave if he's lucky, and a headstone with two names carved into it. . . . What does it require? It requires we open one hour earlier tomorrow. It will be our biggest night of the year."

"Maybe I'll wear a dress."

"Maybe I should ask Mort if his All Electric Band, Stray Voltage, is available to play after the tourney. There should be dancing."

# Chapter 28

Hizzoner took another bite of his sandwich, a sloppy ketchupy sort of a thing, and watched as Jenkins wiped the bicarbonate from his face with a moist towelette, then blotted dry with his handkerchief. "Tomorrow at noon, you say?"

"Yes, sir. I thought, perhaps, the fishing tournament would be an excellent opportunity to announce the completion of your circumnavigation. The similarities with Magellan could be quite nautical: Two captains of the open seas, surrounded by their faithful, passionately leading brave men in search of mythical treasures . . . Two peas in a pod, sir."

"Hmmm." Hizzoner pondered. He licked the ketchup from the side of his sandwich and made a slurping sound as he stared out into space. He finished the last bite.

Jenkins could tell that the mayor was not completely convinced. He was about as opaque as cellophane. "You could give a speech, sir," he said. It was a thinly veiled attempt at coercion and he knew it, but he let it fly anyway.

The mayor pondered a few seconds more. "Jenkins, I like you. You've got a good head on your shoulders, and in some small way, I see your logic. However—and this, I believe, is the difference between you and I—is that you fail to see the bigger picture, the grand panoramic scope of things, the prize in the Cracker Jack. Where you would have me present myself and reveal a monumental accomplishment to a group of registered voters at a sporting contest, it is I who recognize that the attention of those precise same voters would needlessly be diverted from the true object of their desire: the sporting event itself. It's simply bad form to command that they hold two disjointed thoughts in their mind at the same time. It just isn't done. These are simple people with a simple goal in mind: to win the sporting event. It is the American way. And in America, it is champions who are revered, held in the highest esteem and immortalized with bronze busts and streets in their name. They even open supermarkets. Let's be sensible, Jenkins, no one remembers who sang 'The Star Spangled Banner' at the World Series."

"No, sir."

The mayor was quick to continue. "But that doesn't mean we shouldn't participate."

"Participate, sir?"

"By all means, Jenkins. I propose a two-part plan. Part One: All the world loves a winner. There are ticker-tape parades and golden trophies awarded by comely young women from local cosmetology colleges. Cub reporters from the local newspapers will fall all over themselves for a scoop they can shout in 72-point type and even include a photo — DEWEY DEFEATS TRUMAN. Adulation, Jenkins, that's the key; there is nothing like it in the world. It can't be coaxed or cajoled, but only given of free will—a moment to accept, a lifetime to reflect. I declare it will be the spirit of the day and to the victor go the spoils . . . A more fitting reception for a second coming, wouldn't you agree?"

Jenkins was not prepared for the mayor's comments. Words stuck in his throat, and for a split second he couldn't decide whether to speak or swallow. "Win, sir? Do I understand you mean to win? Surely circumnavigation will suffice, sir."

"Big picture, Jenkins. Big picture. What did you say first prize was?"

Jenkins could not provide an immediate response. He was too busy backtracking each word he had spoken since returning from O'Connell's in an almost archaeological effort to unearth where he went off the trolley. This could not end well, he feared. "$50,000," Jenkins said after an uncomfortable silence, a hint of defeat in his voice.

The mayor hadn't noticed the change in his aide's demeanor. "A princely sum, indeed, and one that is altogether not unfamiliar. Be that as it may, we need only look to the history books and to the bursting creels of a man who has attained the highest office of our land —Silent Cal to be specific —for angling techniques befitting a man of my stature."

"Calvin Coolidge, sir?"

"Naturally, Jenkins. You'll recall that in the days before he was to give a speech at the dedication of Mount Rushmore, he put on a bit of a trout fishing display at a local lodge. Granted, some would have called it a spectacle (the ease with which his natural talent oozed remains highly dubious, pulling in brightly colored trout one right after the other, seemingly without effort), but a fishing display nonetheless."

Jenkins nodded. As the mayor referenced Coolidge in the context of Mt. Rushmore, the memory of a National Geographic article he read aloud from many years ago resurfaced. "I recall, sir. I seem to remember that in that specific instance, it was the townspeople who trucked fish in during the night and netted off portions of a stream to ensure the president's success."

The mayor, as if conjuring up pleasant visions from his past, smiled gently. "Yes, it is a blessed thing to have supporters. Sometimes they appear like elves in the night."

Jenkins was very deliberate in his response. "I believe the likelihood of that scenario repeating itself tomorrow on Lake Lulu is highly unlikely, sir. Your presence is not anticipated."

"It was just a thought," the mayor responded quickly. "Please don't think for a moment I was suggesting . . ." The mayor stopped midsentence as if to rethink his direction. He scratched the top of his head in a nervous gesture. "Never mind," he said with a wave of his hand. He then pursed his lips and rubbed his pointy chin for several abrupt seconds as he turned from Jenkins to stare out the window and into the square, an exploration. "Do you . . . Do you know anything about fishing?"

Jenkins recognized the need for a cautious response. He didn't want to suggest in even the slightest way that he could be of assistance in landing a species of fish that hadn't seen a frying pan or the light of day since The Civil War and Reconstruction. "A bit, sir. It can be a lot like waiting around."

"And this tagged fish? Do you know of this prized fish?"

"The blue walleye, sir?"

"Yes. Are you familiar with it?"

"My understanding is that O'Connell has put a specially numbered tag on one of its fins. You must catch the fish with the tag to win the prize."

"Ah, yes." He nodded. "That would make the prize more elusive."

"Yes, sir. It is a very elusive fish, indeed. More so than most."

"Have you ever caught one?"

"No, sir, I have not."

"Are they common?"

"No, sir. I can say with a high degree of certainty they are not."

"Yes, of course," the mayor said. "That makes sense. A prize of that magnitude should require a little extra effort, maybe even some luck."

"That is the way of worthwhile prizes, is it not?"

The mayor began to pace with uneven steps, his fingers neatly interlocked behind his back, his thumbs furiously twiddling. He mumbled something about the long odds once again favoring his old associate O'Connell, and he let out a quiet and almost inaudible sigh. "Jenkins?"

"Yes, sir?"

At first, the mayor postured in an authoritative manner, as if addressing the aldermen in chambers over a particularly thorny zoning issue. He then just as quickly relaxed, his rounded shoulders evidence and wordless testimony to his change of heart. The mayor asked, using his most non-official voice, "In your honest opinion, what do you think are my chances of being the one to catch the big prize?"

Jenkins noticed a look on the mayor's face that he had not seen before. It was one that suggested in a compassionate way that he did not want the honest answer, but the answer that best fit the grandiose scenario in his head of a victory, an adoring and welcoming crowd, the warming sun of an early July day, and the opportunity for oratory —a stirring and potent speech given to rapt constituents. He didn't want to hear odds. He didn't want to think that there was a chance that he was the long shot. "Sir, I can say with all honesty, and in the most egalitarian of ways, that your chances rival those of all others."

"Thank you, Jenkins. That was kind."

"Sir?"

"Yes?"

"Part Two? You said you had a two-part plan."

"Yes, that I did. You are quite right." The mayor fumbled for the right words. "I'm afraid now that I'll have to admit that Part Two was contingent upon the success of Part One. I may have put the proverbial cart before the horse."

"I see."

"Somehow, I got all turned around."

"Back on track tomorrow, sir."

"Right, yes. The circumnavigation will be just the thing. Everything will be back to normal tomorrow. We'll get up early to prepare for our hike out to the lake."

"Prepare, sir? I believe one of the fellows from O'Connell's has made his bus available. We could ride, sir."

"No, the hike will do us good. One foot in front of the other, that sort of thing. The miles will pass more quickly than you'd suspect."

# Chapter 29

With Lyle's first knock on the door to Janet's apartment, he felt grateful. It had been less than twenty-four hours since his revealing display in the square, and he was eager for the opportunity to begin again, start fresh. Her gracious lunch invitation was offered in the true spirit of companionship and friendship and forgiveness and, more than anything, Lyle wanted all to go well, smooth sailing, with perhaps a touch of high adventure thrown in for hopeful good measure.

It was the second knock that caused the problems.

Lyle used the knuckles of both hands to rap out a playful tune on Janet's door when he realized that he had come empty-handed. He brought no candy or flowers, no sparkling water or cheesy dessert, no ceremonial small plant as a token of his gratitude and thankfulness, nothing. Janet extended the first hand for a second time, gone the stereotypical extra mile for him and what had he shown up with? His appetite.

The door opened with Lyle caught in the middle of his perplexed thought. Janet smiled warmly. "Hello, Lyle. Come in," she said.

"Thank you," came the partially distracted reply. He attempted clumsily to hide his hands in his pants pockets as he stepped in.

"I've set some things up at the kitchen table," she said. "Please, have a seat."

"Okay, sure. That sounds great," he said. Lyle stepped toward the kitchen, past her sofa with the soft velour, which only yesterday teased the hair on the back of his legs as he paged through her photo album. He acknowledged with a miniscule nod of his head the ceramic animals on her bookshelves, the lions and tigers and elephants and giraffes, whose territorial glances seemed once again directed his way, even more so than yesterday when he swore their eyes followed him around the room. He remembered quite clearly how he felt it inappropriate to enter her kitchen yesterday, her all-too-pristine white kitchen, with its sparkling appliances and satiny tablecloth he dare not smudge. Now, clearly without debate, he walked right in and sat.

"Do you like maple-glazed salmon with pineapple salsa?" Janet asked. "I've made polenta hearts, as well."

"Mmm-mmm," Lyle replied approvingly. In truth, he had no idea. He'd never eaten salmon, and he couldn't begin to guess what a polenta was.

"The marinade has teriyaki sauce in it. I hope that's okay. And there's a little jalapeno and some bell peppers in the salsa," she said. She began to bring the food to the table.

Lyle didn't know what to do. The white kitchen he dared not enter the day before had suddenly taken on stunning new characteristics: there were peach-colored cloth napkins folded like fans and bound with sterling silver napkin rings; dinnerware so keenly polished that he could see his eager face reflected clearly in the bowl of a serving spoon from a foot away; a utensil he was reluctant to touch for fear of leaving a premature and imperfect fingerprint; fine bone china like the kind he saw in magazines his mother used to buy—someday, she would say in a hopeful voice, someday. There were foods of bright yellow pineapple and red and green peppers on serving plates temptingly within his reach, and a golden brown salmon grilled to such perfection that, had that fish been prepared during his employ at Grossman's, a fistfight would have broken out among the waiters as to who among them deserved the privilege of serving it.

"Can I get you something to drink?" Janet said. She offered a pitcher of iced tea she took from the refrigerator.

"Thank you, yes," Lyle said. It was an honest thirst.

Lyle watched Janet pour the iced-tea into his glass, a crystal goblet, so foreign to him in elegance that as ice cubes would fall from the pitcher and into the goblet, they would clink, clink, clink against the sides of the glass and coax notes of such perfect pitch into the air that they would somehow linger before him, wavering, hovering over the table like some carefully orchestrated musical mist. Lyle took it all in with a deep breath before having a sip.

Janet poured herself a glass of iced tea and sat to join Lyle. "I just love the sound the ice cubes make when they plop into the glass, don't you? It always reminds me of the lemonade stand I had as a girl. My mom always said it was the sound of the poor man's dinner bell and that she had to make the cubes bigger and bigger year after year as my father developed selective hearing loss. When she gave me the goblets as a gift last year, she said Father had gone almost completely deaf and that heirlooms belong to the children anyway. Isn't that funny? What do you think?"

Lyle was slowly sipping his iced tea, an ice cube pressed against his upper lip. "We drank milk," he said, lowering the glass. "Look, no mustache."

Janet returned an easy smile, and the two began to serve themselves and eat. For the next several minutes, pleasant glances were served and exchanged, and the only sounds that were heard were those of flatware on china, ice cube against crystal. "What should we talk about?" Janet then asked in a very casual way.

"Anything," Lyle replied in between bites. "I'll talk about anything. What would you like to talk about?"

Janet watched Lyle enjoy his salmon in a hearty and particular way; he was careful to marry a piece of pineapple to every bite of fish. She even noticed he took an extra helping of polenta hearts for balance. "I have an idea about tomorrow—a picnic," Janet started. "We could go on a picnic out to Lake Lulu. We can rent a rowboat from the Lincoln Lodge and have fruit and sandwiches out on the lake. I can bring grapes and strawberries, and we can feel the cool lake breeze in the morning before the sun rises all the way up over the top of the pines. It'll be sweet as pie. Don't you think that sounds like fun?"

"Sure," Lyle said, scooping the last pieces of salmon and pineapple into his mouth. "Lakes are neat."

"Great. It's a date."

Janet's terrific lunch left Lyle full and satisfied, and the prospects of the next day on the lake with her took on bright and wonderful new dimensions—there was anticipation for an event like none other he had experienced, and as Lyle projected himself into that rowboat, pulling mightily on the oars, the wind at his back as Janet playfully dropped red grapes one by one into his mouth, he prayed that thunderclouds would have no part in that day and that they would instead be blessed by the warmth of the summer sun. He even thought about using the word "girlfriend" for the first time.

It was the next few minutes, however, that brought the uncertainty.

Lyle recognized that he had said few words during lunch, and he hoped he had done the right thing. He tried extra hard not to speak with his mouth full and felt fortunate that he was able to squeeze out a brief acceptance to the picnic between delicious bites. He didn't want to make a regrettable mistake of etiquette, or anything else that might suggest to Janet that he was impolite, rude, discourteous, or, least of all, common. Best behavior was to be on the agenda and at the top of the list.

Lyle quickly recalled a memory of his father to guide his actions. It was spring, Saint Patrick's Day, and Lyle thought he must have been nine or ten. He recalled his father at the dinner table, devouring a corned beef sandwich as big as his head and washing it down with the largest glass of green beer he'd ever seen. And when his father was done, when that last drop fell from mug to gullet, he groaned a baritone belch and pushed himself away from the table and proudly proclaimed, "Fit for a king! I shall honor you all with The Nap of Thanks." And then he lay on the couch, asleep in a wink, and proceeded to saw logs loudly into the night.

Lyle always thought his father to be quite proper, and, several days later, discovered he was quite noble, as well. One late night, as Lyle was lying in bed, he heard his father come into the house and into the kitchen, where Mother was waiting up for him. The loudness of their voices stepped all over each other, until a brief silence, a rest, when he heard his mother finally say, "If you're such a swordsman, why don't you go fly off and fight the Spanish!"

He would not see his father again.

Lyle excused himself politely from the kitchen table. "Fit for a king! I shall now perform The Nap of Thanks!" And Lyle lay on the couch in a fetal position and closed his eyes, waiting for sleep. He could not manage a belch.

When he woke, he discovered a note pinned to his shirt. It said:

Dear Lyle,

Thank you for coming for lunch. That was a very unique 'thank you.'

Is it European? I tried to wait until you woke up, but I had to go to work. Please be here at 10:30 tomorrow morning for the drive out to the lake. We'll talk.

Janet

# Chapter 30

Hizzoner and Jenkins woke early the next morning in preparation for the hike out to Lake Lulu. The mayor, using his most persuasive interpersonal skills and official voice, convinced Jenkins of the need for both of them to attend the day's event incognito, just on the oft chance he was unsuccessful in reeling in the catch of the day. No sense in calling attention to oneself before absolutely necessary, he argued. He sent Jenkins down to the janitor's closet to retrieve the sodium bicarbonate.

"Here it is, sir," Jenkins said. He carried a medium-sized box of sodium bicarbonate and a bucket of water. "I've found it applies best when mixed with water. It's a little like wearing toothpaste on your face, but, in my experience, yields the best results."

"And you feel satisfied that concoction will mask our identities? Our constituents will not recognize our features?"

"Yes, sir. I have discovered over the years that when most people see me coming, they turn away. Granted, I haven't always been able to tell without my glasses, but that was my overall impression. On occasion, small boys have pointed fingers, and once I was asked by an elderly woman if I was exfoliating, but the general reaction from the voting public has been to look the other way."

"Good."

"I also have this, sir," Jenkins said as he reached into his pocket and removed a black-and-white bandana. "I thought you could tie this atop your head. It looks as if the morning sun will be quite hot today. There is not a cloud in the sky. I wouldn't want you to get a burn, sir."

Jenkins tied the bandana atop the mayor's head. He stepped back.

"It doesn't make me look too much like a pirate?" the mayor asked.

"Not without an eye patch and earring, sir."

"Right, then. Bandana it is. Thank you."

The two took turns applying the pasty bicarbonate to their faces. The mayor found it an easy task; Jenkins said he hoped it was for the last time. Upon completion, the two stared into the whiteness of each other's faces and at the lumps in the paste, which were so pronounced and obvious when seen from up close that they had to resist the urge to pat each other smooth.

Hizzoner sensed they were almost ready. He also recognized in a hopeful way that his time in the Hall of Records was growing short. It was his transplanted home, as well as his office away from the office—more sanctuary than exile, really, when he recounted the many contemplative unspoken thoughts—and one day he knew it would be time to leave and move on. It was, for him, and he hoped for Jenkins, always more wayside than destination.

"Sir?"

"Yes."

"I've calculated the seven-mile hike to the lake should take somewhere between two and two-and-one-half hours."

"Yes, good."

"If the average person can walk at approximately three miles per hour, that would be approximately six miles in two hours and seven miles in two hours and twenty minutes. Now, that assumes a sampling of individuals whose gait, most likely, would range anywhere from twelve to twenty minutes per mile. I am also assuming that those individuals who would require the full twenty minutes per mile would be those persons suffering some type of ambulatory ailment, or those miraculous souls who genuinely suffer no sense of urgency. We are neither."

"No."

"I am also assuming that we do not fall into that group of individuals who could traverse seven miles in a lickety-split twelve minutes per mile as if our hair were on fire. Such individuals either picture themselves Mercury reincarnate or have been genetically predisposed to possess long limbs and the stride of a gazelle. Again, we are neither."

"No."

"Taking the mean and eliminating any undue wind resistance for complete lack of baggage, places us somewhat comfortably in the middle . . . barring any unforeseen events."

"Things do come up."

# Chapter 31

Janet rented a rowboat inside the lodge while Lyle stood outside on the end of the pier overlooking the lake. The midmorning sun had not yet made it over the top of pines, and there was barely a breeze to ripple the lake's glassy surface. A fish would jump and Lyle would watch the splash and the ensuing waves, concentric circles that would get broader and broader, their amplitude declining until they disappeared altogether as they came close to shore. It was, just as Janet said it would be, sweet as pie.

When Lyle was a boy, he heard stories of a wide and deep crooked creek that began from parts unknown and snaked through a vibrant marsh and emptied into the four-hundred acre kettle known as Lake Lulu. He heard swamp thistle and common cattail, northern bugleweed and bright marsh marigold, giant goldenrod and horned bladderwort, poison sumac and tufted loosestrife all edged along the creek sides and followed the flow to the wide opening of the lake, a fine home to a nesting pair of sandhill cranes, a bald eagle, and some lake loons, abundant curious reptiles, as well as the rare pickerel frog with its odd rectangular markings and timid, droning mating call.

He knew the Lincoln Log Lodge, and the exact place he stood, were some distance away from that opening, well past

263

the point where the marshy bottom morphed into fine beach sand and the thin-stalked marsh grasses gave way to towering white pines rooted firmly on shore, the summer morning air rich in their sweet smell.

Many years ago, he heard, it was rumored that the very spot on which the lodge sat had been cleared by immigrants using only two-man bucksaws and elbow grease, their skill at felling the mighty pines that became the bones of the lodge so keen that they would often labor well into the moonlit night, their sonorous cries of "Timberrrr!" echoing across the lake and into the darkened countryside, the sound carrying like the elongated yips of a pack of howling coyotes.

They crafted a magnificent structure.

More than a dozen birch bark canoes and a lone rowboat, all bearing the hand-painted initials "LL," were tied to round wooden posts along the pier, waiting. Lyle, too, waited for Janet and continued to think about the conversation they had in the car on the ride out to the lake and the friendly and inquisitive way in which she repeatedly asked about The Nap of Thanks. She seemed particularly interested in its origin, the context in which it was used, and how many times —exactly —he had done that before. Lyle shared what he could remember. He did, however, choose not to mention the little black book, or the way it went flying out of his hands and into the night air of the celebration. He considered it an oversight he could live with.

Janet walked out of the lodge and waved to Lyle at the end of the pier. She carried a wooden picnic basket and wore a white summer dress with small red polka dots and a stylish red belt, comfortable sandals, too. She added a floppy straw hat to fight off the sun, and Lyle could see her smile as she stepped onto the creaky pier.

"I think we're ready," Janet said, as Lyle approached her.

"Okay. Good," Lyle said. He carefully stepped off the pier and into the rowboat. It took a moment for him to get his balance, the boat rocking side to side even in the shallow water. He steadied himself with an oar into the sandy bottom and extended a hand to help Janet into the boat. "Here, let me help you," he said. "Give me your hand."

Janet handed Lyle the picnic basket and he set it on the floor of the boat. She reached for his hand. "Thank you," she said, as Lyle guided her safely into the boat.

Lyle loosened the mooring line from the wooden post on the pier. It came undone easily, and with a hefty push of his hand against the pier, Lyle set off onto the lake with Janet.

As Lyle gripped the long spruce oars and set them deliberately into the water, he took special notice of how neatly each oar fit into its oarlock, fixed and locked into place at a single point on the hull, yet unrestricted in its to-and-fro motion —a simple lever with which to propel him through the water.

The ease with which he took to rowing startled him a bit, the basic motion of extending his arms in front of him and then returning them smoothly to his chest producing remarkably rhythmic and efficient results. It was easy and kind of fun; he wondered why he hadn't tried it sooner. With each long successful stroke, he smiled in a Cheshire way at Janet sitting aft, the midmorning sun sprinkling his confidence with gentle warming rays.

Stroke, stroke, stroke, Lyle continued until he felt he was almost to the middle of the lake. He could still see the Lincoln Lodge in the distance with each pull of the oars and a jarring revelation soon followed: He was not looking where he was going.

# Chapter 32

It was about 11:45 a.m. when O'Connell and Stella arrived at the Lincoln Lodge to set up for the tournament. From the previous year's experience, O'Connell learned that arriving any earlier was of absolutely no use (there had not been a rush of early bird entrants, nor any looky-loo interested spectators to contend with), and that waiting in the hot sun for a group of starry-eyed anglers to show up, intent upon catching a nonexistent fish, was a bit of a hot, sweaty bore —nothing good was to come of it. Fifteen minutes would be plenty of time, he felt.

O'Connell directed Stella to take the two wooden sawhorses from the bed of his pick-up truck and set them up on shore about six feet apart just next to the entrance of the pier. He waited by the truck while she made two short trips from the parking lot, and then he helped her with a large piece of plywood they took from the back of the truck. They carried it to the sawhorses where it made an efficient —if not somewhat flimsy and cheap-looking—tabletop.

O'Connell sent Stella back to the truck for the rest of the supplies. On her return, he could see her lumber to carry an overstuffed cardboard box marked "Lunker Lotto," and as she got closer to him, she plopped it on the ground near a sawhorse, an exasperated sigh her not-too-subtle way of suggesting that help of some kind could have been offered.

"Thank you," O'Connell said simply, as he began to rummage about in the box. "Don't forget the folding chairs," he added. Off she went.

O'Connell removed a large, white bedsheet from the box and spread it out over the plywood. He grabbed four nearby rocks from the shallow water of the boat landing near the pier and used each to weight a corner of the bedsheet, the bottoms of the rocks smooth and slippery and wet from where they had rested in the lake, undisturbed and unnoticed for eons.

The other necessary items for the day's event he inventoried from the box: a clipboard for logging each entrant's name and special tag number; a small plastic trophy adorned with a golden jumping fish, its mouth wide open as if about to strike (it was, naturally, the same trophy that had gone unclaimed the year before); a stack of topographical maps purporting to show the various depths of Lake Lulu, its thermoclines and its underwater springs and ledges (For Sale: $10 each); a bullhorn for announcing the official start and completion of activities; and the specially numbered tags themselves, brass buttons the size of quarters, O'Connell's name and likeness stamped on one side, a formally engraved numeral on the other side, making them so official-looking that, had it been another time, they could have been confused with coins of the realm.

Stella returned with two folding chairs and gave one to O'Connell. "Thank you," he said, as he opened the chair. "I think we're ready."

No sooner had O'Connell popped open his folding chair, the legs settling into the sandy shore under his weight, than

Mort's school bus tooled sharply into the parking lot, the bally-whooing hoots and pips and several stout "Ole!s" heard above the honking horn and the squeaky brakes.

The doors to the bus opened and out poured the O'Connell crew: an impatient Nick; the panic-stricken man, his arms swatting at invisible insects; Clancy; the disbeliever; the man in the sharkskin grey suit; and a collection of various rogues, mercenaries, thrill-seekers and treasure hunters. A rubber-gloved Mort was last off the bus, preceded by a lone figure, an albatross, an ersatz angler, an individual whose image —mutton chops, button-popping paunch, and long-tailed waistcoat —conveyed about as much fishing acumen as the thought of Little Lord Fauntleroy prancing about on the decks of the *Pequod.* It was Alderman Peabody. None other than Lester I. Peabody, in the flesh.

O'Connell picked up the bullhorn and aimed it at the mass exiting the bus. "This way, everybody," he announced with a hint of ringmaster's flair. "This way. Follow the sound of my voice," he enunciated, his measured tones and even delivery skillfully avoiding the unpleasant feedback squeal of the casual bullhorn operator.

"Is that Peabody?" Stella asked O'Connell in a genuinely surprised way as she stared at the group. The crowd moved toward them in a swarm.

O'Connell squinted in the sunlight. "I believe that it is. Looks just like his father."

"Hmmm," Stella remarked. "I wonder if Deb's coming?"

Nick was the first to make it to the table, where his eyes immediately locked onto Stella. He puffed out his chest and sucked in his gut in a single motion. "Hi, Stell," he said confidently. "First prize has my name written all over it."

"That's the attitude, son!" O'Connell interrupted with a hearty enthusiasm, as he slid the clipboard in front of Nick. "There's a completely empty space on line number one and, by coincidence, I was just thinking that your name belonged there. Cast your lot, son. We'll have you paired up and ready to go in no time flat."

O'Connell set the pen in Nick's hand and watched him legibly print his name. A rather orderly line formed behind Nick, the anglers and the miscreants, the patrons and the opportunists, all willing to assemble peaceably if it meant a chance at the big cash prize. There were twelve canoes and space on the clipboard for twenty-four names, and even the most mathematically challenged of the group could understand the relevance of being the twenty-fifth entrant. Funny, most didn't bother to count heads.

* * * * *

"Have you a lucky number, lad?" Clancy said. He was at the end of the line and had addressed his comment square into the back of the head of the fellow in front of him.

There was no response.

"I say, have you a lucky number, lad? Like twenty-five, perhaps?" Clancy added a tap on the man's shoulder.

"It's six," the man spoke, while offering only a casual and slight turn of his head toward Clancy. The line was moving quite slowly.

"Ah, yes, a delightful number. One well suited for children's birthday parties with piñatas and toy horses, some sticks of bubble gum, too. 'Tis one of the few lucky numbers you can count on your fingers."

"I've had it my whole life."

"D'vil, you say? My, the successes you must have had! Riches aplenty! All these years, the same number! Good fortune must follow you around like a relative wanting to borrow money! Rainbows at every crossroads end! Every picnic beside a hedgerow of four-leaf clover! I envy you, lad . . . What in the name of Saint Brendan did you do with last year's prize money?"

The man turned to face Clancy. "What prize money?"

"Why, the prize money for winning last year's tournament. Surely a man with a blessed figure as yours would not have missed an opportunity to showcase the magical digit upon the sea, to feather his own fiscal nest, to siphon the currency from his spiritual good tidings. Was it six fish you caught? Was that how you did it?"

"Why . . . no. I didn't catch any fish last year. I don't think anybody . . ."

"Not the big prize? Not a strike or a nibble?"

"No, you see, O'Connell told me he thought I was fishing the wrong thermocline at the wrong time of day. This year, I'm going to buy a map."

Clancy shook his head in a disapproving manner. He put his hand on the man's shoulder. "Lad, what manner of fish would this be to coordinate his own capture by arriving at a preordained spot at a predetermined time? Fish have small brains, lad. 'Tis all they can manage to swim right side up. I'm afraid the skunk in your creel can be traced to an obvious error of ethos, an unfortunate misapplication of the powers of coincidence."

"Huh?"

"In layman's terms—your lucky number is wrong."

"But I've had it since I was a kid."

"Sure enough, there's the proof. I'll admit I was a bit skeptical when you told me you've had but the one, but I'm not a doubter by nature. I am, however, a bit of an expert on lucky numbers, a guide of sorts, an aligner of the mystical orbits of the prime and the not-so-prime that surrounds each of us every day, an aura, like the fine country air that we breathe. And of this one thing, I am certain, lad: As a man counts his blessings, he'll have a lucky number to match, and from those blessings, all bounty will flow and he'll not know an empty creel a day in his life. That's how I know your lucky number is wrong."

"So, what's your lucky number?"

"'Twill be thirty-six next year."

"And where's your prize from the tournament last year, if your number is so lucky?"

"Last year at this time, I'll admit to having me head on a soft pillow, me supple arse enjoying the support of a fine hemp hammock, the pleasant chirping of a family of yellow-rumped warblers overhead filling the summer air with one of nature's original symphonies—F sharp, I believe. As luck would have it, those thin-beaked songsters would swoop down from above at the first hint of mosquito or chigger, allowing the finest nap I may have ever known, the rapid workmanlike flutter of their wings a cool breeze upon my cheeks on a balmy day. I'm blessed."

"Are you saying I shouldn't buy a map?"

Clancy smiled and spread his arms in a welcoming gesture. "Look at us. Two philosophers debating the success of each other's day in the sun. My cool serene symphony and your dry and empty . . . well, day. My cup runneth over, and I'll admit to being embarrassed by me own gluttony. I only ask your forgiveness and beg your indulgence for a meager act of atonement."

"Are we still talking about the map?"

"Your lucky number is a maestro at mapping out a blank and empty path, and she'll do it again. She's an ugly mistress, lad, not fit for the light of day where friends may see her. I only suggest you stand in my stead, so that the good tidings I've known will wash over you as if you were me. 'Tis the least I can do. 'Twill be a gesture I don't think you'll soon forget."

"Do you have a map?"

"No, lad. What I offer is not found on any map, but a place all the same. I offer a different place entirely —my place—in line that is, and I'll take yours. And of this one thing, I'm most certain: You'll see with eyes not your own your borrowed luck linger and before you wet a line, your wee thoughts of maps and fish will be whisked away by a warming glow in your belly and a delightful sense of F sharps to make you want to sing out loud for all to hear. In fact, I'm sure you'll be full of it—not to mention, of course, all the cash prizes."

Clancy smiled, as the man returned a skeptical glance. He could not turn away. Somewhere in the back of Clancy's mind, he remembered offering various whispered barroom conversations about sunken treasures, buried booty, half-naked native girls, secret elixirs stirred with monkeys paws, and mysteriously arrived-at fortunes. Each and every story included, at the very least, a hint of the outlandish or the mention of a foreigner and a far away land (usually Hungarians, Russians, or Gypsies) and always happened to someone somebody kind of heard of (but never him). He hoped the man was part of the crowd at the fringe, always listening. If he was, all in all, with maximum possible rewards figured in, he would reach no other conclusion than to believe the scales tipped in favor of providing the benefit of the doubt.

After making sure no one was looking, the man whispered, "Okay," in Clancy's general direction.

The two switched places with a manly do-si-do; Clancy added a wink, the cherry on top to seal the deal.

Clancy turned away from the man and lightly tapped the new shoulder in front of him. "Are you a seafaring man, lad?"

# Chapter 33

"We're almost there, sir," Jenkins said in a horrifically unintelligible way. The long, dusty walk in the hot sun had caked the pasty substance around his face and mostly around his mouth, paralyzing the muscles necessary to produce well-formed and linguistically recognizable sounds. Instead, the words came out like those of an entry-level ventriloquist, someone who mastered the art of keeping his mouth closed but was not yet able to produce a readily identifiable syllable.

"Mmmm?" responded the mayor. His mouth worked no better.

They were, in fact, close. Jenkins had done a commendable job of forecasting their travel time; it was a sporty two hours and fifteen minutes on the dot, and O'Connell and the entrants' table lay just seconds ahead at the end of the parking lot in front of the pier. He had, however, seriously underestimated the physical toll meted out during two-plus hours trekking in the hot, midmorning sun over asphalt, as their breaths were now pantingly short, legs weary, and a dense fog of fatigue making its way like kudzu through their frontal lobes, muddling most rational thoughts. A fine condensation had also formed on the inside of Jenkins's lenses, adding a dripping visual to his heat-induced disorientation.

By the time Jenkins and the mayor approached the

entrants' table, the line had dissipated and reformed into a huddled mass on the pier, the men staring at the empty canoes like expectant fathers, wondering which seat was the lucky one and which would be theirs.

Stella continued her duties, eyes front, and Jenkins couldn't help but notice the curious look on her face as they neared. She focused one-hundred percent of her rapt and flabbergasted attention on their appearance and looked at them as if they were some kind of creatures that had just crawled out of the marsh, the stark whiteness of their faces and the wobble in their step offering little in the form of normalcy.

"Who are you guys?" Stella asked, quite dumbfounded, as the two stood in front of her.

"We're here for the tournament," Jenkins tried to say.

It was no use. All Stella and O'Connell could hear were mumbles and a high-pitched hum.

"Must be mimes from the circus," O'Connell said. "Maybe they're here for the lotto." O'Connell pantomimed a long cast and quick retrieve, at one point mimicking the strike of a large fish with a jerk of his imaginary rod and emitting a whiny squeal meant to imitate the line of his reel being drawn out at breakneck speed.

Jenkins and the mayor nodded in unison.

Stella looked to O'Connell. "We only have one spot left. We were more than full a minute ago, but two guys left running, screaming something about sea monsters. I have no idea where they went, but I think they ran down TBNL."

"Just as well," O'Connell said. "We shall not have an empty ship today. One of the mimes will take his place." O'Connell looked over his clipboard. "I shall write him in as 'substitute man #1.'" He addressed the two. "So, men, who will it be?"

Jenkins understood the situation at once, and there would have been no debate between the two as to who would remain and compete in the tournament, even if they could speak and understand each other clearly. Jenkins, in a clearly improvised moment, signed an 'o' to the mayor using his thumb and index finger to signify that the mayor was to stay and complete his circumnavigation as planned, while gesturing with his free hand that he would begin the long, hot walk back to town, preparing all that would be needed for a new beginning. It was, after all, his job—heat and journey and inconvenience be damned.

Jenkins had no concerns about leaving the mayor to fend for himself; in fact, he believed in the strongest possible way that once the mayor became part of the flow of the event, that he would surround himself with men of eligible voting age to renew his vigor, and that the old rhythms and speech skills would return to him like riding a bike, or like boomerangs flung from over a decade ago, only now returning to their proper hand. All would be as before; and, if the mayor was lucky, there would be time for a rousing speech to stir the heart and punctuate his return with an elegant and triumphant soliloquy. Jenkins could almost see the eagerness in the mayor's face beneath his lumpy white veil.

\* \* \* \* \*

O'Connell saw Jenkins pat the mayor on the back and head off. "Looks like it's you," he said to the mayor, as he wrote in and then double-checked his clipboard. "Onto the pier, you go," he pointed. "Stella, prepare for the lotto."

Stella took a deep breath and blew it out between her teeth. "Listen up!" she let out toward the men on the pier. "Listen up! I will give each one of you a brass button with a number between one and twenty-four on it. If you are odd, your partner will be the man with the next highest even number. If you are odd, stay put and an even-numbered man should find you quickly. I repeat: If you are odd, your partner will have a better chance of finding you if you remain in your place and do not jitterbug about like a crazy person. One will be partnered with two, three with four and so on. This man will be your partner for today; your fortunes will be linked. Once you have found your partner, you are free to launch your canoe and begin the Lunker Lotto! You may paddle away! Good luck, gentlemen! The blue walleye await!"

The men on the pier cheered loudly and waited for their buttons. As Stella passed them out randomly, the men swarmed around her like she was a queen bee handing out choice pollen-collecting assignments. Nick stood by for a second before deciding to use both elbows in a liberal manner to get as close to Stella as he possibly could. When she gave him his button, he looked at it for his number, smiled from ear to ear, and froze in place just as he had been instructed.

The all-male partner dance moved along quickly, aided by each odd fellow chirping out his number in a unique way, and in no time at all, each even-numbered man located his counterpart.

O'Connell had seen this act before. The men paired up

in a flurry of activity, without so much as a nod to the smallest of pleasantries or the narrowness of the pier. Just as last year, he saw the rush to occupy the empty canoes reach fever pitch, the blind enthusiasm, the spectacular carelessness, and he was certain it was only a matter of time until . . .

SPLASH!

And, suddenly, there sat the mime in the lake, up to his chest in twelve inches of water.

Perhaps it was that his vision was obscured by the paste around his eyes, or that he had lost his footing on unfamiliar ground. Perhaps he had been inadvertently shoved or nudged in all the excitement an inch too far over the edge of the pier that caused him to lose his balance. Or perhaps it was the tremor of sudden and uncontrollable shock it looked like he felt when he heard Alderman Lester I. Peabody's voice say, "I am number two. I am your partner today."

Or the aftershock, when he looked into Lester's eyes and it seemed as if he wanted to speak, yet was stymied by the mutton-chopped face that looked back at him with consummate politeness, but without recollection.

"Somebody help the mime!" the panic-stricken man called out. He was fastening his life vest while Mort loaded his dry cell batteries into their canoe.

One of the rogues threw an imaginary rope.

"Nothing like damp britches on a hot day," Clancy said fondly. "Ah, the memories . . ." He and the man in the sharkskin grey suit were all set to paddle off. The man muttered something about a girl from long ago, something that Clancy ignored.

Alderman Lester I. Peabody offered aid as best he was able. He knelt on the pier and steadied the canoe with one hand as his partner stood in the lake and attempted to shake off his embarrassment. The mime climbed into the canoe with an appreciative nod to his partner; he sat with a squish. Alderman Peabody cautiously stepped into the canoe amid a round of applause from those who were still safely moored to the pier.

"Was that so hard?" the disbeliever asked his partner. They sat in their canoe, watching. It was a rhetorical question, but Nick shook his head anyway. They pushed off.

Dozens of paddles dug earnestly and simultaneously into the lake, as splashes of lake water flew in all directions from various and inconsistently applied strokes.

Several drops hit the panic-stricken man in the face, and his attention immediately turned to the collection of dry cell batteries Mort had brought on board, to the series of colorful wires that connected them in parallel, and to the uncertain reasoning for their presence.

"Should we cover those batteries?" the panic-stricken man said from the front of the canoe. He tried not to sound nervous. "I mean . . . water and electricity don't mix, right? There could be an incident."

Mort pondered as he paddled. "Anything's possible. But then again, electricity, I know. Bzzz. If I were you, I'd be more concerned about snapping turtles. Snapping turtles, I don't know."

"Snapping turtles?" the panic-stricken man replied sheepishly.

They paddled on.

\* \* \* \* \*

O'Connell and Stella watched from shore as the group, much to their amazement, somehow managed to collect in a single spot about fifty yards from the pier. Stella couldn't help but think it unusual, four hundred acres of mostly wide-open lake and a dozen canoes coincidentally stopped paddling within earshot of each other, as if permission to continue had been unilaterally revoked by powerful and unseen forces.

Within seconds, the fishermen grabbed for their rods and hurriedly attached their bait of choice. The Lincoln Lodge had agreed to provide all equipment for a small fee to O'Connell and delivered on a promise to provide a variety to suit all tastes. There were fat nitecrawlers impaled on hooks dangling beneath red-and-white bobbers; plastic insects—crayfish and grasshoppers and leeches—with tiny hooks protruding from their heads and thoraxes; colorful lures shaped like minnows with painted eyes and fins and gills and even freckles in the shape of The Big Dipper, a series of treble hooks not-so-inconspicuously suspended at regular intervals along their underside; some rubber fish that jiggled, too. There was even an oblong thing with a small metal propeller attached on one end, a lone barbed hook sticking out of its midsection.

Whatever the bait, and by whomever's hand, it was flung.

In the eyes of O'Connell and Stella, the proximity of canoe to canoe, as well as fisherman's cast to fisherman's cast (ironically, each perceived optimum landing spot was almost identical), yielded rather predictable results.

Lines became tangled almost as quickly as they hit water, fishermen yanked on bent rods with both hands to free themselves, and someone screamed, "My eye!" There was also some bad language.

"Look at them," an astonished Stella gasped. "They're nuts."

O'Connell cocked his head and flashed his famous gold-toothed smile. "The Spanish Armada it's not."

# Chapter 34

High noon can be an inhospitable time for a summer stroll—the sun has reached its highest point in the sky, and its rays are most intense, the high angle unable to diffuse any of the powerful radiation coming from directly above. Still, Jenkins had a broad smile on his face as he walked on rubbery legs down TBNL toward town, the waves of heat rising up from the asphalt in front of him looking like a watery oasis in the desert just beyond his reach.

He kept on, confident in his beliefs that the mayor would find a way to satisfactorily complete his much-needed circumnavigation and bounce back to the position of prominence he had deserted so long ago. He also thought that meant things would soon be back to normal for him as well, better even, though he couldn't provide an exact reason why, other than to suggest to himself that there must certainly be some type of reward for competence, hard work, and loyalty. He didn't think he was asking that much.

By midafternoon, Jenkins arrived back to an empty town square, the newly dedicated statue, "The Patriot," holding court to a flight of pigeons and no one else. He sat by the statue and reached in his pocket for a moist towelette to wipe the bicarbonate paste from his face for the last time. He was anxious to put all forms of disguise behind him.

As the last of the bicarbonate was wiped from his face, he breathed a sigh of relief and at once looked forward to his second chance, when he noticed a small black notebook at his feet.

He picked up the book and read:

> Sparelli, Nick:
> Very proud of his chest hair (singular). But I loved the eyebrows. Also wouldn't payoff on the arm wrestling bet. Says he slipped.

He turned back a few pages and read:

> Grossman, Leo:
> Competent. Efficient. Sturdy. A well-oiled machine with relatively few breakdowns. Tendency to bark out commands, though. But I kind of liked that part. Fun.

His natural curiosity forced him to turn to the 'J' section. He read:

> Jenkins:
> Smart. Kind. Helpful. Cute. Shy. Employed. Somewhere down the road, he could be the one. Deb Jenkins sounds kind of nice.

A rush of adrenalin surged through him. Seeing his name in the book was a shock of ten thousand volts, and seeing kind words written about him was an immeasurable joy. Seeing his name linked to Deb could only be described as breathtaking and, in an instant, he could only hope that it was written by the Deb he remembered—that bewitching red hair, the pure-as-heaven white sparkle in her smile, the forever azure sky in her eyes.

He basked in the recollection of her features and in the way he always felt a little jittery flutter of excitement in her presence until he realized, in the most honest way, that those words would have been written quite long ago, perhaps too long ago to be of any consequence. They weren't, after all, carved in stone.

Jenkins knew of no rational next step. As he rose, he chose to look for her, and he let it go at that.

\* \* \* \* \*

Deb was seated at her desk in the Chamber of Commerce, preoccupied with the latest version of Lester's Redevelopment Plans, when Jenkins walked in. He walked bravely toward her and looked at her with hopeful eyes, not certain of what to say. He stood not four feet from her, waiting for her to look up, and readied a smile in the most heartfelt and genuine manner. She was as pretty as he remembered, for all these years.

Deb finally looked up, and began with, Jenkins felt, an uncomfortably long silence. "Hiya, handsome. Where ya been," she finally said.

"I've come back," Jenkins said without thinking. In his ten years in exile, he had a multitude of well-practiced speeches at the ready for this precise moment, none of which began, "I've come back." Now he couldn't remember any of them. He tried to re-focus. He went on. "I've been helping the mayor. He's coming back, too. He's going to start fresh. You'll see. He's going to take his place again. Right now, he's fishing, but I'm sure he'll be walking back into the Chamber at any minute. I don't think he'll have any fish, though. But I'm certain he's come about in the right direction. You see, there's been this long circumnavigation . . . and then I found this book with my name in it," he said, holding up Deb's little black book. "I found this book and . . . and there are so many things I'd like to say. And I don't know if I should, if it's been too long. I don't know where to begin. I don't know if I should start with all times I went to get the mail, or help with your errands, or brought you lunch, or all the times I thought about you, or the time away, or the circumnavigation, or the walk down TBNL, or all the things I wanted to say, but never did. I'm a little lost."

Deb returned an easy smile. She looked him straight in the eye and winked. She let out a long breath. "All I can say is, it's about time. I was beginning to think you forgot about me. That was a crazy thought. Lunacy. Absolute lunacy. After all, I couldn't begin to think that someone would forget about me, especially someone like you, someone who walked around my desk in circles like a satellite every day bringing my mail or asking for some stamps or an envelope. You would not have been more noticed had you worn a cowbell around your neck and blown retreat on a bugle, I can tell you that. It was cute," she added with a reflective smile. "And there I was, trying to play along, just as polite as you please, waiting and waiting and

waiting and waiting for you to make some kind of next move. Everybody else always did. All the nitwits. At first, I figured you must be shy. But, then, I'd hear you speaking to the mayor, trying to coax and steer Schuyler with your way, leading him on, and I knew there was something else beyond your words, something more. Then I figured you were up to something. And then one cool autumn day, Mayor Schuyler A. Peabody himself walked up to me in Town Square, and, proud as a peacock, told me he thought you were a gem and that you reminded him of Abraham Lincoln, loyal and devoted and honest. He was quite proud of you. That was the last I saw of the mayor. He must have shoved off soon after. And that very next day, when I walked into the Chamber and found it empty, I felt like I was alone on a deserted island, and I instantly knew that you had set about on your own arc, at your own speed, that sort of thing, and that it would be some time before you returned. I can't put my finger on it, but there was something about you, some unspoken thing, that seemed to come flying in from outer space to land in my view and catch my eye—you drew me in without a word. Funny, you never said anything."
She paused for a brief second. "You watched. You watched like I was a fragile sculpture of the Venus de Milo, with the funny broken-alligator arms. Sometimes, you stared from a distance, like you were looking through a dime telescope, but your eyes paid no toll and rambled on, as if they were flying down the highway at supersonic speeds to scream big, sappy things into open spaces, things a girl needs to hear. But for some reason, your mouth put on the brakes. A girl can tell about these things. A girl knows when she's being watched. A

girl knows when she's the sparkle in someone's eye. And, yet, you came by every day to sparkle in silence. My daily sparkle. You came by every day to ask for silly things until one day you didn't come by. You were gone without a clue, no trace, no vapor trail in the sky, nothing, and so were the little things, the wordless littlest of things, the things I'm sure you never thought of, the things I'd grown accustomed to, the things you miss dearly when they are no longer there—so much, so much that these things you pine for—these things I've missed, these precious absent things, like the priceless sparkle in your eye. Each day since, was as if the sun set and gave birth to a black starless night, not a light in the sky—not a twinkle. There was only the smoky haze of the moon, and you vanished like a puff of that smoke in a cheap magician's trick, and I couldn't begin to guess where you were or where you went. At first, I thought you had run off on some flight of fancy, some boyish whim. But without a note, that would have been rude, and I had never seen rudeness in you. Only devotion. Only loyalty. You were always at the side of Mayor Schuyler A. Peabody, a right-hand man, if ever there was one, and if the mayor was gone— and he was truly gone—you were surely at his side; he would have granted no leave and you would have taken none. That much I knew from watching you. So I waited. There is, after all, no expiration date on true loyalty, which makes patience a worthy suitor. And I believed that one day, when enough starless nights had passed, you would return and I would see that sparkle again. My sparkle. I believed it so much, in a way that defies all natural science and explanation that the silliness of it made me want to giggle whenever I thought of it. Have you religion? Can you believe that? It's true. Did you know that it was my mission to seek out every man in this town, ask them questions, hear their tales, have some tea, all to try and divine any bit of information that would tell me where you went? Where the aldermen went? Where the mayor went? When or where you might show up next? Nobody said much. Not much at all. What an unbelievable collection of the uninformed. Polite, and a bit dim, but uninformed. Everyone so far out of the loop. It's quite a fraternity. Oddballs, mostly."

"You did that? You did that for me?"

"No explanations. Come on. Let's get a cup of joe. I know a place. A girl can only wait so long, you know?"

Jenkins held out his hand to help Deb out from behind her desk. They took the elevator down to the first floor and walked out of the building and into the square.

He didn't know where she was leading him.

# Chapter 35

Clancy and the man in the sharkskin grey suit extricated themselves from the mess in front of the pier and spent the better part of the last two hours paddling around in search of a secluded and promising fishing spot. Little fishing was done, and the man in the grey suit was feeling more than a bit anxious, his frustrations manifesting themselves in wild and rapid thrusts of his paddle into the lake.

"Easy, lad, 'tisn't escape velocity we're after," Clancy said from the stern.

"Why aren't we there yet?" the man whined.

"I wouldn't think just yet," Clancy said, his eyes skyward. "The right spot can be a d'vil of a thing to pin down—you can ask Galileo Galilei on that . . . You wouldn't, by chance, be able to lend me a sextant, now, would you, lad?"

"A what?"

"Never mind . . . Just as well . . . I believe we are here."

Clancy used a nifty and mostly unknown paddling technique to stop the canoe on a dime, the sudden halt of forward motion catching his partner by surprise and almost launching him over the bow.

Clancy watched the man in the grey suit right himself. The man said nothing. "No shame, lad. We are quite alone."

Clancy had navigated to a spot of perfect tranquility,

no canoes in the distance, the mouth of the creek over the horizon and out of sight, absolutely nothing to fix a point or catch a bearing, the eyes of no other man upon them. The tall pines, the scotch and the white, the Douglas fir and the sturdy hickory ringed the edges of the oddly shaped lake and cast great shadows onto the still water, the unmistakable hoot of a great horned owl, the short clear whistles of the tufted titmouse, and the tweet-er-reee of the wood thrush the only sounds of intelligent life. The boat landing and the Lincoln Lodge were also now lost somewhere, beyond the line of sight and tucked somewhere back into the pines.

"I wonder where everybody went?" the man said. "I wonder where that mime went? That guy was all wet and paddling around in Alderman Peabody's canoe. I wonder if he's dry yet?"

"Don't know."

"I wonder where they could be?"

Clancy reached for his rod. "Judging by their previous display of seamanship . . . I would guess the bottom," he said confidently, as he readied a cast.

The man acknowledged the possibility with a quick nod and readied a cast of his own. He attached a large rubber frog with bright red eyes to his line, its twin barbed hooks supporting its abdomen like a razor-sharp cage, and cast it out as far as it would go. It landed with a belly-flopping plop of a sound, and the man immediately began a slow retrieve, the frog riding the surface, its wiggly legs rippling the water and forming a gentle wake.

"I see you've a frog," Clancy said approvingly.

"Yes."

"Right fine choice, that."

"Thank you."

"Would that be a local frog, do you know?"

"No. I don't know."

The man retrieved his frog almost back to the canoe. In a single motion, he jerked the bait out of the water and re-cast it out as far as it would go, the belly-flopping plop of a sound on impact the signal to start the slow retrieve once again.

"You see, I'm a bit of an expert on frogs. In Ireland, we have both frogs and toads —as well as the newt (rascal of an amphibian) —and most people don't know how to distinguish between the two. It's all in . . ."

"Yes, yes, yes," the man cut in, most agitated. "This is all very interesting, but can we please be quiet while I'm trying to fish? I don't want to scare the lunkers. I plan on winning the big prize."

After a brief and digestive pause, Clancy conceded an, "Oh, I see." From an earlier conversation in front of the pier, it was clear he hoped for a more leisurely afternoon, one filled with whimsy and sunshine, the occasional interruption by bluegill or perch. And even though O'Connell's poster promised a handsome purse for a special fish, he had not seriously anticipated a fierce and competitive agenda searching for big game —he just hadn't. Now, however, he watched the man track every movement of his frog in the water, the plops and the wiggles and the big red eyes staring back at him, every second a hopeful opportunity to witness the big strike.

Plop!

"You know," Clancy started, "It's a bit of an ol' wives tale, that ol' saw 'bout not making any noise in a boat. Why, when I was a lad, I can remember stories of me Granda' MacNamara hauling in stringers of Atlantic salmon while simultaneously playin' the fiddle and singin' 'The Rocky Road to Dublin.' He may have even tapped his foot on the bottom of the boat t'keep time to the music, though that part was told t'me by his brother, Shanny, who was known t'drop a pint from time to time."

"Please," the man implored.

"Now, now, I know what you think, but I've simple science on my side. Of this, I'm most certain. You see, lad, fish have no ears."

The man turned to face Clancy. He deadpanned, "Then why do they swim away when you make a noise?"

"Sure enough, that would not be for me to say. Flight is an awkward enough thing for the landlubber to explain if he had the words. Fish thinking, now, pardon the pun, is all wet . . . Now, were I a clear-thinking man, a man of letters and prose, I'd call the urge to go an impertinent sneeze of the central nervous system, a split and silent second of hurried inconvenience in the motherly name of self-preservation. 'Tis at best a directionless scamper. A cerebral knee-jerk to perceived danger is all, no less terrifying and unpredictable than the thought of a bolt of lightning to the tip of your nose—and 'tis often no noise required, not a peep or a pip. A prolonged silence pining away might do just as well, the cogs and gears of grey matter spinning like a gyroscope 'til they shake loose from their moorings and set one stumbling

on, rudderless. An errant bang, a pop, a crack or a splat—
these things haven't a fiddler's fart to do with why. A man
goes because he goes. He moves on with purpose or not, the
empty road before him not his path until he's set foot upon
it and can look back at his tracks and wonder how in blessed
blazes he's gotten to be where he's at. Now, the fish with no
ears and no feet moves on because he moves on for reasons of
his own. The sainted Heavenly Father has, perhaps, given him
a gentleman's sporting chance at his own new path. There's no
tellin' for sure, but I've me own suspicions as to why he goes."

The man stared blankly at Clancy. He seemed to weigh
his words as if they were some form of imponderable Gordian
Knot, his slack mouth begging a clarifying question. He cocked
his head as if trying to think.

"Guppies," Clancy spoke in a lyrical way, a pleasant smile
in tow like a comet's tail. He lofted a cast into the lake, an arc
like a rainbow, and began a patient retrieve.

"The little ones?"

"Aye, lad, the wee ones. They know what causes them now.
I told you I've science on my side. A right powerful thing: men
in white lab coats gone to university."

The man shook his head in a halfhearted way and once
again lobbed his frog out as far as it would go. He asked Clancy
for quiet and had been offered the central nervous system,
lightning bolts, gyroscopes, and fish with no ears and no feet.
Any further request for quiet—in any of its forms (silence, calm,
shhh) —might open discussions as varied as the infinite origin
of the cosmos or the mating habits of the North American
game fish. There would, assuredly, be no quiet today, just as

there was no peace two days ago when he sat under that tree, sobbing with his head in his hands. He thought of the guppies and turned to Clancy. He introspectively offered, "I had a girlfriend once . . . Maybe if I could win this money . . . Did I tell you what happened? She left me."

"Bootless cries, lad, and they'll not get far in this boat. Time to get your sea legs."

"But I've . . ."

FA-WHAP!

The man in the grey suit's complete lack of attention to his task caused him to miss the great strike, the unmistakable proof a rod bent like a banana, the high-pitched squeal of his reel giving line to the escaping fish sounding off and assaulting his eardrums in a knife-piercing way. The rod shook in his hands, and he could feel the weight of the sturdy fish on the other end as he set the hook with a forceful and instinctive yank, the line becoming taut and zigzagging in the lake before his eyes. The powerful fish even managed to turn the canoe as it fought valiantly, the bow jerking back and forth like a compass point, fighting to find true north. "Hey!" the man cried.

"Fish on!" Clancy bellowed.

The man shrieked, "What do I do?"

Clancy stared ahead at the man and at the oblivious look upon his face. "HOIST THE GREAT FISH, LAD!"

The man struggled to control the rod as the mighty fish tugged powerfully from the other end, the unpredictable jerks violent distractions as he tried to crank the reel and bring the fish closer to the boat. He could feel the tension in his forearms as he pulled the rod high to avoid slack on the line, a line so taut that, had it been plucked, it could have sounded a perfectly pitched high C.

As the man cranked on the reel, the mighty fish was being drawn nearer the boat, the serpentine swirls of surface water providing the men the first glimpse of the hooked one.

"There!" Clancy pointed. "She's a two-footer, at least!"

"Maybe more!"

The nearer the boat, the greater the hooked one splashed and thrashed, its steely blue dorsal fin breaking the surface and catching the sun's rays, reflecting a prism back to the men in the boat.

"Did you see that?" the man yelled, his excitement palpable.

"Aye, lad! She's the one!"

"I've almost got—"

PING!

The man in the grey suit felt the tension leave his rod in an instant, a frayed and broken line dangling helplessly from the tiptop end of the rod.

As quickly as it appeared, the thrashing was gone, the serpentine swirls and the shiny blue dorsal fin breaking the surface committed to new memories, their images vivid enough to grab and hold in your hand—but gone all the same, vapors.

Clancy watched the man, motionless, staring with a sullen expression at the broken, limp line as if waiting patiently for the inanimate object to provide a rational explanation.

"A darn shame," Clancy consigned. "She could've been the one."

"Gone. Just like that."

"A darn shame. 'Tis my pleasure to have been in the boat."

"Gone . . . I thought she was the one. I was seeing stars . . ."

"'Tis the way."

The man looked at Clancy with watery eyes. "Is this the part where you tell me there are more fish in the sea?"

"No, lad. I'll not insult that fish or cheapen the heartbeat of a moment when you thought she was yours. 'Twas your moment and yours alone, and only you will ever be able to tell if another is its equal. And with me hand upon all I know to be holy, and from the bottom of me aged 'eart, Godspeed, lad."

# Chapter 36

Hizzoner had resisted the urge to wipe and chip away the pasty bicarbonate from his face for two straight hours. From the bow of the canoe, he paddled dutifully ahead and listened to Lester's familiar voice make pleasant, but uneventful, attempts at conversation. There were comments about the accommodative weather, the calm and waveless lake, as well as polite asides as to the geniality of circus folk.

Not a single line hit water.

"What say you of the redevelopment?" the alderman asked after a while. "Have you noticed the progress? Mind you, I understand that you are a mime. A nod will do."

The mayor nodded.

"I've tried my best. I've tried to decide on the right things."

The mayor pulled his paddle into his lap and lightly bowed his head. The canoe coasted forward.

Lester, too, pulled his paddle into his lap and listened to the water break in tiny waves as the canoe glided to a quiet stop. "It can be a difficult thing to know, the right thing," he said. "There are endless choices. But I've people depending on me. I've decisions to make."

The mayor again nodded.

"Sometimes," Lester continued, "some of them are easy. Sometimes it's as easy as saying, 'Slap a new coat of paint on the

Chamber,' or 'I'll have the usual,' when ordering lunch. And some of them are more difficult—like what to name that road, TBNL," he said. He smiled easily and breathed a tiny laugh to himself. "Deb's suggestion of 'The road Les traveled' was too corny even for me. A nice young fellow, proud patriotic lad, suggested 'US Highway America,' and I might have taken him up on that suggestion had he not just won the Fourth of July essay contest. I didn't for a moment want anyone to think I would play favorites."

The mayor shook his lightly bowed head no.

"Yet, the harder I thought, the more I pondered names and suggestions to avoid a show of favoritism, the more I knew I would not succeed. My thoughts were diverted elsewhere by a recurring allegiance, I'm afraid. I am, after all, an honorable man, and I should say that is the least that I am . . . I am a thoughtful man . . . I am also not a forgetful man whose memory is an inconvenience to him. And I should think it rude to ignore the very circumstance I find myself in, and I will not be discourteous to those who have gone before me: elected officials and voyagers alike, Pilgrims with square buckles on their shoes."

Lester paused for a deep, contemplative breath. He drew another.

Hizzoner looked to the sky, a blueness as far as the eye could see. In Lester's silence, he felt profound resignation.

"There can be no other conclusion. One step leads to the next; it has always been the way. It has been right in front of me the whole time." He cleared his throat. "It is, therefore, for lineage sake (and the will of the voters) that I am here in this place —alone to decide—and decide I must. Decide, I shall . . . I have therefore decided to show my favoritism and wave that banner as if it were Old Glory flapping in the breeze in Town Square on a windswept Fourth of July. It is simply best for all. A thing well named is named forever. I can do no more than that. It *is* my best effort. Resolved, I *have* decided: In recognition of the longstanding familial dedication to public service, for the efforts made, for the missteps just as easily forgotten, and mostly for the seed of redevelopment planted by my father, Schuyler, I shall name that road, 'The Peabody Skyway.' When you stand at one end and look out along its path to the horizon, it shall look as if you were heading off to infinity and into the blueness of distance, where all growth and prosperity is found."

Hizzoner felt a proud moment swell within him. His first thought was not to cry out in joy or to embrace his son in a warm and loving way but to reach into his shirt pocket for the index card he had been carrying for two days. He delicately drew the card from his pocket, careful to not crimp an edge or put the slightest crease across the face of the neatly printed words, and read to himself:

> We have chosen to become a brave and passionate populace; it is both the breath which sustains us and the bright starlight which illuminates our paths. When faced with great obstacles, it is the soothing and guiding hand of our forefathers on our backs and the lightning strike of our courage. When we are lost, It is our way. And when we are loved, It

is our bounty. It is the invincible cornerstone of our Great Nation, and the foundation upon which we—we patriots —build our futures, and align our boundless fortunes.

Lester I. Peabody
July 7th     5 Stars

"What's that?" Lester asked.

The mayor slipped the card back into his shirt pocket. "First prize," he said to himself.

# Chapter 37

Lyle eagerly watched the summer sun rise up and arch over the pines, then pass directly overhead, reddening his cheeks at midday; and now, at midafternoon, as it eased its way over his shoulder and headed decidedly and predictably west, he wished it would slow its pace to the horizon.

He watched the sun and remembered the night when he stood alone on TBNL, the dark and ancient sky above him, the constellations in their shapes and the stars too numerous to count. He thought of Caesar, Napoleon, Alexander—and Speckman, and he wondered then if those great men ever wished upon a star. Now he wondered whether it was ever in their good fortune to sit in a rowboat with a pretty girl, the sun in its radiant glory, and not have a care in the world.

Lyle looked at the picnic basket on the floor of the boat between himself and Janet. He remembered setting it there when he offered his hand to help Janet into the boat, but now, after the better part of a day on the lake, he could not recall if it had ever been opened. Janet promised picnic sandwiches and grapes, fresh fruit, green apples, and maybe even some watermelon, he thought. Now, he couldn't remember for sure if he had taken a bite of anything, nor could he recall the smallest specific detail of their conversations of the day. His thoughts were lost in a sea of smiles and tiny laughs, red polka dots and a floppy straw hat, the ache in his arms from pulling on the oars (he didn't care) and the way Janet's toes crinkled in a cute fashion whenever she said his name.

"Lyle?" Janet asked, "Where did all these canoes come from?"

"Ahoy! Ahoy there!" called out the disbeliever. He and several other fishermen formed a semicircle of canoes around the rowboat. "Are you catching anything?" he added, using his hands around his mouth like a megaphone.

"We're not fishing," Lyle yelled back.

"We've been watching you," the disbeliever said, as he readied a cast. "You've been in the same spot quite a long time."

"But we're not fishing."

Plink! A blaze-orange lure in the shape of a torpedo landed near Janet, its stainless steel treble hooks clinking against each other as they entered the water with barely a splash.

Plunk! Plunk! Poink!

Each succeeding cast landed closer to the boat than the next. The last one skidded across the water and bounced into the hull, then floated upside down on the surface like a child's forgotten and abandoned pet goldfish.

"Lyle, I think we should leave. These men have fishing to do. Let's be on our way," Janet said.

"Yes, of course," Lyle agreed.

Lyle pulled on the oars and began to put some distance between the men in the canoes. A soft breeze began to blow and rippled small waves across the lake and into their path, while the disbeliever watched.

"Hey! Where are you going?" yelled the disbeliever. "We think you know something!"

Lyle didn't respond. He pulled on the oars and watched the incredulous look on the disbeliever's face as he retrieved his cast.

The soft breeze from only seconds ago suddenly stiffened, and a light chop on the lake now broke wave after wave after wave head on against the bow. Lyle pulled harder and watched the distance between he and the disbeliever grow.

"Hey! Hey!" yelled the disbeliever. He and the other canoes offered a halfhearted pursuit, their efforts stymied by the wind and the waves. "We think you know something!"

Lyle's arms ached as he continued to pull on the oars and put a greater distance between him and Janet and the men in the canoes, their images now a speck on the horizon, so far back as to be almost invisible to the naked eye. Lyle had not realized the distance he covered, that he had crossed the lake one stroke at a time, until he found that he and Janet were at the mouth of that crooked creek that fed Lake Lulu.

Upstream, they rowed.

# DANCE

**Book 3 of the Lovers Dance Series**

---

**by Deanna Roy**

Six-Time *USA Today* bestselling author of
*The Forever Series*
*The Lovers Dance Series*

---

Sign up to be notified about new releases via email or text.

Casey Shay Press
PO Box 160116
Austin, TX 78716
www.caseyshaypress.com

E-ISBN: 9781938150661
Paperback ISBN: 9781938150654

Library of Congress Control Number: 2017905598
eBook version 3.0